her SHADOWS
his SECRETS

USA *TODAY* BESTSELLING AUTHOR
CC MONROE

HER SHADOWS, HIS SECRETS
Copyright © 2022 by CC Monroe

Edited by Kayla Robichaux
Cover Designer & Interior Design by Juliana Cabrera, *www.jerseygirl-design.com*

All rights reserved. No part of this book may be reproduced in any form or by any electronic or mechanical means, including information storage and retrieval systems, without written permission from the author, except for the use of brief quotations in a book review.

I hid in the shadows all my life until you found me.

other books by cc monroe

ALWAYS AND FOREVER SERIES
Always The One • Always Us
Forever The One • Forever Us
Lana (A Novella)

LOVING SERIES
Loving Ben Cooper • Loving Kate Beckett

HAPPILY EVER ALPHA WORLD
from AURORA ROSE REYNOLDS
Until Kayla • Until Mercy
Until Brew

WRITTEN w/ KD ROBICHAUX
Steal You • Number Neighbor
Bad Medicine • To Have and to Hold

STANDALONES
Protecting Her Honor

Hanna, many things have come and gone in the last two years, but one thing that lasted in some of the hardest times is our friendship. I had to give a character as unique, kind and yet fiercely badass like you, a name like yours.

You deserved a real friend and many betrayed you. But may Brenda never betray you. May she always be there and protect you with so much love and a shield of Armor.

And to Salvatore Randazzo, rest easy with light and love. You will be missed.

Prologue

HANNA

THE DOOR HANDLE MOVES, GENTLY AT FIRST, BUT the sound is oddly loud in my small New York apartment. I take a slow, deep breath, and yet to me it sounds heavy, as if the person on the other side of the door would be able to hear it.

Tonight marks the third week this has been happening to me. Whoever stands outside my door never fully makes it in, no attempt other than to maybe spook me. It's not an upscale place where I live, so all it would take is a swift kick with gusto to tear that door apart and step inside. Hell, the person could make it in if they just used a card, most likely even a piece of paper folded up a few times.

"Who— Who's there?" I finally call out. Weeks of restless sleep and nightly visits from the stranger have led me here with no choice but to let them know I'm here and doing my best to be unafraid. I fail miserably, because I'm chilled to the bone. Every noise arouses such fear in my blood that shadows haunt me.

I look over my shoulder, feeling the constant eyes boring into me. Waiting for me to be unalarmed, unprepared, and absolutely vulnerable.

After my voice rings out, it's silent, the echoes the door makes and the jiggling ceasing. Loud footsteps move away gradually, the sound of something scraping along the walls as the person leaves making me grow cold. They know that I know, and now, my fear has only multiplied.

My shadows have only grown more haunting.

One

HANNA

THE CITY BUZZES AROUND ME, PEDESTRIANS' FEET moving at a rapid pace to get from one place to another. I do my best to stay on the outside of the crowds, dangerously close to the busy street with ruthless taxi drivers and worse—everyday New York drivers. My work is only twelve blocks away from where I live, so I leave an hour and a half early each day to make it.

Sure, I could take the subway, but lately, there has been this uncanny feeling of danger nagging at my stomach. And although the subways are usually busy—full of people, so lots of witnesses—I feel safer above ground, in broad daylight, and shoulder-to-shoulder with people who I can hide behind, yet I have open room to run.

The logic makes zero sense, but nothing has lately. I grew up in this city, I was in the foster care system at eight years old. My parents—not druggies, not dead, not anything—just didn't want me. I was an inconvenience, and that molded me and how I view myself today.

I'm...more than curvy, my body unlike most New York women. I wouldn't say I'm a linebacker or something grotesque, but in today's world, I'm no Cinderella. I have curves that accentuate my waist, and my thighs have no gap. My breasts are large, and my bottom is generous.

But for most my life, this has kept me hidden and unbothered by men, society, and anyone who might want to get close. I have no desire to have a large group of friends nor enjoy the idea of going out on weekends to whoop it up. I'm a plain Jane, with a plain, lonely life.

God, listen to me. How pathetic does that sound? "Woe is me" is the story. Or so I thought. But recently—the past three weeks—things have...shifted; something has changed in my life.

I'm being watched, followed, harassed, or, as the cops say, "delusional or hearing things." But I'm not. There is always someone watching me. I feel their every gaze; I hear them outside my apartment every night. On occasion, they will cut me some slack and give me a damn break, but he or she returns and taunts me more.

The police, I gave up calling eventually. Whenever they came, there were no actual threats being made, so I was written off as just a "scared, lonely woman hearing things in a rundown neighborhood."

I'm not crazy. There are a lot of things I am—shy, timid, insecure, and yes, lonely—but I am not crazy or hearing things.

Someone is out there, and for whatever reason they would want to harass someone like me, it's beyond my comprehension. I'm not anyone or anything special.

My thoughts can no longer linger on this as I walk through the revolving doors of the small, derelict magazine company I work for. This is why I live in the neighborhood I do. I make barely above minimum wage, and half the time, the magazine cuts our hours, because—let's face it—we aren't doing well. We mainly focus on local eateries or places to see and visit when in New York. We write glorified tour guides, and no New Yorker wants to read that.

Everyone local knows this information already, but we are only published in New York, and our online presence suffers, because the cheap man upstairs doesn't want to pay for a marketing team for our website.

Stepping into my small cubicle, I remove my purse, then hang it on the small holder I have Command-stripped to the small box I call a workspace and fix my dress. I wore my Monday dress. I only have seven nice work outfits, so I repeat them frequently—another New York no-no. I live in the capital of fashion, but this black sundress with cap sleeves was eight dollars at my local thrift store and gets the job done. It's not like I'm working for *Vogue*.

"Hey, Hanna, it's good seeing you."

The pleasantries I share with Chelsea in printing are about it for me. I know I'm a little shy and never the first to initiate a conversation, but this place is stuffy. There is one person who is persistent though—Dax in editorial. He's a nice guy, clean cut, and seems to be like me, wears the same few outfits and tends to keep to himself.

He asked me out a few weeks ago, and I turned him down. I could tell it hurt, but he didn't seem too upset. In fact, he stayed pretty normal if you ask me. Still stops by when he's on my floor, says hello, asks me about my day or the past weekend, and then he smiles and is off. But other than that, my face is in my computer, researching, writing, and editing final articles.

My days pass like this. They come and go, and as a twenty-three-year-old, I realize just how pathetic it is. Do I need to be more social? Probably. Should I consider dating? Maybe. At least I don't have a bunch of cats—hell, not even one.

Go me!

I have no idea where to start though or even what I would do. This whole harassing thing has definitely made me leery to go outside and trust people. But what could they want? Money? Are they druggies looking for a hit? My apartment complex *is* that kind of place.

Nothing exciting jumped out at me at work, per usual, and once I head off, I'm only three blocks away from home when my stomach starts to sink. The closer to home I get, the less foot traffic there is, leaving a nagging, spine-tingling sensation that I'm not alone.

I risk looking back yet see no one there but a few locals I've seen around. I pick up speed and get inside to the mailboxes. Hurrying, I open my box with my keys in my shaking hands, looking behind me and over my shoulder. Messily, I grab the few envelopes, then rush up the stairs. Once inside, I lock the door and release a deep breath.

"Relax, Hanna. You're starting to sound insane even to yourself now," I whisper into the room. I want to rinse off; the muggy summer day and long walk to and from work have me dying to clean myself up, and maybe the brief spray of hot water that will last at most ten minutes before going cold can help settle me down. I complained for over a year now that my water doesn't stay hot, and they do nothing. But hey, beggars can't be choosers, especially when you live in a place like this.

Putting my purse and keys down along with the mail, I start to undress. I wait until I'm fully naked before starting the water, making sure I save every second of warmth I'll get. Stepping in, I make work of cleaning myself from head to toe, and closing my eyes, I daydream of a luxurious shower and hours of hot water…or maybe a nice bubble bath. By the time I'm clean, the water goes from lukewarm to bite-you-on-the-ass-with-snow cold. Shivering, I turn off the tap and grab the towel hanging over the shower rod, covering myself up, followed by my robe.

Stepping onto the mat, I tremble a bit while putting on my nightly face moisturizer. The sun is almost about to set, and I plan to eat a microwavable Lean Cuisine and curl up with a book in my bed. Whenever I have extra money to spare, I go to the local used bookstore and purchase whatever novel intrigues me. Usually, the cover is all it takes to get me hooked, but when I can't find one that catches my eye, I spend over an hour reading blurbs on the back until I find one I like.

The latest one is a romance. Not my usual, go-to genre. Thrillers like *Gone Girl* or *Girl on a Train* tend to be my favorite, but with the nightly stalker showing up at my door, I don't want to add to my building paranoia.

Looking at the clock while my dinner heats up, I pull out my romance novel, and my Diet Pepsi from the fridge, and walk to my nightstand. My studio apartment is small and as cozy as it can be. It's not much, but I've done my best to make it a home.

It's nearly 7:30 p.m. when I finally sit to open my book and eat the heated-up dinner. I try not to anticipate the late-night visitor, hoping they take the occasional night off tonight. Honing in on my book, I get lost in the pages. This is definitely not a book I would normally read, but I hate to admit I'm a little obsessed with the insta-love trope.

"Wonder what that's like," I murmur into the empty space. I'm at the part where they kiss for the first time, and unlike most romance books, it's dangerous, all-consuming, hot, and possessive, something I know nothing about but suddenly feel intrigued, wishing I could experience that just once.

To be with someone who loves you so deeply, with such force and desire that they would do anything to keep you as theirs and theirs alone. To be the center of their world and touched in a way that shows you just that—bordering on obsession. I wouldn't know, nor will I ever, because the men in these books would never go for a woman like me. Curvy plus a little extra. My brownish-blonde hair, green eyes, and certain facial features are the only things I find somewhat appealing about my entire self.

The night passes on, and I slowly drift off, my eyes heavy. But my short-lived luck passes when I hear it. The very thing that haunts me nightly and keeps me from sleeping.

Them?

Him?

Her?

Someone.

I stand slowly, taking small steps until I'm a few feet from the door.

The handle moves, gently at first, but the sound is oddly loud in my small New York apartment. I take a slow, deep breath, and yet to me it sounds heavy, as if the person on the other side of the door would be able to hear it.

Tonight marks the third week this has been happening to me. Whoever stands outside my door never fully makes it in, no attempt other than to maybe spook me. It's not an upscale place where I live, so all it would take is a swift kick with gusto to tear that door apart and step inside. Hell, the person could make it in if they just used a card, most likely even a piece of paper folded up a few times.

"Who— Who's there?" I finally call out. Weeks of restless sleep and nightly visits from the stranger have led me here with no choice but to let them know I'm here and doing my best to be unafraid. I fail miserably, because I'm chilled to the bone. Every noise arouses such fear in my blood that shadows haunt me.

I look over my shoulder, feeling the constant eyes boring into me. Waiting for me to be unalarmed, unprepared, and absolutely vulnerable.

After my voice rings out, it's silent, the echoes the door makes and the jiggling ceasing. Loud footsteps move away gradually, the sound of something scraping along the walls as the person leaves making me grow cold. They know that I know, and now, my fear has only multiplied.

My shadows have only grown more haunting.

When enough time has passed and my heart rate has settled, my fight-or-flight instinct calming. Looking around—for what, I don't know—I try to think of what I should do now. For weeks, the phone calls to the police have left me with nothing. No change or security—I'm the crazy one. In fact, the last officer said it's most likely a cracked-out addict looking for his dealer. *"That is to be expected in this type of neighborhood."*

No. I'm not crazy. I haven't lost my mind.

So I move fast, going to my purse, but in my frantic state, I hit the small table with the front of my thigh. I curse out from both the pain and my things falling to the ground. Rubbing out the ache, I finally bend and make quick work of cleaning up what fell to the ground: mail, junk mail, more junk mail, another piece of jun—

I stop, the last envelope catching my attention. Addressed to me from a South Carolina Law Office. That's where my parents are from. That is one of the things I do remember before they left me to start their life without me.

Trembling hands open the cream-colored envelope. What if it's them? My parents? I stop once the lip of it opens. Do I want to read this? Is this even something I'm ready for? They never wanted me. I was a waste, unlovable, and an inconvenience in their lives. Is this just going to be another punch to my gut, a blow to my already fragile heart?

I grew tough skin, but there are still wounds unhealed beneath the surface. Can I take more? Maybe it's still the nerves and fear molding into a mess inside me, but I give in and pull out the letter. The words are typed out with a generic font, and my eyes slide across the page, sentence by sentence.

> **Dear Ms. Hanna Whittington,**
> My name is Jack Loweson. I'm the attorney for your grandfather, J.D. William Whittington. I'm reaching out to you in these unfortunate circumstances and after great work. You are one hard woman to track down. Your grandfather has recently passed, and per his Will and Testament, he has named you not only as his Power of Attorney but has left all fortune and physical assets as of his passing.
> There are multiple physical possessions left as well as his estate. I would like to get in contact with you to discuss further instructions and manners of his Will and Testament. We are able to conduct a phone call or plan a time in which we could fly you to my location. Money has been placed aside for travel expenses if needed. A funeral has been held already, but due to the lengths it took in

order to find you, the burial has come and passed.

I'm very sorry for the loss of your grandfather. He meant a great deal to us in Cherry Hill, South Carolina. I am sending you thoughts during this hardship. I look forward to hearing from you.

All my best,
Jack Loweson
Loweson's Legal
621 E. Southern Rd.
Suite 203
Cherry Hill, South Carolina 84555
Phone: 555-215-5555
Fax: 555-215-5554

My body feels frozen in time. Everything suddenly loses color, and I'm convinced this is a dream and that the nightly visitor is upping the ante in my head. There is a sharp ringing in my ear, so piercing I'm almost brought to my knees. The words on the page echo in my mind, and now...my body responds, and she chooses flight.

I move, grabbing the suitcase from the top shelf of my tiny closet and begin packing anything I can. Clothes, shoes, all I can fit in one suitcase. I leave everything else, knowing full well I never intend to return.

How? I don't know.

Am I thinking rationally? No.

But I need out.

Changing into some jeans, a bra, tank top, and hoodie, I slip on my shoes and grab the letter. With my free hand, I grab my purse and keys.

I want to say I open the door and, with one dramatic, long pause, turn and look at the life I'm leaving behind, but I don't. Slamming the door shut and locking it, I move fast.

Time will catch up and logical thinking will take precedence, but now.

Right now, it's just time to run.

Two

HANNA

A NOISE JOLTS ME AWAKE. THE MORNING LIGHT IS playing peekaboo with the horizon in some farm town as I look out the window of the bus I'm on, which only has four other people, including the driver. When I left, I went to the bus station, grabbed a ticket, and within forty-five minutes of reading the letter that changed my life, I was on a Greyhound to a town called Cherry Hill.

Realizing the noise that woke me up was the bus hitting a pothole, I straighten up and look around. The other passengers are sleeping still.

I crashed within minutes, my rash decision and draining adrenaline finally catching up, and I couldn't keep my eyes open. I left everything—my job, my home, and what little I had—in New York because of some letter.

What if it's not real? What if this is a scam?

But why would someone do that to me, and how would they

find me and my information? My parents never mentioned a grandparent, and the foster care system never found anyone, but how could they not?

Suddenly, I realize it's most likely the first option, and I am being scammed.

"Shit," I say under my breath, shaking my head and cursing my lack of logical thinking. I reach in my purse and grab the letter, which I read over and over again. Each time I do, I analyze it and come to a conclusion—one most people would disagree with.

This has to be real. And in all honesty, I hope it is. I want to know where I came from. Maybe I have more family. Cousins? Aunts? Uncles? It's unlikely, since no one ever claimed me. But a lonely woman like me who's had no family nor a place to call home, I can only pray there's someone waiting in Cherry Hill for me.

The day passes, the night after that seeming longer, my short bouts of sleep not lasting long, when we finally arrive. The bus station isn't at all what I imagined. Envisioning a dirt road and cows mooing a welcome at me isn't at all what I'm greeted by. I'm charmed by the small town, which is alive with people, window shopping, outdoor coffee conversations, and the occasional bench with friends hanging out. Everything is so very different than New York, which I knew to expect, but seeing it, being in it—it's homey.

I hold the letter tight in my hand and make my way toward the host of the closest café. The stand is outside, and I approach the young man who looks to be no older than sixteen.

"Hi, um...I was wondering if you know where Loweson's Law Offices is located."

He gives me a friendly smile and nods. "I sure do, ma'am."

Ma'am? I really am in the South.

"If you walk up this main street for about five blocks, Jack's office is just on the corner of 5th and Southern, ma'am."

He said Jack's name, so that's a good sign—he's known as a lawyer, so we are one point for no scam.

"Thank you so much. Have a good day." I smile and head in that direction.

It's not a long walk, maybe three minutes or so, before I'm standing outside the exact address and law office stated in the letter. As I step in, a bell rings, notifying the receptionist of my presence.

She's young, her face buried in some gossip magazine. Looking up, she smiles at me. "Hello! Welcome to Jack Loweson's office. Can I help you, sweetheart?"

Better than ma'am.

"Um, yes, my name is Hanna Whittington, and I received a letter from Mr. Loweson about my grandfather's will."

Her face drops, sadness taking over. "Oh, sweetie, we all loved JD. I'm so very sorry for your loss. We were expecting you to call, but it's even better you're here. Let me go see if he's available."

Just like that, she scampers off, and I look around. I take notice of all the pictures of what I assume is this small town over the years, going from black-and-white, to sepia, and then full color, new buildings added each time. Her words echo in my mind as I take in the photos. Was my grandpa some kind of small-town royalty? Even though I knew I had to have grandparents at some point, it does feel weird saying it in my head.

"Ms. Whittington?" A male's voice pulls me from my wayward thoughts. Turning, I'm met with the sight of a man who's about five-foot five, with thick glasses and a sweet smile. There is a hint of sympathy behind his smile, but I don't call it out. I'm not sure who my grandpa was, so the pain of his loss isn't hitting me hard, as it seems to be doing to those in this town.

"Hi, Mr. Loweson?"

"Please, call me Jack. Come on back. It's so good to see you." He glances at my suitcase but doesn't address it, thank God. I don't think there is enough time to get into that baggage. Literally. "I'm sorry we're meeting under these circumstances. Your grandfather was a wonderful man. I'm greatly sorry for your loss."

He stumbles at the tail-end of his apology. He must know I never knew who my grandfather was. Though Jack seems filled with pity, he's probably trying to imagine how I feel. All these years, I've felt lost and like I had no one. Now, I find out there was a grandfather out here, one who loved me enough to leave me his belongings in his passing.

Trauma. More trauma to load onto my already packed shoulders.

"Thank you. If I'm being honest, I don't know why he would leave me anything. I didn't know him." Mumbling the last part,

I look out the window for a moment before continuing. "I didn't even know he existed. My parents left me and took everything with them, including family history." I don't need Jack thinking I'm some sort of entitled brat who made the choice to not be in my grandfather's life. Especially with the way he speaks so highly of the man he seems to have been.

"I understand. There is no need to explain yourself." When I choose not to respond, he picks up on my cue and continues. "We are going to go over the monies and property that were left to you in his will first, and then we will sign all legal documents. You can ask me any questions you have. Do you have a lawyer you would like present?"

I shake my head. I barely have two pennies to rub together, let alone enough to afford a lawyer.

"There isn't anything here that I believe you would need to have counseling for, but I always ask, and I can also act as your lawyer, seeing as I was JD's." His warm smile invites one onto my face.

"Thank you, Jack."

We carry on. The entire time he's speaking, my mind is whirling. I'm overwhelmed, to say the least.

"He left you his home and acreage along with his two dogs."

"Dogs?" I want to curse myself. Finding out about the million dollars he left, the land and estate, didn't get me speaking, but dogs? Maybe I should plead insanity and just leave.

"Yes, his two Great Danes." He smiles, no doubt reading me

like an open book.

"Oh, names?"

"Dorothy and Clyde."

"Adorable."

When I say nothing more, he continues, ignoring my lapse in sanity. He must be a really good lawyer to pick up so well on awkward exchanges. Hours later, we are finally at the end of the meeting.

"Now, we went over a lot of information. Do you have any questions for me? You haven't said much." What really is there to ask? Twenty-four hours ago, I was living a life in New York, a nobody with nothing to her name but her romance novel and a closetful of thrifted clothing.

I start simple. "How did he pass?"

"He had a heart attack. He had some health problems with his heart prior."

"Oh." I never met him, but that hits something in me, making my own heart hurt.

"Why didn't he find me?" *That's good, Hanna. Go zero to sixty.*

"I'm not sure. I wish I had more answers for you on why he didn't. But that is one thing he never discussed with me. Kept conversations about you scarce."

"Okay." I don't know what else to even say.

"How about I give you a ride out to the house? Show you around the town a little bit?"

Peering up from my nails I didn't realize I was picking at, I'm met with his soft gaze. "Thank you. That would be great."

We finish initialing everything, and I grab the small folder with copies of what I signed and JD's will, as my other hand grabs my suitcase.

My old life in one hand, worth nothing more than twenty dollars, while the other hand holds my new life...worth millions. The comparison is heartbreaking yet filled with hope. I have so many questions, some I will try to find answers to and others that were buried with my grandfather.

Nevertheless, I'm going to find something here in this small town—the dream I had of running away and living a new life, where I wasn't just a lonely girl. Or maybe a chance to reinvent myself. Maybe even find myself. Being a child of the state, an orphan, it leaves you empty sometimes—or *filled* might be more accurate, with questions, pain, and a constant longing for something more. Something you can't quite place, but here in Cherry Hill, South Carolina, I hope to find it.

Three

THEO

One Week Later

THE SOUND OF THE COFFEE STEAMERS PULLS MY attention off my phone in my hand.

"Black coffee with two sugars for Theo," the barista at our local coffee shop calls out, and sliding my phone into the back pocket of my jeans, I walk up to the counter. She gives me a knowing look, one I'm not new to.

"Here you go, Theo. Is there anything else I can grab for you?" She presses her breasts together with her biceps as she leans over the counter. If I had time, I would possibly entertain her obvious idea, but I have to get to work, and I'm already running behind from the fiasco that is my sister, Brenda, today and the new guy she started seeing.

"No, sweetheart, maybe another time." I wink, and she practically turns into a melted pile of goo. With that, I walk out, climb into my truck, and leave, making my way toward my house.

It feels weird being back in Cherry Hill, yet it's good to be home. A few years ago, I moved to New York for my job.

Now, I've been called home to do a job, which is ironic. What are the odds that a job would call me to the small town I was born and raised in. Coincidence? Or fate. I'm going with fate. Means the job will be easy. The big man or whatever is out there must be on my side, giving me a break and rewarding me for the years of shit work I've had to do. This will be my best paid job yet.

My phone rings, pulling me from my thoughts.

"Brenda, I just left there. Is that piece of shit back again?" This morning, I got a call that the guy my little sister just started seeing is really married with a family of his own, and when Brenda caught on to his sleezy ass, she ended it. But he didn't like rejection.

"No, I just wanted to call and tell you thank you. It's good to have you home."

I pull the phone away and look at it as if it isn't real.

"Was that a compliment from my little sis?" I prompt when I bring it back to my ear.

She scoffs. I can tell she rolled her eyes with that one. "Don't be a dick about it. I'm serious. I'm glad you're home, but you're still annoying." She grew up with me always hovering and protecting her like she was made of glass. She felt suffocated by me growing up, so when I left Cherry Hill, she was able to gain her own freedom. She gained freedom, yet I went mad with knowing I couldn't always be there for her. That the control I have to have with all things slipped out of my hands when it came to her. But I trained her well. I love her and am proud of the kickass, take-no-shit firecracker she has become. But I will still be first in line to defend her with no mercy and would protect her against anyone and anything.

"You're welcome." I choose not to give her too much shit. It's been a hard morning; she's had enough for one day. When he wouldn't leave her house and threatened her, she called me, and I had to come put the fear of God in him with my pistol, taking the butt of it and rearranging his nose. That seemed to do the trick. I think being back here, hating the idea of it, and combining it with my pent-up sexual frustration made me snap in a way. I fight daily to contain it. Poor schmuck—not really—was at the receiving end. Should have learned how to listen better.

"Anyway, how long are you here for?"

"Until the job is done."

"Hmm."

"What?" I ask.

"Nothing, just seems random that you are *here* for a job. What kind of tech job would bring you to Cherry Hill?"

I take a second to respond. "Sis, what's really going on? Since when do you care about my job?"

She lets out an exasperated sigh. "Fine. Listen, Mom and Dad have been fighting a lot. Mom is constantly calling me to cry, and I've just felt...lonely since you left."

Straight punch to the chest. "Why didn't you call and tell me this, B?"

"I don't know. It's like you left to get away from all of us. I didn't want to bother you."

Damn it. Did my leaving really create such a gap, an absence in her life? I didn't leave because of her. I left, because I outgrew Cherry Hill. This small town is just that—small—filled with rumor mills, lack of opportunities, and a dating pool of barely any fish. I wanted to get out, see the world, chase my dream job, and I couldn't do that here.

"I didn't leave because I wanted away from you. That was never the reason. Okay?" I soften my approach, pulling onto the dirt drive of my small two-bedroom vacation home I bought last year. I had intended on coming around more, so buying a place for me to stay when I visited seem logical. Shutting down my truck, I wait on her response.

"I'm sorry. Today has just been shit. I really liked him, and he turned out to be another douche like all the men I've dated before him. There aren't that many fish in this little sea anymore. I'm probably going to die alone, with cats. Cats that will feed on me, because I'll have no one to come check in on me." I laugh.

"Whoa, cut the dramatics. You are not going to die alone and be feasted on by cats." I open the door and step out of my truck. "You could come to New York. You would love it there."

"No. No way. I don't fit in, in a big city."

That has me nearly stopping in my tracks. "Brenda. Come on. Your personality is too big for this Podunk town. The city is just the right place for you to be yourself."

"You're just saying that because I put the disturbing image of me being eaten by cats in your head. I don't need the pity."

"I'm serious." Opening my front door and dropping my keys onto the table in the entryway, I make my way toward my home office.

"Yeah, okay. Anyway, don't tell Mom I told you about their fighting."

"I won't," I lie. I don't know why she hasn't called me to tell me they're having problems.

That's not like them. My parents have always been the town's star couple. High school sweethearts and all that shit.

"I will see you at family dinner on Sunday. Love you," she says.

"Love you too. See ya then." Ending the call, I finally get my ass in gear and work.

Opening my email, I click on the assignment information. It's easy, just like I told my client back in New York. I will be done in no time, back up north within a month.

While I work out my plans to complete the job so I can ensure I'm not here too long, I can't help but think about my parents and what I plan to do about them. I can't just ignore what Brenda told me. Something tells me she knows that, and though she asked me not to say anything, a part of her wants me to.

Maybe after dinner, I'll take each of my parents aside and find out just what in the hell is happening between the two of them. How much did I miss while I've been away, and what the hell else is this month going to bring?

Four

THEO

Standing in front of my bathroom vanity a few days later, I peer up at my reflection under hooded lids, my brown eyes darkening. Today was a shit day, so bad it consumed me, and I felt like every little damn thing could set me off. I felt rage boiling over into each activity, work email, job task, and more. I know why it's this way; there's no reason a normal person would feel this way, but I'm not normal.

No, I have tastes, a hunger that has to be met, and since I've been here, it hasn't. Leaving me violently in need of it.

Control.

Lust.

Venom for my veins.

I need to bury myself inside a woman, lose my mind in the control and dominance I would claim from her. But I can't do that here. Everyone is either married or we went to high school together. Besides, they wouldn't satisfy my needs. This dead space isn't the only reason I left for the city. It didn't hold the amount or the variety of women I need in order to sate my cravings, to please the palate.

A decent man would say that is cruel, but I'm not a decent man. I'm a devil among saints. There is a side of me that no one sees, not even the women who submit to me. On their knees, peering up at me, praying I show them who I really am. Little do they know, I already have. I'm a monster, and no one would ever know.

Looking at my naked form, even I notice I'm more defined than I usually am. I've always been fit, but the new dips, muscles, and cuts along my skin are proof of this pent-up need. I've been working out whenever I get the chance, using it as a way to get my...aggression out. My eyes trail the length of my tense body, ending at my hard cock.

"Fuck." I need to release some of this frustration or this dinner with my sister and parents is going to be murderous. Closing my eyes, I wrap my fist tightly around my stiff shaft, the head wet with pre-cum. I smear the warm liquid around the head and down the length, my veins throbbing with my pulse.

I close my eyes and begin stroking myself. Slow at first. So fucking slow. Doing this on purpose, knowing the buildup will make the climax that much more intense and satiate me enough to get me through.

"Oh yeah," I moan, the sound filling the bathroom. I try to imagine a woman here with me, but it's no use. I just need a release; no time to try to play a highlight reel of all the faceless women I've fucked. I pick up speed, chasing the oblivion I know can never truly be reached. It's a temporary fix for a man like me. Never fully satisfied. Never able to settle.

"Fuck yeah," I growl, the sound feral.

Get the job done.

Go back to New York.

And fuck the first willing woman you see, I tell myself, the climax building. Just the knowledge that I'll be able to go home and find a plaything is all I need to shoot violent streams of cum onto the bathroom counter and into the sink.

I keep my eyes on the mirror as I come down from the top of my pleasure. The blackness in my eyes begins to fade as the brown in them returns.

The monster is silenced…for now.

* * *

YOU READY TO BE BOMBARDED WITH A MILLION AND one questions?" my sister asks two steps ahead of me as we approach my parents' front door.

"Yes," I respond.

"What's with the dark and broody? You okay?" Brenda eyes me inquisitively.

Snapping out of it, I open the door and nod for her to go in. "Nothing. Work was busy today. I'm distracted."

She chuckles. "Who knew IT could be so tiring? You would think you were doing illegal stuff."

Furrowing my brows, I laugh at her as I shut the door and remove my jacket. "What?"

"You know, like hacking systems to find bad guys. That would be stressful. Helping companies get their systems up and running doesn't seem like it would be this taxing, I guess." She shrugs.

"Then it's a good thing you aren't in IT. You wouldn't be able to keep up." I tilt my head, watching her roll her eyes.

"Smartass." She turns and heads to the kitchen.

Rolling up the sleeves of my flannel, I follow her, a cocky grin on my face. I love when she can't think of a better comeback. The only thing I miss about this town is seeing my sister.

I don't like people. I have some male friends back in New York, but for the most part, I don't like many. They seem boring, lacking anything to add to my life. Oh, I know it sounds cruel, but once again, I never claimed to be a nice man, a gentleman. Self-serving isn't a negative term to me. Brenda—she is the only one who doesn't make me want to plug my bleeding ears because of boring conversation. Maybe it's because she and I are cut from the same cloth and tend to act like it. She can be just as fierce and controlling, not as deeply rooted as me, but she is very much a hardheaded, strong-willed person, just like her brother.

"Theo! Baby!" my mother screeches.

I exhale, not ready for a night of her giddy behavior. I love my mother, don't get me wrong, but she is terrible at knowing when to knock it down a few pegs, to stop overcompensating with volume and cheer, when really something in her life is in shambles. Like her marriage.

Knowing my parents, they are going to act as if everything is fine. That's where Brenda and I differ, why she asked me not to say anything. She can separate her feelings at times, treat different people with more care than others. Me, I straight-shoot everyone. Maybe Brenda doesn't want to confront my parents and call them on their bullshit, but me? I won't hesitate.

I don't want to be a father and never will be, but I will say it doesn't take a genius to know that lying and putting up a terribly hidden façade that your marriage is great so your children don't suffer is far more damaging than just divorcing. They have to know that, right?

Clearly not.

"Mom. Hello." I kiss her cheek and stand tall again before moving to my dad and giving him a sideways hug. That's enough affection for the night.

"Son. Good to have you home. We didn't think you would make time to come spend with us." Ah, there it is. Maybe my father has learned. Or maybe he has hidden this part of himself all these years and has reached the peak of not giving a fuck. He wouldn't normally call anyone out on things like that. I can't say I'm mad. I'd rather have honesty than whatever it is my mother is trying to pull tonight.

"Rob," my mother scorns.

"What? He's not a child, Kerrin. We don't have to baby them anymore."

Cracks. There are the cracks. Clearly, my father is bending and breaking faster than my mother is.

"Mom, Dad, can we not? Not tonight," Brenda somberly begs next to me. Mom releases a deep breath, and my father follows suit.

"You're right. Kids, let's eat. We need to talk about some things with you."

"Oh no," Brenda responds, and turning my head to her, I see her eyes are watering. Fuck. As if today wasn't already bad enough. Now, I have to watch my baby sister fall apart.

"Cut the shit, Dad. What do you two want to say?" I don't even blink or flinch when I ask this question. Instead, I take a seat at the table and rap my knuckles against the tablecloth-covered wood—a habit of mine, something I do when I'm trying to decipher something.

"Don't be so crass, Theo. We haven't seen you in almost a year. The least you could do is act like you love this family," my mother scolds like I'm a petulant child.

Taking in a deep breath through my nose, I release it after a brief hold, collecting myself and remembering my control. I can't snap, not with Brenda in the room. She's already tearing at the seams.

"I do love this family. Don't play such a childish card, Mom. But Brenda and I don't need to be fed, told we are loved, and that it has nothing to do with us. We're grown, so sit and tell us what I'm sure we already know." I cut the thick air with my even, low timbre.

My mother sighs, and my father shakes his head, using his

hand to massage the back of his neck, an attempt at relieving the tension.

"Okay, you're right. Your father and I have to tell you kids something, and we want you to know—"

"Mother," I cut her off. Did she not hear a word I just said? My parents have always had a predictable marriage. Robotic, if you will. I'm not shocked the cracks are showing and the dam is breaking.

"Fine. Your father and I are separating." She finally lays it out.

"No, can't we help you two work this out?" Brenda cries.

I place my hands in my lap, my fingers laced as I let my sister work out and come to terms with this. I'll intervene when needed.

My parents and I have never been super close. There wasn't any one thing that happened; I just grew up with a different outlook on life, and it showed. I love my parents, make no mistake, but affection, love, adoration—those left me a long time ago. It stayed here when I went to New York. I would be the first person at their aid, but that doesn't mean I'm the first to break bread any chance we get. Relationships in all forms have never been my forte—except in the sexual nature.

"No, sweetie. We want to attempt to remain friends. We tried for a long time. Therapy and more. It just isn't our time." My mother leans over and places her hand atop Brenda's, and my father rounds the table to comfort her as well. Standing beside her, he stoops and kisses the top of her head.

"We know this is hard to see, but marriages don't always work."

I fight the urge to voice out loud that prolonged monogamy *never* works. But I bite my tongue. This is for Brenda to process. I'm just here to make sure they don't overstep and push her too far. Brenda is passionate. So are my parents. And they all will fight for dominance. I guess all of us got that trait. If things got too impassioned, it could lead to a world war.

"But what does that mean? Are you both going to stay in this house? This town?" She wipes at her tears. The sight of her hurting has my jaw ticking. I don't like watching her break like this.

"Yes, we will be staying here in this town, but your father is getting his own place in the next couple of months. We are so sorry, sweetie."

"I don't even know what to say." My sister sniffles.

"We know. It will take some time to process this, but we are here to help in any way. We love you both," my father adds.

"Theo?" Brenda calls out to me, seeming to beg for me to prove this is all a bad dream.

"I'm sorry you two couldn't make it work. Brenda, if Mom and Dad aren't happy, we can't and shouldn't force that on them. It will be okay. You will be fine," I reassure her.

Dropping her head, she nods at her lap. "Yeah, I know you're right. I just don't want to stop our dinners and these moments where we can come together and unwind. Be an actual family."

"We can still and should still do that." My father glances back and forth between the three of us. I nod, agreeing to it, because I will most likely be gone before we even have another one of these…lovely and lively dinners. The job will be completed, and then I will go back home. It's Brenda I worry about most. But as long as she has me, she won't need to worry.

The only person I have a soft spot for is her. I'd never admit that to her, because her ego is already big enough when it comes to who is the superior sibling, but it's true. I have a space open in my closed-off heart that is reserved just for her.

The night carried on peacefully, no tables being flipped, no having to play referee, so all in all, it was a nice dinner, and even I enjoyed catching up with my family. I ended up not needing to take my parents to separate rooms to talk, which worked in their favor. I'm too pent up. Too enthralled with the stresses of my job, and being back here and celibate, that I could detonate at any moment. This dinner played out in the best way it could for not just me but for my family.

Five

HANNA
One Week Prior

"YOU GRANDFATHER HELPED BUILD HALF THIS TOWN." Drawing my gaze away from the storefronts and to Jack behind the wheel, I smile sweetly.

"Really? Is that what he did? Construction?"

"Oh yeah, and many other things. He was in construction, investments...hell, he was a man of many trades. That's why he is so well known here."

"It's a small town. Doesn't everyone know everyone?" I question.

"True. I guess it's more like, that's why he was so well *loved*. He was always the first in line to help when anyone needed anything. Very selfless."

I don't respond to that. I can't help but feel a tinge of resentment. Clearly, he knew of me. How come he was so willing to help and be the town's shining star to everybody but his own flesh and blood?

He had to have known about my parents. He had to know

they left me behind and that I grew up in the foster care system, occasionally staying with families until they'd have kids of their own and didn't want me anymore.

"That's the town grocer, not too far from your house. Walking distance. However, I know the owner of the car dealership on the other side of town if you're wanting a new vehicle."

"Thanks. It looks like my grandfather has a couple of cars in the paperwork. But I'm not sure yet. Still trying to process everything. I will let you know what I decide to do."

"No worries. Most places here are within walking distance, so you should be good for your basic needs," he informs me.

"Anything else I need to know about Cherry Hill?" I question as we pass the final building and drive past beautiful open fields with different crops—flowers, cotton, and so much more. I've never seen anything so beautiful. Truly. Most of the time, all I see is people, high-rise buildings, and trash thrown all over the ground.

"Not much. Everyone here is friendly and willing to help with whatever it is you need. I will leave my cell number with you, and you can call me whenever." He pauses. "JD was one of my dearest friends. I know he would want you to feel as safe and comfortable as possible. You can count on me. Know that you at least have one friend here so far."

He gives me such a sweet smile I almost feel overwhelmed by it, because today is just a lot. I can't really say much or offer any means of appreciation for his hospitality, because I really just need a second to breathe. "Sure. Thank you."

Just like he stated, the place isn't too far from the city limits. "We're here," he says as we pull up to what I can only describe as a beautiful masterpiece. This place is like one you see in the movies, a two-story home painted white with black shutters and accents, and the best part is the wraparound porch.

"It's perfect. Truly perfect." I didn't mean to say that out loud.

"He built it just a couple of years back. It's the gem of Cherry Hill."

"You don't say. This is too much. Are you sure there isn't someone else he would want to leave this to?"

He laughs. "No, ma'am. You are the sole person named in his entire will. Welcome home."

"I—I can't accept this. It's too much," I repeat the second we're out of the car.

"You are welcome to sell it to someone, but other than that, it's yours. Come, I'll help you get inside."

I follow slowly, unable to take my eyes off of everything. The home is truly a work of art; I can't believe this is happening. I would pinch myself, but I don't want Jack to think I've gone mental. Though, could he blame me?

"Here are the keys. There is a shed just a few feet from the back steps that has yard tools and equipment in there if you need anything. And here, take my card." Pulling out his wallet, he pulls out his business card and hands it to me.

"Thanks, I'm sure I will use this. I'm just a little overwhelmed today. Thank you for everything, Jack."

"You are more than welcome. We will talk soon, I'm sure, but have a good rest of your day." With that, he's off, and I stay standing in the middle of the entryway, the sound of the door closing deafening.

"This is your new life, Hanna," I whisper to myself. "Where do we start?"

I finally set into motion, walking into the first room on the left, which is a sitting room. The furniture is homey, surprisingly modern and not outdated. I don't know what I was expecting—maybe floral couches with plastic on them? There's some art hanging above the fireplace, the shiplap wall and black brick fireplace contrasting perfectly. My grandfather must have paid someone to decorate. This looks like it was done by professionals who know styles and art.

There is an open passage that leads to the kitchen, and I head there next. This is even more stunning than the front room. The cabinets are painted white with glass doors so you can see everything inside. And everything in them is organized and monochromatic, leaving it to look clean yet effortless. The countertops are a gray, white, and black marble, and the backsplash is glossy white tile.

The kitchen island is shiplap and marble, with a vintage, western-style canned light hanging above it. There is a window above the sink, and stepping up to it, I peer out into the wide-open green land. The hills are rolling in the distance, and I'm stuck in place, looking at the beauty.

Peace.

This is what that must feel like. True and utter peace.

Willing myself to step away to explore some more, I still hold onto that feeling that peering out the window gave me. Hoping it will bring me some comfort and understanding during all this. Stepping back into the hall, I head back toward the front door. There is a living room to the right and stairs. I look into the living room, seeing a TV and a sectional couch with a coffee table. There is a bay window that looks out to the front of the house.

The upstairs is next. The stairs are a dark wood on top and accented with black on the front panels, and the rails are white. Details—JD must have been anal retentive, very particular, and detailed. I'm not that way. Sure, I'm no slob, but I'm in no way this attached to perfectionism. The hallway at the top of the stairs is lined with windows; it's unique. I would have never thought to do something like that.

Detailed and talented. I'm learning something new about the man who was my grandfather. It's feels weird saying that, but I guess I can't deny it or run from it now. I'm in the middle of the beautiful farmhouse home he left for me with millions of dollars now in my name. Each bedroom is simple. Beds, dressers, closets, the typical, but the master bedroom, this is anything but typical. The entire right wall, facing the back of the house, is floor-to-ceiling windows. And I do mean the entire wall, in height and width.

What on God's green earth is this? It is beautiful. I would never have thought to do something like that, but I'm thankful he did. The peace I felt looking through that much smaller kitchen window returns, and I realize in this moment that I will be sleeping here, and that will be my view from sunup to sundown.

I step into the bathroom, which is all white—white and silver marble countertops, white vanity, a separate all-glass shower, and a large jacuzzi tub with a window above it.

"Grandpa must have loved windows," I whisper, walking through to the attached closet. Flipping on the light, I'm hit with a scent. It's a cologne and fresh linen smell. For some reason, it brings tears to my eyes, especially as I look at all the clothes and shoes surrounding me. All this time, I had someone. Someone out there who I could have called family. A solace I could have leaned on when everything was dark.

And believe me, everything was dark, often.

I had no one and nothing, while there was a man here who could have loved and accepted me. That's when it happens. I sink to the ground and sob in the middle of a stranger's closet. Feeling pain and loss for someone I never knew, but moreover, what he could have been to me and how I will never have the chance to know. I officially have no one, and that is a reality.

I cry because of the life I fled from. I hated my life there, wished so often for an escape or alternate reality, and now I have it. Here in Cherry Hill. I have it, and yet I can't pick a side to be on. Happiness or loneliness.

Suddenly, I'm interrupted by the sound of the doorbell. I wipe frantically at the tears and snot running down my face. Attractive.

Standing, I stop to look in the mirror and see it's useless. Even cleaned up, my face is red and swollen from crying. Oh well, might just be Jack who forgot to give me something.

Hurrying down the stairs when the bell rings again, I nearly miss the bottom step, catching myself on the front door. Shaking my head, I stand up straight, righting myself, and open the door.

"You all right? Sounded like something fell!" A woman stands in front of me with two Great Danes who must be Dorothy and Clyde.

"Oh yeah, I'm fine. Just tripped. I'm not very coordinated." She's stunning—tall, auburn hair, green eyes, and a figure I would kill for.

"Oh no. Well, I'm glad you're all right! I'm Brenda. I live two houses east of here. I was watching the pups while waiting for your arrival." Her smile is genuine and soft, very welcoming.

"Thank you so much," I tell her, and she lifts her brows, still smiling at me. "Oh God, sorry. I'm just having a long day. I'm so rude. Hi, I'm Hanna. It's nice to meet you."

The dogs are sniffing me, their tails wagging rapidly.

"They like you. They are great guard dogs but also very sweet. You will love them."

I stoop down, and immediately they are on me, attacking me with kisses. "Ah! Oh my gosh!" I laugh, trying to save myself, but they're huge, and I'm outnumbered.

"Clyde, Dorothy, come on. Give your new mama a break." Brenda helps me up, and once I'm free and back to my full height,

I give her a thankful smile. These dogs are anything but pups. They must be nearly my height when they stand on their hind legs.

However, no complaints here. I know I'm a long way from New York, and that is now in the past; I'm in a new place, in the middle of farmland, and alone. They might bring me some peace and make me less afraid of the things that go bump in the night.

"Thank you. I've never had dogs. They may be more of an undertaking than this house."

"They seem it, but I promise they are the sweetest yet fiercely protective. I passed a pedestrian on my way here, and they nearly chased him to the other side of the road." We share a laugh.

"Good to know. Um, I'm not sure if there is anything here to drink. Would you like to come in?" I don't usually socialize like this, but it's the least I can do, and wouldn't it be nice to know at least one person besides Jack?

"I would love to, but I gotta work in the next thirty minutes, and my car is in the shop, so these feet are my ride. But how about I bring you some groceries after work? That way you can get settled, and then this week, I can give you the juicy details of the town and everything you need to know in Cherry Hill." She winks.

Smiling, I tuck my dirty-blonde hair behind my ear. "I couldn't ask you to buy me groceries. I have to find a bank and set up all my finances here, so I don't have any cash on me."

Waving me off, she scoffs, turning to head down the front porch steps. "Please, I don't need your money. Consider it a welcome gift. Where you from anyway?"

"Oh, uh, New York."

"Oh yeah? You're a long way from the city, babe. Get used to favors, small acts of kindness, and an ungodly number of pies. The people here are way different than those city types. See ya tonight!" And like that, she jaunts off down the paved driveway and back onto the road toward town.

"Well, okay then." Shutting the door, I turn, and I'm met with two sweet sets of puppy dog eyes and wagging tails. "Dorothy, Clyde, what do we do now?"

Six

HANNA

WHEN I HAD A MINUTE TO REALLY SIT DOWN AND collect my thoughts, which didn't get collected or even the slightest bit unraveled, I decided to make work of the closet upstairs. Taking the small amount of clothes I brought with me, I fit them onto a rail, taking up nearly no space at all. Could I clean out the closet? Yes. Am I ready or feel like it's right? Absolutely not.

I just got here, and I can't tell my head from my ass. So taking on that type of project just seems...futile. Another day, another time. But looking at my clothes in the closet, I feel it's more noticeably pitiful, given the house it's in. That's like rags sitting in riches, literally. Does this town even have a place to shop for clothes?

Money—the next point nagging my brain. I have loads of money now. More than I care to admit. Spending it, knowing it's mine, seems daunting. Just because I didn't know the man, it doesn't mean I don't feel bad or as if I'm using him. Is that my intention, no. But come on. That's madness, sick almost.

"Hey, Grandpa I knew nothing about, thanks for the millions. Sorry 'bout your death. I'm going to spend all your money now and live in your home and act as if this is all just another day!"

Crazy. I'm officially insane. I'm talking to myself, and the audience that watches me is just as much on the crazy train as I am, as Dorothy and Clyde stare at me, not judging me, just... staring.

Releasing a sigh, I pat their heads again and pull down some distressed jeans and a black off-the-shoulder Def Leppard tee I found at a thrift shop, then take my long hair and throw it up in a loose, low-hanging bun. Setting the clothes on the bathroom counter, I then start up the bath and moving back to the sink. I open the drawers and cabinets, looking for some sort of bath salts, bubbles, or even just some body wash.

The fourth drawer is the winner. I find some scented bath salts and dump them into the rising water. The aroma fills the bathroom, and I sink into the hot water, blowing out a deep breath. I release as much off my shoulders as I can, almost dissociating, which is something I'm good at. Seeing as I grew up in foster homes, making temporary connections in which I had to sever more often than I wish I ever had to do.

The troubles of my life just seem to fade, like the heat of the water as it grows cold after an hour. Finally, I will myself out and get dressed, preparing for Brenda to return.

THE DOORBELL RINGS, AND THE DOGS START BARKING, running to the door with wagging tails. I see Brenda with some bags in her hands and a giant smile. Opening the door, I greet her, "Hey! Welcome back," moving aside to invite her in. I take some of the bags from her hands, and we make our way into the kitchen.

"I'll never get over how beautiful this house is. My mother and JD really made this place something special."

"Your mother?" I question, placing the bags on the kitchen counter next to the fridge.

"Oh yeah, sorry. My mom, Kerrin, she's an interior designer. She helped your grandfather design this place."

There it is. I knew he had to have some help; this place is literally flawless. "That makes sense. I mean, I didn't know JD, but I couldn't believe he'd do all this alone."

She nods, and the smile that seems to never really leave her face widens just a bit more. "Yeah, he had expensive taste but terrible execution, so insert my mother. And hey, we don't have to talk about him if it's too much. I can only imagine all you are processing after losing a loved one."

I swallow thickly, past the lump that has formed in my throat with that statement.

"Oh, um…I don't know how much you know, but I never met JD. I wasn't even aware I still had any living family." That makes her smile finally leave her face, and I hate the pity.

"Oh, Hanna. I'm sorry. I shouldn't have said anything. I can go. I don't want to overwhelm you, and I basically just shoved my own foot in my mouth."

"No, no. Please. I don't expect you to know a stranger's whole life story. It's no big deal." I pause, shocked that I'm about to admit this aloud, as it is very unlike me. "Besides, I could use the company. Today really has been a lot."

Her features soften, and she reaches out, placing her hand on my forearm. "Listen, I may be a stranger, but I don't have to be. I'm here to be a friend and get to know you, and in time, if you feel like you wanna talk about it, you so can."

"Thank you." I give her a nod, my tongue clicking as I shift the conversation. "I will be going to the bank tomorrow, and I really insist you let me pay you back for all this." I wave my hand over the bags of food we begin to unpack.

"Not a chance. I told you it's a welcome gift."

Rolling my eyes, I sigh. "Fine, at least let me order us some pizza tonight." I have a credit card with a little room on it; it's the least I can do for her kindness.

"I won't say no, and check it out! There are still some beers in the fridge," she says, and I turn with my hands filled with items and smile. Sure enough, there are some beers left in the fridge. "Oh, and some nasty molded leftovers. Those need to go."

"Ew."

She pulls out some glassware with moldy food that looks like lasagna—or what used to be. "Yeah." Moving to the trash, she dumps it out. "Remind me to take that out before I leave tonight." We both laugh.

"For sure. Now, pizza joint recommendations?"

"Yes! The only pizza shop we have in town, Mama Zeppa's." She pulls out her cell and makes work of typing something. "Here's the number. I'm simple; pepperoni is my favorite. But they have some really good ones. I know New York is famous for pizza, so I bet you have better taste than me."

"No, pep is good. A personal favorite of mine as well."

"Look at that, already one thing in common." Winking, she pops the tops on two beers.

Placing an order and finishing up putting away the groceries, we finally make it into the living room with beers in hand.

"So what do you plan to do now that you're here?" Brenda asks.

Debating, I quickly think over if I want to tell her everything. Sure, she has shown me kindness and seems like she would be able to handle the story, but is it too much?

"Hey, you can talk to me. I promise I'm a great listener. My parents and brother can attest to that." She laughs, and I return it with a sheepish smile.

"Well, I think I need to just figure out as much as I can about JD. Find *myself* a little bit in the process," I mumble off the last part.

"You really didn't know about him at all?" Her brows furrow.

"No. I mean, I knew there had to be grandparents at some point, but whether they knew of me or if they were still alive was the question."

"Your parents never kept you in contact with him?"

I scoff, messing with the neck of the beer bottle. "They didn't even keep me in contact with *them*. I was a foster kid."

"Holy hell, Hanna." It isn't a shocked response; no, it's filled with empathy.

"Yeah. My parents didn't really want to be parents. Dumped me in the state's hands and skipped town."

"Grade-A parenting there," she mocks, and this actually makes me chuckle a bit.

"The best."

"So, clearly, JD knew of you. How come he didn't make himself known to you?"

I shrug. "You and I are wondering the same thing." I take a swig of my beer. "I think that's been the hardest pill to swallow with this whole thing. Not the house or inheritance but the why. Why did he never come to me when he knew I was out there this entire time?"

"I wish I had those answers for you." I can tell she wants to ask something, but she hesitates.

"What? You can ask me."

"Well..." Readjusting herself, she sits on her feet, tucking them under her. "Do you know where your parents are? Can you ask them?" Okay, maybe I don't need to be so willing to just take questions about my life. That one hurt me more than I anticipated it would.

"No, I don't. I could probably pay to find them with the inheritance, but I would really have to think about what would come with all that."

"That's true." Pausing, she looks around the room. "Listen, this is heavy. I don't want to overwhelm you more, so let's talk about something else. The rest can come when you're ready." Brenda isn't dumb. It's obvious she picked up on my internal reaction to her last questions.

"Ditto. So what about you? Who is Brenda?"

"Well, I'm five ten, and I like to— just kidding. What do you want to know?"

"You said you have a brother? Younger? Older?"

"Older. And he never lets me forget it. Super overbearing and protective, more so than our own father. But what's new. Isn't that what all big brothers do?"

"So I hear." I chuckle. "His name?"

"Oh shit, yeah, his name is Theo. He actually lives in New York too. He works in tech."

"No way! Small world. Where in New York?"

"Brooklyn."

"Seriously? I don't know a Theo, but that's not far from me. Doubt we've crossed paths though, as there are basically a hundred people per square foot." We laugh in unison.

"True. Yeah, he hated it here, did damn near anything to get out of this town. We never pinned him for a tech guy, but I guess he found his calling." She shrugs.

"Hey, we all have hidden talents. And your parents? Your mom is an interior designer. Dad?" I leave this very open-ended. Given my history, I know never to assume that everyone has a whole home, and nothing is more awkward than having to take your own foot out of your mouth.

"Dad is the owner of the car dealership in town. They have been married for thirty years, high school sweethearts. Adorable. But really almost all couples in this town are high school sweethearts—small town rite of passage."

"Yikes. So you must have someone then?"

Her face drops. "I did. I thought he was going to be the one. But alas, he wasn't."

"Was he an idiot? You're like...the perfect catch."

"He had a whole-ass family. So yes, an idiot—complete fucking moron." She takes a swig. Before she continues, the doorbell rings, and I stand to go get the pizza.

"Hold that thought. We are definitely going to talk about that. I mean, if you want!" I holler over my shoulder as I make it to the door. Opening it, I grab the food left on the bench on the front porch and move to the kitchen. Thank God for the glass cabinet doors or I wouldn't know where the plates are without having to hunt.

"One piece?" I call out.

"Two and some of the cheesy bread!"

I match her portion and head back in, another round of beers under my arm as well. "Okay, can't leave me on a cliffhanger. What happened? How?"

"We met in Charleston; it's about an hour away. I was there for a girls' weekend, and we hit it off. Exchanged numbers, spent weeks texting, Facetiming when we could, and then he came to visit when work let him. This was about six months of truly falling, and I mean *falling hard*.

"Then one day at work, I was minding my business, and a woman approached me—his fucking wife. She was livid, showed me pictures of them with their children and told me to stay away."

I can only imagine. That's awful. "Oh shit. I'm sorry; that's brutal. So you just stopped talking to him?"

She chews her pizza, swallows it, then responds, "Yes, but I gave him a piece of my mind. I told him he was garbage, that I hope his dick falls off, and to never call me again."

I grimace. "I agree. I hope his penis falls off too."

"He keeps calling, but I ignored him, and when I blocked his call, he just called me from another number."

"That's a bit much. When did this all happen?"

Laughing around her next bite, she answers, "It's been seven days exactly." She looks down, sadness trying not to take over her face, but I see it crack through a bit. "Not like I'm counting or anything." Her tone changes, and she laughs it off. I debate asking her about the obvious heartbreak she's wearing in her heart but decide we aren't there yet, and from what I can tell of her so far, she wouldn't be much of an overshare type of person.

"Seriously? So this is fresh. I'm sorry."

Waving me off, she shrugs. "It's okay; it doesn't hurt yet. I'm too mad. I'm sure when that all wears off, I will show up here with beer, ice cream, and a PowerPoint of how I want to destroy his car."

I like her. Brenda is a breath of fresh air, one I hope to continue to get to know. Moving around all the time, and eventually becoming a recluse, I never really made friends. "I'm down. Listen, thank you so much for tonight. I needed a reprieve, and you're really kind."

She reaches over and gently pats my arm. "Anytime, girl. I'm excited to have you here. How about next weekend, you come out with me and my girls? We are just going to Dean's Bar and Grill. They have live music and beer. Come hang out?"

I hesitate for a moment. Crowds? More people? Socializing?

New life, Hanna. A chance to reinvent yourself, I repeat the mantra I declared earlier.

"Okay, but I need to get some new clothes. Is there anything in town?"

"Yes! We can go shopping Friday. I can actually drive us to Charleston. It's an hour away, but they have the best shopping mall."

"Perfect, I also need to work on getting a job here. Will you keep your ear to the ground for me?"

"No need, come work at the market. We need some extra help. I know it's not ideal, but we could use it!" She gets giddy over this idea.

"Your bosses are hiring?"

"Yes, I am."

"Huh?"

"I own the grocery store. It was my grandpa's, and he left it to Theo and me, but Theo moved, so I took it over."

"Really, Brenda, thank you. I'm a fast learner. I appreciate it."

"No need to thank me. Just be there tomorrow morning at eleven, and we will start your training."

"Deal." We shake hands, then spend a couple more hours chatting before we call it a night.

Maybe Cherry Hill will be even better than I anticipated.

Seven

THEO
Present

I HATE IT HERE. THE MOMENT I DROVE PAST THE CITY limits sign, I was reminded why I left. I always told my friends and family that Cherry Hill is a place people go to get old and die. I've already had ten people stop me while running errands in town to tell me about all the things I've missed while being gone, none of it meaning a single thing to me. No thanks.

I've been here for almost a week, and it feels like it's already been a month. This one-month assignment is most likely going to seem never ending at this rate. My week was eventful, to say the least. I could have castrated my sister's ex-boyfriend, but that would have ended with me in the sheriff's chair. No thanks. Breaking his nose with the butt of my gun will just have to be enough. But if he comes back around, I won't hesitate to do worse. My sister is a pain in the ass, but she's a fucking saint and didn't deserve to be played by a liar with a family.

When she confided that his wife showed up at her place of work and told her all about his secret life, my blood boiled. I've always had a short temper, a thirst to lay hands on anyone who does wrong to good people. But my temper isn't the only aspect of my personality. I demand control, need to feel like I'm always in charge and ten steps ahead of everyone.

This is also why women are just a quick fix and not a permanent deal. At least they all know it before sliding into bed with me. I feel like this is cliché. Most men today live by this philosophy. I'm part of a living, breathing breed that sees women for one thing and one thing only—fuck toys.

My mother would be proud.

Not.

Finished with my work day, I make my way into the grocery store, needing to pick up a few things and check in on my sister. She owns this store—well, we both did, but I gave her my share when I left Cherry Hill. Hopping out, I lock the truck and head in. A few locals say hi and share pleasantries, while I try to short stop as many conversations as possible. Rounding the corner, I bump into someone, and at the same time I curse, "shit," under my breath, the person I ran into begins apologizing profusely.

"Oh no, I'm so sorry. I didn't mean to run into you. I'm sorry. Gah, I'm just a klutz. I'm sorry." How many times can a woman apologize in one breath? Our eyes finally lock when I place my hand on her chin and lift it.

"Don't worry about it, gorgeous," I tell her, and I swear when her green eyes meet my brown ones, I nearly lose my footing. This woman is fucking breathtaking, and I don't say that about women. Her eyes are a vibrant green, her long dirty-blonde hair contrasting with them perfectly, and her body, though hidden behind the store's uniform polo, cannot be disguised. She's thick, curvy, her body winding and dipping like it was sculpted for a hungry man, and fuck me, I'm starving.

There has never been a woman with a body like hers that I've salivated over. But a thousand and one thoughts about seeing her naked run through my head.

Focus.

"Um, sorry?" Her eyes are doe-like. God, she seems like she would submit easily. I guess I'll need to find out...and soon.

"You heard me. No worries. You can make it up to me another way, beautiful." I wink at her, and something shifts in her gaze. It's no longer soft and timid. She looks...pained.

"I have to get back to work. I'm sorry about running into you. Have a nice day."

I tell her to stop, but she doesn't. Instead, she picks up her pace.

"Hey! What are you doing here?" My sisters voice interrupts me, ending my pursuit. I'll catch up to her another time. It's a mission of mine.

"I need some food for my place. This is a grocery store," I respond cockily. She slaps my shoulder.

"No shit, smartass. I just meant it's the middle of the day. Why aren't you working?" I look back at the woman's retreating form, her hips swaying temptingly.

"I am working. Trust me. Don't worry about me. Who is that, by the way?"

"That's Hanna, JD's granddaughter."

"Oh. I heard about his passing. How's the town holding up?"

"Sad." She crosses her arms. "But Hanna's story is brutal."

"And how do you know her story? Breakroom chatter?"

"No, she and I have been hanging out this week. I've been taking her shopping, showing her around, and today is her first day working." She nods in Hanna's direction, and something overtakes me.

The man training her puts his hand on her back. It's low. Way too low. But why the fuck would I care? She's a conquest for me while here; that's all. But seeing her smile shyly, tuck her hair behind her ear, and let him touch her? Yeah, I don't like that.

"Easy, tiger, you look like you're trying to melt off Jesse's flesh. What's your deal?"

I finally look back at my sister, and her brows furrow.

"Oh hell no. Damn it, Theo, you are not going to use her like one of your fuck buddies. She's a sweet girl; she doesn't need another blow to her life. You are a bomb that could implode it. Find a new one-night Betty, and leave Hanna alone. Got it?"

"I didn't say I wanted her," I lie through my teeth. I really shouldn't want her. But here we are.

"Good. Besides, I'm taking her out to Dean's Bar and Grill tonight, and I invited her a guy. I'm trying to set her up."

My head whips back to Brenda, unwillingly tearing my eyes away from Hanna. "With who?" I try to say with finesse, an uncaring façade.

"Jesse's brother Anthony. He's recently single, and I think they would hit it off."

"I thought he was married."

"He was, but they got divorced after his wife was caught sleeping with the pastor."

"Goddamn it. Could this town be any more fucking cliché? Anyway. How you holding up? The other day was rough." She starts to move, fixing items in the aisle, avoiding eye contact.

"I don't know. I'm still really hurt. I just want to forget about him and move on." Her voice cracks. There are tears in her eyes, but I don't acknowledge them. She and I are yin and yang, but the one thing we could say makes us similar is our lack of emotional expression. It's not really our thing. Especially not mine.

"He was a dick, sis. Come on now."

"I know, but can we not do this here? Or like...ever again? I just want to act like he never happened." She wipes at her errant tears before turning on me. "Finish your shopping. I got some paperwork to get to. See you Sunday at family dinner." She hugs me, catching me off guard, and by the time I realize it's a hug, she moves, leaving me there to watch her walk off.

I wait a minute, debating what to do, but if I know anything about Brenda, it would be to leave her alone when she needs it. And now, more than ever, she needs it. That guy must have really meant something to her.

I grab the rest of my items and head to the register, looking around me to see if I can spot Hanna, but she isn't up at the front. I in no way want any type of relationship other than a physical one. It's like pursuing a one-night stand; you see something you like, that you're physically drawn to, crave them, entertain them, buy them a drink, and then you share a flood of orgasms. This is no different. I want to use her body and bring her pleasure while selfishly taking mine. I guess I know where I will be going tonight.

Dean's.

* * *

IT'S BUSY TONIGHT, THE DIRT PARKING LOT FILLED, AND the grass banks along the highway are also lined with cars. I walked here, seeing as this place is less than a mile from my home. That's the thing about this town—basically everything is within walking distance unless you are way on the outskirts.

When I step in, the loud country music blares, people hollering their conversations, drunk people whooping and making scenes, and it's like redneck heaven. Sad that this is the highlight of nightlife here in town. In New York, everywhere is a happening place; there is so much to do. How pathetic is it here?

I spot the table I need and make my way straight there. I can only see her back, but I can tell right now that her outfit was picked out by my sister. Legs—her legs are long, tan, and beautiful. My cock is going hard just watching her from across this bar. She's wearing over-the-knee black boots, a long T-shirt-like dress, and her hair is down her back and curly.

That doesn't seem like the timid woman who said sorry a hundred times in a row for simply bumping into me. I wonder how much convincing it took from my sister to get her out of the house and in something like that. I don't know her, but you can tell by her body language that she isn't exactly comfortable or in her usual element.

Walking up to the table, I greet, "Sis, want to introduce me to some of your new friends?" I don't know any of these women. My sister is constantly making new acquaintances, and I've been gone for years. So new faces.

"Oh hell no. Are you really here? I told you not to ruin girls' night for me. Why are you that brother? The one who has to always be there?" Brenda groans, taking a sip of her drink.

"Come on now. Most people would say I don't ruin parties but better yet make them quite fun." I look around at the ladies, my eyes landing on Hanna. She is avoiding eye contact, keeping her head down and her hands playing with the condensation on her beer. A woman of great taste. I prefer beer myself.

"Hanna. Aren't I a lucky bastard, running into you twice in one day?" I turn my body toward her, and she rolls her eyes.

"Theo," Brenda warns.

"No, Brenda, it's all right. I can handle it," she tells my sister, and my brows lift.

"I love the sound of that. You *handling* me."

"You are something else. How the two of you came from the same DNA is beyond me. You're an ass." With that, she turns to grab her bag off the back of the high-top bar stool. "Brenda, ladies, thank you for the invite, but I'm going to head out. Have a good night. I'll see you girls another time."

"No! Hanna, don't let him scare you off. He's just like this with everyone." She glares at me, then softens her features toward Hanna, reaching out for her.

I take it Brenda told her about me being her brother and Hanna told her about our exchange earlier.

"No, really, I'm tired, and I have a lot to do tomorrow. I'm working out in the garden, to try to see if I can revive it."

"I'll walk you home," I tell her.

"Not a chance," Brenda says.

"No thanks. I think I'm good." Hanna turns to leave.

"It's dark out there, baby girl. I don't want you getting hurt," I say after her.

"I'm not a damsel, doorknob." Doorknob? Did she just call me a doorknob? I smirk, clicking my tongue. I chase after her, giving little goodbyes to my sister and her friends. I came here for one thing, and that thing is hauling ass for the exit.

"Hold up. Did you just really call me a doorknob?" I grab her elbow, and she yanks it back, turning to face me. Her almost-emerald eyes glimmer in the neon lights, my chest roaring with want.

"Yes, I did." She crosses her arms, looking up at my towering frame.

I match her stance, not missing the way she admires my leather jacket molding to my muscular physique. "How in the hell is that an insult?"

"How is it not? Who wants to be called a doorknob?" We both stare at one another, my smirk only widening. Finally, she cracks, chuckling at the fact that she called me a goddamn doorknob.

"Knew I could make you laugh," I say proudly.

She starts walking. "No, I was laughing at my own choice of words. But take the credit if it strokes your ego."

"Ego? Is that what you think I'm doing here?"

"No, I think what you're doing is sick and, quite frankly, cruel. That's two for two tonight."

My mouth curves downward, my brows furrowing. What is she talking about? "I'm sorry?" I prompt, and she turns on me again, this time halting me before I topple over her.

"Is this some sort of fetish? Or is there a fun little bet where you flirt with the fat girl in town, make her all gooey-eyed, then laugh about it with your buddies? If that's the case, you can take a flying leap. You *and* the guy your sister brought who took one look, shared less than one drink, and left because no one likes the big girl." Turning on her heels again, she takes off. We both look shocked by her admission. She seems like she wouldn't be the type to share such a vulnerable part of herself.

I'm stunned silent. Sure, I wouldn't usually find women like her attractive, but she is different. Call me a prick, but it's true. I have never been attracted to big women, but she makes it look like a delicacy. How could Anthony not see it? Fuck that guy, Tony. I knew he was trash. It's no loss for her. He's a small-town waste of breath with no experience good enough to handle a fucking body like hers.

Finally, I get my ass in gear, moving to catch up. "Hey! Wait a minute."

"No, leave me alone. I have nothing to say. It's not funny, and I already have a laundry list of insecurities and self-degrading thoughts, so I don't need some small-town dickhead adding to it."

"Hanna, I said stop," I demand, my voice a growl. I'm angry now, wanting to regain the control I always must have. And with her, I don't just crave it; I am breathing for the sole purpose of having her succumb to it.

"Listen, I am not in on some bet. I'm not a child. Second, I am honest with what I say. I don't have time for games." My front is to her back, my body heat matching the temperature of hers. I arouse her too. I know it, and this little chase has made me want her even more. Her chest is rising and falling; I can see it as I tower over her, her breasts playing peekaboo with me. I can't wait to take her like this, her lush ass taking my cock as it disappears between the thick creamy cheeks.

"Then why are you...I don't know...flirting?"

She can't tell? How is she even phrasing that as a question? Isn't it obvious?

"I will work on making you lust after your own body a different time. Until then, you're going to be a good girl and let me walk you home. Got it?"

Her breath hitches as she hesitates to answer me. She turns her head and looks up at me over her shoulder. "Sure. Okay."

Submitting so easily. Fuck this is going to be fun. I have to restrain myself, physically and mentally control my palm from flying forward to smack her ass and get her moving. "Move, greens."

She does, slowly at first, most likely making sure she doesn't fall on her shaky legs. A few moments pass, and she finally speaks, "Why did you call me greens?"

"Your eyes. They're the first thing I noticed. They are fucking stunning, Hanna."

She tucks her hair behind her ears. "Oh, thank you. People tend to compliment those…on the rare occasion I get one." She laughs, but it's fake, because she's clearly been berated and belittled by so many but doesn't want to give them power, so in a sense, she takes on the idea of laughing with them.

I hate her insecurity. Can't she see it—how that body entices people, her heavy breasts, her round ass, curves that look like something to bite, suck, and brutally grab onto while she takes a good fucking?

"So you just moved here?" I shift the topic, saving my plans for a different time.

"Did you know JD Whittington?" she asks.

"Who didn't?"

She snorts. "Yeah, well…me. I'm his granddaughter. He passed away, and I was left his house. So I moved here."

"Brenda mentioned that earlier at the store. I'm sorry to hear that. But you didn't know him?" I knew this, but I decide it's best to act as though I don't.

"No." I think she's going to continue, but it clearly isn't something she wants to talk about with a stranger.

That's fair.

"You like it here so far?"

"Sure. I mean, I definitely like it better than New York."

"Oh really? I live in New York, and I would say the opposite."

She laughs softly. "Well, you and I are very different. New York accepts people like you with open arms. I just take up too much space."

I make a mental note—that's the third time she's talked down on herself.

"Give it enough time and you'll start to see what a hole this place is."

"Someone sounds bitter. Did this town see your ego was too big, so they stopped feeding it?" She mockingly pouts her lips.

"No, but who honestly wants to come here when they're younger than retirement age? You saw this town's nightlife. Dean's Bar. Exciting." Shrugging and wiggling my fingers with heavy sarcasm, I grin when she returns with a roll of her eyes.

"I don't know. It's nice. New York was way too much. No one should like being drowned in seas of people and barely any privacy."

"I won't complain." I watch her carefully. She's exquisite, a mystery, and it's thrilling, the thought of breaking her under my hands, getting her to bend and spill all she is.

"Welp, here we are. Thanks for the walk. It wasn't needed but wasn't the worst. See ya around." She starts up the driveway, and my feet are planted, surprised at how she isn't fawning over me or leaving subtle hints to come inside with her.

Ego-crushing siren...for now.

"Oh, you will be, greens. I plan to see a lot of you." I leave no room for her to read into what I'm saying. I lay it all out. Hanna will be in my hands, in my bed, and at my will. We won't have a relationship beyond that, and I intend to make her see just how fucking thrilling this town can be now that I'm here. Before, it was dull, and after me, she will regret ever meeting me. And I'm the bastard who knows it but don't care. I want her. Crave her. Want to taste that skin against my tongue.

"In your dreams, doorknob." Like that, she's gone, letting herself in and shutting the door. I watch the house for a few moments longer before I finally turn and head home. I had planned for tonight to be spent on more time with her, but that will have to happen another night. If I'm going to get her where I need her, I may just have to turn on the real charm, the romance I will regretfully have to tell her isn't for anything other than respect for her, while I plan to disrespect her in the bedroom.

And I know she will love it. No matter how hard she has to fight her inner warnings. I will break her under me.

Eight

HANNA

WHAT THE HELL WAS THAT?

Hanna, do not—I repeat—do not let him get in your head.

He's messing with me. He has to be. I internally fight with myself as I undress and turn on the shower, still not used to not having to worry about the hot water running out. I've been here a short amount of time, and it's been a hell of a ride already, especially today.

Brenda's brother, is...God, he's hot. Attractive, and not just the normal, decently attractive kind. I'm talking out of this world, someone who you see in movies or have modeling careers. Not someone who could ever be seen with me. Definitely not someone who would want to place their perfectly masculine hands on my imperfect body. He is just playing a game. A cruel one, and I won't let him in.

But it doesn't make it any less painful. It hurts. Why do women like me have to be belittled, shamed, and mocked? Can't we just be left alone...or better yet, loved? Aren't we deserving? Do the lines stretching across our skin mar us to the point of repulsion? Are the curves so disgusting that they don't deserve the intimate touch of a man who we desire? Whether they be men like Theo or men just like us? From *all* types of men. Why are women who look like me so hard to love for all the imperfections we carry instead of all the other things we have to offer? Better yet, why are bodies like mine considered imperfect at all?

I stare at myself in the mirror, now stripped of any fabric. Even I can't stand the sight of me. The world has made women like me seem so undeserving and abhorrent that even *we* can't see anything worthy of touching, loving, or desiring. What a brutal world, and how pitiful that people will always find it acceptable to hurt and tear us apart until all we are is skin, bones, fat—just bodies. Not humans. We are at the mercy of a world so cruel.

Shaking my head, I let those thoughts go.

He's just as shitty as the rest the world. Don't let his nice talk fool you.

Stepping into the water, I ignore anything else but the task of washing away the night and preparing for sleep. I've still been sleeping on the couch downstairs at night. I haven't been able to feel settled enough to make myself at home yet. I've really just been working, spending time in the garden, and reading on the porch, with Dorothy and Clyde running around the front yard.

Maybe one day I'll find the reason JD never came to me or

reached out but left everything he had to his name to me. That's reaching; I doubt I ever will, but it's nice to pretend, isn't it? The water feels nice, I'm exhausted honestly, and I'm thankful I have the next two days at home, because my trainer had these days off prior to my starting there. Now, I can spend time outside in the garden. I also picked up a new novel I'm dying to devour. A mystery thriller romance. Yes, please.

Climbing out, I dry my feet on the shower mat and wrap the bath blanket around my body. Dorothy and Clyde stare up at me as I put on lotion and face moisturizer. They truly have not left my side anytime I'm home. They must miss my grandfather; you can see it in their eyes, I swear it. But the gentle giants protect me like no one nor nothing has before.

"You two hungry? Let's have a snack, huh?" I drop to my haunches and pet their heads before moving to get dressed.

I put on a camisole nightie that reaches midthigh, the white silky fabric cool against my freshly heated skin from the shower. I put my hair up in a towel and head downstairs, the pups in tow. Opening the fridge, I pull out some of the special dog food I got this week. It's supposed to be super healthy for them, and they are already on their second bag.

They start to devour it, and I leave them to it, heading toward the living room. I leave the light off, the kitchen's giving me enough illumination to see everything I need. Laying out the blanket, I make the couch up for the night, turning to grab my pillow off the chair in the corner. Suddenly, I'm stopped when the room brightens from headlights hitting the wall as someone pulls up the dirt driveway.

It happens then, for the first time. The anxiety rises into my chest, causing my heart to beat at a rapid pace.

New York.

I see myself in that small apartment, afraid of who was on the other side of the door, trying to get in. The familiar sensation of being watched anywhere I went creeping in. My chest rises and falls quickly as I try to calm myself enough to walk to the window. I fail miserably...until warm fur hits both sides of me.

This brings me back into the moment, aware of my surroundings. All doors are locked, and I'm safer in this house than I was in that apartment. And to top it off, I have the alarm system.

"Shit." I forgot to set it, like I often do. Moving quietly as if they can hear me, I go to the front door and set the alarm. I release a deep breath, close my eyes for a moment, then peek out the window beside the front door to see a black truck with headlights and a spotlight on. But whoever is in there isn't getting out, and with all the lights shining directly on the house, I can't make out who it is. My heart is running rampant, and my palms are sweating, my nails digging imprints in them. I pick up my phone to call Brenda, and right as she answers, the truck backs out and heads off down the highway.

"Hey! You okay?" Loud music plays, telling me she's still out.

"Shit. Yes, sorry, I just freaked out for no reason. Someone pulled into the driveway and stayed there without getting out.

They just got back on the highway. They probably got lost." Placing my hand over my heart, I step back and head into the living room to take a seat on the couch and attempt to calm down.

"Oh, hun! You're okay! Want me to send my brother back?"

Instantly, I'm able to take my mind off what happened, and I blurt out, "No! I mean, no thank you. It was nothing. I was just a little spooked for some reason. Maybe the beer got to me. I haven't drank in a while." I awkwardly laugh.

Seriously, I sound mental. Brenda doesn't know anything about the whole situation back in New York. After telling her so much already, this one seems like it should be a couple months of knowing each other before I drop a "yeah, so I think I had a stalker," or "something weird, when I found out about my grandpa, I left in the middle of the night, ditching everything without a word and brought only a few things with me."

I have yet to call the landlord and tell him I left. Right now, I'm focusing on getting settled, and with a new job and some of his inheritance, I'll be able to pay the rent there until I feel I can go back, get rid of everything, and end the lease.

One overwhelming task at a time, Hanna.

"Are you sure? He would be more than happy to. It was most likely a lost out-of-towner, but you can never be too sure."

"They left, so there isn't anything he could do. If they come back or it happens again, I will take that raincheck. Thanks, Brenda, and I'm sorry I left so abruptly."

"No! Don't worry! I will come by after work tomorrow, and

we can have dinner and chat a bit more. I hope Theo wasn't a total shithead."

"No, he wasn't. He was surprisingly decent." I leave out the part where he dropped hints of wanting to hook up with me, because it's too hurtful, and I think she and I both know he's doing it to be a dick. I don't need to cause a family feud over it. I'm a big girl. I got it.

"Good. I'll see you tomorrow. You fed me last time, so I will bring the dessert—store bought, because I can't cook nor bake, so that's the best way I can repay! Unless you want me to order takeout?" she hollers as the bar-goers and music seem to get louder and rowdier.

"Sounds good, and no, I can cook! I love it! See ya then, and have a great night."

"Oh, I'll try. The townies who get too drunk and a bit handsy showed up, so I might be calling it a night as well. See ya, girl!"

"Bye-bye." I laugh at her comment, ending the call.

I really need to get a grip. This is not New York, and clearly whoever that was who always tried to get in my place isn't here. We are thousands of miles away. Can't start this new life if I'm constantly reliving the old one.

My head starts to pound. All the night's events and constant battle in my head have collided and taken me down. I shut off all the lights, double checking first that the alarm is set, and then I get to the couch, my eyes shuttering within minutes. Tomorrow is a new day.

● ● ●

I WAKE TO THE DOGS BARKING, AND IT'S STILL DARK out. Looking at my phone, I see I've slept maybe an hour. What in the hell? Then it hits me.

Did they come find me?

Shooting up, I start to freak out again, and that's when there's a pounding on the door.

"Hanna! Open up. It's Theo."

"The actual hell?" I fume, standing and moving to the door in a rage, ready to rip him a new one. Swinging the door open, I see he looks angry, glancing around the house as if someone else is going to come popping out. "Um. Can I help you?"

His eyes land on me, and they travel up and down the length of me, his fists balled and clenching hard, making the veins in his arms pop. I'm ashamed to say the throb between my legs returns, and there's now a damp spot in my panties. Holy hell, he looks lethal.

"My sister called and said someone showed up and spooked you."

I curse Brenda in my head. I told her not to call him. He looks angrier than what this news should've spurred. Why does he seem like he wants to kill someone?

"Theo, I'm fine. You can go now, and take a chill pill while you're at it. You look like you want to—"

He cuts me off then, slamming into me and gripping my

throat violently. I go to speak, but I'm silenced when his lips collide with mine. He's brutal with his kiss, taking my mouth like it's something he doesn't care if he breaks it. I hesitate at first, but then something happens.

My body takes over. Not my brain, because if it did, I would be pushing him away. But hell, this kiss. God. It feels so good. Incredible, and I don't want it to stop.

I've never been kissed like this before. He's brutal, demanding, skilled, and when his tongue hits mine, I moan. He tastes like a man. A real, feral man who wants to devour me with this one kiss. And I don't want to tame the beast. What is happening?

Reaching up between us, he pinches my peaked nipple, and I gasp, dropping my head back and losing his mouth.

"You keep fighting me, believing I don't want you. You're such a bad girl, and I should take you upstairs, slap your pink pussy, and make you understand just what I want," he growls, stepping back and peering down at me, hunger bleeding from him, and right before he's about to lean back in, the dogs start barking again.

I shoot up from the couch with a gasp, my body covered in a hot sweat, my core aching with desire...and that's when I realize it. It was all a dream. It was just a dream.

What is happening? What was that? Why did I have such an intensely sexual and crude fantasy about Theo? I stand and head to the kitchen, getting a cold bottle of water from the fridge and taking sips.

He's not the guy who's going to do those things with you. He is an enigma, Hanna. You can't be feeding into that or fantasizing about it. Let it go, and act like it never happened, I scold myself, stunned that my subconscious did that. He's hands-down the most attractive man I've ever known...and he's unreachable.

Let it go.

I say it again and take my water back to the living room. The pups are no longer barking; I'm assuming I was making God knows what kinds of noises in my sleep. It must have startled them and had them waking me up. Thank the good Lord above they're animals and can never repeat whatever noise I was making, or worse—the words I was saying.

I lie awake for another hour or so, my mind ruminating that dream repeatedly. That can *never* get out. No one can ever know I had this fantasy about Theo. Ever.

● ● ●

"COME ON, DOROTHY. LET'S GO, CLYDE," I SAY TO THE pups, opening the front door with my bucket of gardening items needed to work on the white roses I want to plant along the front of the house. I have no idea what I'm doing, but the picture online was too stunning to not attempt it, and the how-to blog with was pretty clear. So, I'll put all my faith in it. Worse thing that'll happen is I'll have to pull out dead bushes.

The dogs run out and start playing in the yard, running, smelling, and rough housing with one another. It's a sunny day with just the right amount of breeze mingling with the low-70s temperature.

After working for nearly an hour, making great strides, I stop when my phone buzzes in my back pocket. Pulling it out, I see Jack's name.

"Hey, Jack. Thank you for calling me back."

"Of course, I got your message about the locked room. None of the keys are working?"

Sitting back on my calves, I use the back of my hand to move the hair that's fallen from my ponytail out of my face.

"Correct. I was hoping to go through there and the attic next week to see if I can find anything. Family photos, anything really." A few days ago, I found a door in JD's study, and no keys that were given to me worked to unlock it.

"I don't have anything. I'm sorry; I gave you all the keys I had."

"Shoot. Okay, I will have to call a locksmith. Do you have a number or name for one?"

"I sure do. I can send you the info. How's everything else? Settling in okay?"

I pause, thinking of how I want to answer that. "Yes, I'm doing all right. I got a job at the grocery store in town. So, it's been a nice distraction. Still feel a little weird being here, taking up his space, not knowing who he was. There's a daunting feeling a bit."

He hums. "Yes, that makes sense. No need to rush it. Take your time adjusting. I will stop by next week when I'm back in town from visiting my son. You need anything else until then, let me know."

"Yes, of course. Thank you for all your help, Jack."

"Certainly, and hey, Hanna? Your grandfather was a great man. I don't know the whole story of why he didn't come find you, but I do know he would want you to be happy and comfortable here. So, try to settle in. The rest will follow."

I look down at my hand, picking at the frayed hole in the knee of my jeans. "Yeah, sure. Thanks again, Jack. I'll talk to you soon."

He says goodbye, and I take in what he said.

"Who are you talking to?"

I jump, shrieking, my phone flying into the dirt I just planted seeds in. Spinning, I see Theo towering over me. He looks sexy as sin in his worn jeans, Henley, and boots.

Hanna! I scold myself.

"You know, doorknob, you're like a mosquito. Can't see ya coming, and then—bam! There you are, to cause hell. What are you doing here?" I drop the tools, stand, and remove my gloves, turning to face him.

"Ouch, greens, I was coming to check on you. My sister said you seemed spooked last night when a random person off the highway got lost in your driveway."

"Brenda," I huff out. Thank God I only told her about the truck and not the dream. "I'm fine. Just got a little jumpy."

"Why so jumpy? You have nothing to be afraid of, right?" He places his hands on his hips, the stance and his question coming off like an interrogation.

"What's with the whole cop vibe?" I flap my hand at him, and he readjusts, standing normally but this time crossing his arms over his chest.

"Just want to know why you were all jumpy. This is a small town, but we get a lot of people passing through, and they tend to get a little lost with all the random turnoffs. Don't get too up in arms, greens." I roll my eyes.

"Can you not call me that?" I put my items in the bucket and head up the stairs to the front door, Theo on my heels. What is he doing here, seriously?

"Listen, I wanted to check in. That's all. So are you all right?" He sounds genuine. Turning before I step inside, I release a slow breath.

"Yes, I'm fine. Thank you."

"Good. Here, hand me your phone," he says, reaching out his hand.

"What? Why?" My brows furrow.

"Hanna. Hand me the phone." His voice is curt, the demand sticking to me in a way I'm afraid to admit. It was...hot.

"Um, okay. Sure, here." I fumble to grab my phone from my back pocket, hating that I let him see even an ounce of me interested in him. His fingertips brush against mine as he takes it. He doesn't see me or my reaction, but that sent an electric bolt straight to my core. How embarrassing that I'm reacting this way.

Undoubtedly, Theo is extremely attractive, and I do mean *extremely*. In fact, I would say he is the most handsome, well-built man I've ever laid eyes on. Which is why it's important I nip this in the bud. Fawning over a man I could never bag isn't good for my self-esteem or my lady bits.

"I put my number in. You can call me if you ever get spooked again or if something happens and you need someone to check it out."

I take the phone back, an inquisitive look on my face when I see the name he put. "Sirius. Your name is Theo? Sirius—like Harry Potter?" I prompt, a chuckle bubbling to the surface. Finally looking at him, I admire the sideways smirk adorning his face. "What?" I'm suddenly nervous under his gaze.

"Harry Potter? No, greens. But you'll find out soon enough." With that, he turns and is gone, leaving me confused and, frankly, annoyed. I need some sort of repellent to spray and ward him off with.

Doing my best, I try to leave that conversation in the past. I won't be using his number to call anytime soon. I don't need him, and he isn't my knight in shining armor.

My phone dings in my pocket as I pour a scoop of dog food into the pups' bowls. Pulling it out, I see a text.

Sirius: You don't need to be so tense around me, greens. I'm just trying to get to know you

Rolling my eyes, I tap aggravatedly on the screen.

Me: How did you get my number?

Sirius: Easy...I got it while you were ogling me. Called myself from your phone.

My face flushes instantly, my chest heating as well. Shit. He knew I was checking him out? How humiliating.

Me: I wasn't. I was trying to read your mind and find out just how psycho you are. Don't text me, please. I really am tired of this whole thing.

I think as wittily on my feet as possible.

Sirius: You are wrong about my intentions. Which will be revealed soon enough, when I feel you're ready.

Me: I'm rolling my eyes. You know that sounds like something a serial killer would say, right? Seriously, Theo. Enough.

Setting the phone down and getting a glass of water, I expect that to be the last of the conversation with him, but when my phone chimes and his name previews on the screen, I know I got ahead of myself.

Sirius: Easy, puppet. I'm not a serial killer...I don't think.

I roll my eyes at the ending of that comment, but my stomach still runs wild with him calling me puppet. It does something I hate to admit. So, I need to shut it down, or I will crumble in a way I don't want to.

Me: I'm not a puppet. Seriously, maybe I shouldn't have been so jumpy over the random truck last night but more so the creepy guy in town who tends to not know when to back off. Turning my phone off now, serial killer.

Before I can even give him room to respond and I see it, I turn off my phone and go up to shower. I have Brenda coming over in a couple of hours for dinner, and I don't want to deal with her obnoxious, exasperating brother.

※ ※ ※

THE HOUSE SMELLS DELICIOUS. I COOKED A CLASSIC pasta dish and a garlic bread mix that I learned in a cooking class back in New York. The smell of butter, creamy sauce, and comfort food has my stomach gurgling. I was so busy today that I barely ate.

I scoop up some pasta and sauce on my fork and bring it to my mouth, testing the taste. It's so divine I moan into the kitchen, the hot food gliding down my throat. I take a sip of the red wine I bought to wash it down. I'm ravenous at this point.

The doorbell rings then, and I remove the apron molded to my front and set it down on the counter, hollering as I make my way to the door, "Coming!" Two seconds later, the door opens, and the smile I am wearing disappears. Theo stands behind an annoyed-looking Brenda.

"I tried to tell him to leave, but he insisted he was coming for dinner. I'm so sorry. I told him to be respectful and on his best—" She pauses, turning her head and jabbing his rib with her elbow. "—behavior."

Clicking my tongue, I look up at him and stare into his brown eyes. He doesn't seem bothered by his shameless persistence. "It's fine. Come on in." I plaster a smile on for Brenda.

"Thank you. I'm sorry. Maybe I'll talk about sex and

masturbating and he'll want to leave."

"Funny, sis," he retorts. She moves past me, and I stand aside, letting Theo in, not looking at him, and doing my best to not give him my time. He really is like a mosquito.

"Greens, you got some sauce right here." He gestures to the side of his lip. Rolling my eyes, I lift my hand to clean it up, but he beats me to it, and I watch as if in slow motion. Swiping it from the corner of my lips, he brings his thumb to his mouth and sucks the tip. I'm too stunned that even my jaw can't hit the floor. I stay frozen in place.

"You make the sauce taste good. Not the other way around." With that, he's gone, following his sister into the kitchen.

"Whoa," I whisper, my breath tottering. "Ignore it. You have to ignore it. He's playing with you. So, two options—ignore him or get even." I give myself a pep talk. *I'll see your $20 and raise you a hundred.* No way in hell am I going to let him do this, treat me like a pawn in a sick little game. The hottie with the overweight newcomer. Sick fuck.

Slamming the door, I march into the kitchen. Two can play this game. Meeting them in the kitchen, I grab some plates, wine glasses, and silverware and set the dining table.

"It smells so good. I'm starving and would kill for a good New York pasta recipe," Brenda says, taking a seat at the table. I feel Theo's eyes on me from where he stands in the doorway of the kitchen. His arms are crossed against his chest, and if I didn't know better, I would think he's trying to read me. What does he want to know so damn bad? How I plan to make him eat rocks and regret ever messing with me?

"I hope it tastes good. I haven't made this in forever, and I may have been the worse cook in that class," I tell her, pushing past Theo, my shoulder hitting his bicep. As much as that was meant to be a passive-aggressive move, I won't lie; it turned me on. This maddening man.

"I doubt that," she calls after me, and I reach up to grab some wine. I feel him on me, a hard wall against my back and large, firm hands on my hips.

"You're fucking with me. Enough," he bites out, making my blood boil in a mixture of rage and arousal—a deadly combination—but I manage to hide it.

"What *ever* do you mean, Theo?" I turn and bat my lashes. If he thinks he is going to hurt me the way I was hurt in the past....

I stop. Not wanting to think about it. But if he thinks he can, he's wrong. He stares down at me, a looming, towering wall of dominance, muscles, and cocky arrogance.

"Greens, I've tried to tell you to put down the wall and let me in. If you keep at this, I will take you over my knee, smack your ass raw, and make sure you know what my fucking intentions are."

This.

This has my jaw nearly dislocating from my face.

"You're sick. What is your angle here?" I place my hands on my hips, my chest rising and falling in tandem with his.

"You will find out soon enough, but I suggest you chill and

stop fanning the damn fire. I can burn really fucking hot, puppet," he seethes, and I give it right back.

Stepping up to him, my breasts now pressed against his upper abdomen, our height difference is striking in this position. "I'm not a puppet. I'm not a pawn. You think you're going to win or even play this game? Think again." Our breathing is so loud, so prominent, it's the noisiest thing in the damn house. But there is something else lingering. It's—

"Uh, is everything all right in here?" Brenda interrupts, and I snap back into place, turning and grabbing the wine, trying to cool my rising body temperature.

"Everything's fine, sis. Just trying to get this stubborn woman to let me help her. Least I could do after she made us a delicious-smelling meal."

"You can be on clean-up duty, since you're so keen on helping," I bite out, moving past him and handing Brenda the wine. "You pour."

"Uh...okay." She looks back and forth between us, clearly debating whether to say something or let it go. I'm thankful when she decides to ignore it and let it be.

We settle in and start eating. Brenda leads the conversation, but that tension from the kitchen still lingers, and it's driving me mad. I'm aroused. Angry. And dare I say eager to play the game I just told him not to? He has a plan, and I know it's most likely a cruel one at my expense, and that just makes me even more ready to play.

"So you haven't found any more information on J.D. and why he never attempted to come and meet you?" Brenda pulls me from my wayward thoughts.

I clear my throat, needing the distraction and change of conversation. "No. Nothing. I have been working myself up to settling in here. It still feels wrong."

"Why does it feel wrong?" she asks, taking a sip of wine.

"I didn't know him at all. This was his home, and I feel like I'm disrespecting him while he is fresh in his grave."

"How do you suppose that? He left it to you. Surely he knew you would see this place and not, *not* want to settle in and make it home."

I shrug, pushing around the pasta. "Sure, but I've never been the type to just come in and disrupt someone's space."

"Hanna," she speaks softly, placing her hand on mine, "he's gone, and you staying here isn't disrupting his space. It was his final wish. You need to give yourself some grace."

I look up at her and nod. Moving my eyes to Theo, I see he is sitting there, one hand on the table, his knuckles tapping softly. His other hand is being used as a resting place for his chin, held up on two of his fingers as he watches me.

"I just wish I knew why he didn't even attempt to contact me. I've been alone all these years, ya know? It would have been nice to have someone," I admit, a lump forming in my throat.

Hell no. I'm not going to cry in front of him. That's the last thing I need. If he sees me weak, he is one chess move ahead in whatever it is we're playing.

"It's nothing like New York. Even if you knew him, you wouldn't have come here often. I can tell you this—don't get too comfortable here. It's nothing special," Theo says with no emotion at all, still in the same position.

"Maybe for you. We clearly had two different experiences living in New York." I finally take a bite of my food again, not really a fan of eating in front of people.

And there comes a phobia of mine. Being a big woman means people see me eating and think I'm a glutton versus a normal human needing to eat to survive.

"Maybe you come off as cool and unwelcoming. Ever think that may be why people don't come off as friendly to you? Maybe they are mirroring you?"

"Theo!" Brenda scolds, whipping her head to face him so fast.

I scoff. "I'm a lot of things, but cold and unwelcoming is not one."

"Really? That's all you have been showing me since you got here, greens. You sure about that?" he retorts.

"Theo!" This time, Brenda stands. "What the hell is your problem? You said you wouldn't be a nuisance. So instead you decide to be a dick?"

"You know nothing about me. All I wanted was friends. I kept to myself because I didn't want to burden people, since that's all I've been since day one. Hence why JD most likely never came for me." I stand and throw down my napkin. "This has been lovely, but

I think I'm going to call it a night. Brenda, we can reschedule." I look to Theo, and I see something, a difference, a softer gaze. He looks...regretful.

I make my way up the stairs, listening to Brenda scold Theo, telling him he needs to apologize. I pray to God he decides to stay a dick, because I may punch a man for the first time in my life. I pace the room, looking for my phone that I swore I left up here, but I can't find it. A tapping on the door stops me, and lo and behold, Mr. Dick himself is taking up the doorframe.

"What? What could you possibly want now? To insult me some more?" I throw the pillow on the bed, and he steps in.

"No. I wanted to say sorry. I don't know what came over me down there."

I laugh. "Oh really? Because I do. I think you're just mad because I'm the first woman who isn't fawning at your feet and begging for attention. Clearly, rejection makes you bitter." He laughs, and I cross my arms. "Is this funny? To insult me when I'm already a mess? Is this what you wanted? Get the fat girl all upset, make her feel bad about herself so you can laugh about it to your friends?"

"Enough!" he snaps, his demeanor changing. My eyes fly up and meet his. The way his neck veins bulge and move has me gulping.

"Theo! I will come up there and manhandle you myself. Play nice!" Brenda yells from the bottom of the stairs.

He turns, slamming the door and gaining on me, and within a

few strides, he is on me. Gripping my neck, he uses the pad of his thumb under my chin to lift my face. I gulp. "You call yourself fat in my presence again and so help me, Hanna."

"Why does it mean anything to you?" I hate that there are tears welling in my eyes.

"Because the woman I plan to fuck and worship can't possibly be insecure. You will need to love your body when you're with me, or this won't work."

"Wh-What?" I choke out.

"You heard me, puppet." He leans, taking my quivering lip between his teeth and biting.

I yelp, jumping back. "Theo. What are you doing?"

"What does it look like, greens? I want you to be my little puppet. I want to fuck you so hard that my cock imprints your cunt, leaves you shaped for only me."

This is a dream. Yup, all a dream. Just like the other night. It must be.

"You're not real. This isn't real." He's prowling toward me, slowly stalking me as I back up slowly. Eventually, my back hits the wall of windows, and I'm trapped.

When he places both his large palms against the glass on either side of my head, I breathe in and out heavily, a deep throb in the very center of me. "You are so damn tempting. I looked at you the first time and knew you would be my next fuck toy."

I shake my head. "I'm not a whore."

"No. You're not. You will be exclusive to me."

"Exclusive to you? I'm not going to be your girlfriend."

He laughs sinisterly. "Oh, puppet. I don't want a girlfriend. Never plan to. But I do want you and plan to have you."

"You don't know me." How is this happening? I'm not even sure what to say at this point.

"I don't need to know much, other than how to make you scream while you come. The rest is just schematics."

"You're crazy," I whisper.

"You have no idea." Leaning then, he put his lips against my ear. "I will be back tomorrow, and we can talk it out. Be ready at seven." With that, he's gone. Like a thief in the night, taking my breath with him and leaving me with nothing but arousal.

What the hell just happened?

Nine

THEO

I LOST CONTROL. I NEVER LOSE CONTROL, BUT I WANT to fuck her so goddamn bad it's becoming an obsession. She's right. Women are so easy to obtain, but not her. I could have anyone but her, and that makes me want her even more. To tame her, subdue her, control her, and then lick her wounds with aftercare.

I haven't had a sub in a long time, work keeping me busy. And with this job, my assignment just got even more complicated. I was supposed to be in and out, but Hanna—the curvy, green-eyed siren—just fucked that up. All of it.

"You're going to hurt her. She's too nice, Theo, and we both know what you want in women," Brenda says softly as we pull up in her driveway.

"You don't worry about her and me. We are grown adults."

"Yeah, but she isn't the type who should be used like a toy. You hate relationships."

"She's used to not having relationships. What makes you think she can't handle this arrangement?" Brenda doesn't know what the arrangement will be, but she does know I don't wine and dine. I fuck and use. Leave them wanting more and disposing of them when they cling a little too tightly.

"That right there. You have no idea what she been through, Theo, and she's a person, not an object. And she's my friend. Don't make it to where she doesn't want anything to do with me." Her eyes find mine, soft yet filled with worry.

Releasing a deep breath, I glance at her house, then back to her.

"I won't, okay? Don't worry about me. I will tell her the score, and if it isn't something she wants to do—"

"Be a fuck buddy?"

I release a huff, trying not to react by snapping. I'm just as irritated that I'm even in this situation, but I want what I want. "To be casual."

Rolling her eyes, she opens the door and climbs out of my truck. "You hurt her and ruin our friendship, and I'll cut your dick off myself. Make it to where you can't have any more 'casual' girlfriends," she says, air quoting the word.

She slams the door and marches up the stairs, and I wait for her to be inside and safe before backing out and heading to my place. Once I'm home, I go straight for the fridge and pull out a beer.

What have I gotten myself into? Did I really think this was the best idea? This arrangement could complicate things. No, it *is* complicating things. There is no doubt about that. That's the one thing I'm sure of. What if Brenda is right? What if Hanna can't take this arrangement and falls for the idea of us? For me?

Sometimes women can fall for men with my taste, especially when it comes to the aftercare. There is an intimacy for most people. For me, it's just part of the responsibility.

But here we are. My eyes have claimed the prize, and I will face the risks when they come.

The next morning, I work on my daily report to submit to my client on the progress of my work, leaving out the part that things are complicated now and more time is needed because I want to do things to the new girl in town, things one shouldn't speak of.

I picture her then, hands tied behind her back as she kneels on the ground, the carpet leaving indents in her knees as she slowly, lazily licks at my cock, taking me like a good little puppet. Fuck—instantly, I'm hard and ready. I need a release. Need the thrill. Need her to agree to the proposition.

This morning, my sister texted me incessantly, asking me to rethink my whole approach with Hanna, but I can't. I won't. My mind is made up, and it's what I have to do. All alarms and whistles are going off, caution tape layering, and yet I ignore it all, because that insatiable hunger is the most prominent thing in my body.

Logic? Gone.

Sanity? Fucking questionable.

Desire? Bingo.

By the time I've ignored my raging hard-on and completed

work for the day, it's nearing six. Hopping in the shower, I hurry to get ready, picking jeans, brown boots, and a white V-neck shirt paired with a leather jacket. Styling my brown hair, I don't spend more than a few seconds before I put on my cologne and grab the keys, heading out the door. I climb in my truck, make the five-minute drive to her place, and pull up to see the lights on upstairs and in the entryway. The rest of the house is dark. I swear if she isn't ready and is trying to blow this night off, I might just convince her to do it with an angry fuck.

I hop out, leave the engine running, and head to the door. When I ring the bell, the dogs go wild. I can see her at the top of the stairs, and fuck me—she looks delectable. Tight jeans, distressed and hugging her body like a second skin. She wears some type of emerald-green shirt that clings to her chest, showcasing her beautiful breasts with the perfect amount of cleavage before fanning out below them. It perfectly outlines her hourglass frame.

She's wearing brown boots up to her knees, and her dirty-blonde hair is curled and falling all around her. Her makeup is done, and the best way to describe it is she looks like she is ready for it to be smeared and running from a heady fuck. Damn, she looks so delicious.

I can sense her hesitation as she takes each step of the staircase. I don't blame her. We are in every sense still pretty much strangers, and I propositioned her to be nothing but my toy. A fuck buddy. Finally opening the door, she looks up at me.

"I can't believe I am actually giving you the time of day to explain whatever last night was."

I smile. "Off to a great start, greens. Let's go. Lock up."

She steps out, grabbing her keys and bag. I watch her lock the door, then I take her hand and walk us toward the truck. I feel the slight bit of resistance and hesitation as she tries to pull her hand back from me, but I keep my grip firm. It's best she starts to see how much I like control and establish exactly what I want out of this deal.

"Bold of you, taking my hand. I got it," she says when I open the door and help her up.

"Didn't say you didn't have it."

Rolling her eyes, she puts her seatbelt on, and I shut the door, rounding the front of the truck and climbing in.

"Where are we going?" she asks as we back out of the driveway.

"Dean's. We can have some drinks and order some food."

"Okay." The tension coming from her is palpable.

"Greens, it's fine. I'm not gonna fuck you right here, right now."

"Lord. Are you always so crass? Does this sort of thing work on other women? You just saying 'I'm man. Hear me roar. Let's mate.'"

I laugh, actually tossing my head back. "Let's mate?"

Leaning over, she slaps my arm with the back of her hand. "It's true. You were barbaric last night. I've never seen or heard things like that before, except for in the novels I've read."

I look over and catch the blush she tries to hide. "The novels you read? You read erotic novels?"

Snapping her eyes to me, she clicks her tongue. "You're incorrigible. Brenda was right. You can be such an ass."

"No, this is not as bad as I can get. I'm careless. I don't really have any regard for people and how they feel," I admit to her, pulling into the parking lot of Dean's.

"I know. I wanted to slap you at dinner last night," she mumbles.

Putting the truck in park, I lean in. "That was me being decent. I can be a lot worse, puppet. You'll see." It's a warning. Foreshadowing what this will become. I don't want anyone thinking I'm going soft, because I'm not. But if I want to start a sexual relationship with Hanna, I do need to respect her, have her trust me enough to let me in. I don't need to love her, but to enter this type of relationship, you have to have trust and mutual respect. It's a must.

"I'm gathering you have no regard for anyone but yourself, the exact person I'm trying to avoid. Having no humility is cruel. What a sad way to go through life." Her answer leaves me speechless. Hanna is too kind, a soft heart and an even more encompassing soul. She couldn't hurt a damn fly or be okay with making someone feel even the slightest bit of sadness.

We are a match made in hell, but the collision would be like an exquisite bit of burning heaven. One where the ashes fall in perfect tandem. She and I are wrong. Everything should end in disaster. But I don't fear the calamity. Because when all is said and done, I will have washed my hands clean after feeding the beast.

Whatever happens with her…is not something I will ever have to worry about. That's part of this whole arrangement. The best part, in fact—well, besides the animalistic fucking.

"Inside, you can tell me how much you hate me and wish I would drop dead." I wink, earning me a huff and eye roll. Climbing out, I round the truck and help her down. Her scent hits me, and it makes me feral, highly aware of my cock's stiffness and my desire to claim her. Shit. It's divine, her scent. It's an aphrodisiac all on its own. I can't wait to fuck her with a violence that she will crave, with her wearing only that scent—and mine.

"Let's make a deal. You can tell me whatever it is you want in there, as long as I get to throw a drink in your face after?" she offers sassily.

The way she's teasing and testing me is only making me more fucking eager. Damn this maddening woman.

Gripping her neck and pushing her softly against the side of the truck, I shut the door and place my free hand beside her head on the window.

"You are playing with fire. You and I are going to do this, and I promise it won't be a drink you will be throwing in my face. It'll be your wet pussy that wants to be eaten, licked, and fucked. Now, inside, greens."

Her jaw is lax, her pulse quickening under my hand before I release it, and her skin is red and heated.

Control. I sense it, feel it, revel in it. It takes her a minute to set into motion. I watch her hips move. Even on shaky legs, she moves like a dream; a body so curvy can *only* move like that. Sways were meant for women like Hanna, and she does it as if she invented it.

I can't wait to explore every inch of that body. Examine it under harsh hands, care for it when I bruise it and use it. This is going to be one of the best sexual relationships I've ever had, and I'm angrier with myself, because I know the implications—the complications.

Stepping into the bar, I notice it's not as busy as it usually is, which is perfect. The night life here is dull and, if I'm being honest, garbage of the lowest extent. One of the many reasons I prefer New York. If we were back there, I would take her somewhere nice. Put on a show, especially since I'm about to ask her what I plan to.

We haven't said anything since our exchange back at the truck and still stay silent as we are taken to a free table toward the back of the bar. It's a high-top, with a lame excuse for a candle in a green glass. Classy.

"Here you two go. Enjoy, y'all. Your server will be right over."

I nod to the woman who seats us. Hanna gives a soft thanks before opening her menu, looking it over as if she's going to find a portal out of here in the damn thing.

"Hanna?" I attempt to get her attention, but it fails when all she does is just say "hmm," the menu still covering most her face. "Hanna. I want you to look at me."

Closing her eyes tight, she seems to mentally prepare herself to do what I'm asking, and I would be lying if I said I didn't enjoy her torment.

"What?" She finally gives me those green eyes from beneath her thick lashes.

"In order to have this talk, you need to stop looking like a scared dog who just got slapped with a newspaper."

She gawks. "But aren't I? You have now grabbed my throat twice, said vulgar things to me, and now you want us to break bread? How am I supposed to act? A chipper, thankful, good, and obedient doe?"

My cock jumps. She may not see the double meaning behind her choice of words, but that was exactly what I like to hear.

"Precisely," I growl.

"Ugh, you insane man. What is wrong with you? You know that women are not objects or pawns you can play with and then toss aside when they're broken because of your mishandling, right?" She seethes.

That was personal. This is now the third time she has indicated in some way or another that there has been something done to her. Someone wronged her.

"What is that?" I question, moving the menu aside and pushing hers down as well. There is pain engrained in her eyes. "What do you mean?"

She shrugs, dropping her head. Terrible liar—she is an open book, wearing her scars so openly, horrible at hiding it. "You know what I mean."

Leaning back, I cross my arms, and she rolls her eyes again—a staple of hers, I'm coming to learn.

"Why do you always do that?" she asks and mimics my pose, pushing her luscious breasts up in the process. I could suffocate in those gorgeous tits. I plan to be. My face and my cock.

Focus, Theo, I scold myself.

"Do what?" I match her energy, almost mocking her.

"That. You sit there like you're interrogating me. You come off as cool and malicious."

"So?" I sit forward this time, interlocking my fingers and cocking my head to the side.

"It's...intimidating."

"Good. I like that I have that affect."

Clicking her tongue, she leans in, the student becoming the teacher. This time she matches my pose, but with gusto. "I meant to say it's creeper energy."

This makes me laugh. I know what I need to do. Clearly, my approach won't get me the answers and responses I want, so I flip the script. "Did someone hurt you, greens? You can tell me." I soften my expression, reaching over and touching her hand. The move would seem intimate, but there is nothing behind it except for her to find comfort. For me, it's a formality.

"Please. I don't want to do this. I don't know you," she whispers, turning her head to hide the sudden well of tears.

"Shit," I breathe out, feeling like a complete dick.

Why? Why is she so good at making me feel some type of compassion? I'm not one to be swayed or easily turned into a man with feelings and empathy.

"It was nothing. Okay? Just a group of mean boys in high school who saw a chance to hurt the fat loner in the corner. That was a long time ago." Squaring her shoulders, she pushes her long hair over one to fall down her back and tilts up her chin.

That's a good girl. Confident, strong, unbothered. I plan to watch her learn how to do this more often.

"Give me names. Give me that at least," I order, a slight burn that I'm very familiar with rolling up my spine and settling heavily on my shoulders.

"What?"

"Names, Hanna." The anger simmers, but it will rage much harder if she doesn't tell me. I want whoever made a woman like Hanna drop her head and speak about her body in such a foul manner to pay. Simple as that.

"Why? You going to show up and scare them with your throat grabbing and crass words?"

This makes me bark out a laugh once more, lightening the mood just a bit. Which is good. Anger fuels a lot, gives me many things—courage, strength, control—but it also brings me lust and desire. It can be both a pro and a con with me. Depends on which side I choose and who is on the receiving end. And Hanna is walking the tightrope toward my "pin you down and make you scream my fucking name" side.

"No. Maybe. How about you be a good girl for once and tell me what I ask you?"

"A good girl? You really think that works?" I watch her chest turn a light shade of pink, her breathing uneven.

"Given the way your breaths just changed and the flush spreading from your chest to your face, I would say you think that works perfectly. Don't be ashamed of desires, greens; they are what makes life worth living."

She gulps. "You don't know me. Why would you think this is something I would want?"

"And what is it you think I'm assuming?" I question again.

"I'm assuming you want to make love."

I all but topple out my chair with laughter. "Oh, sweet puppet. Making love is for fools and those without a pulse. *Fucking* is for the living. For the feral. For people like us. I don't want to make love to you, Hanna. I want to make sin with you. Make fire. Fire so hot you burn, and as you almost finish healing from that burn, I want to douse you again in my gasoline and burn us both to the ground."

"Jesus," she moans, not even trying to hide it. "You're so intense. It's—"

"Arousing? You like it? You crave it?"

Her eyes search mine, and she nods slowly. "Yes, but I shouldn't. I can't." She shakes her head, trying to recenter her focus. "I won't. Find someone else. You don't know me, and this could never be a thing."

"Casual fucking—mind-blowing fucking—is normal, Hanna."

"No, it isn't. You need to know the person you're sleeping with. Don't you think that? Even a little?"

"No. I don't. Besides, if I did, what better way to get to know someone than getting to know them that personally?" I wink, taking one of the cashews from the center bowl and popping it in my mouth, smiling around it as I chew.

"That seems lonely. You must be a very lonely man, Theo. Maybe that's why you're so cool to everyone other than your sister." She turns to face the waiter who approaches, and I watch her order. "I'm just going to have a water and the house salad, no dressing."

Is that a joke?

"Excuse me, she must have fallen and bumped her gorgeous head. She will have the steak with mushroom sauce, a side of the house fries, and a Coors on tap. I'll have the same," I speak over her. The waiter says something to us both, but I don't hear it, too busy watching my puppet fume again. This is fun. I could play this game all fucking night if she let us.

"I was fine with a salad. You didn't have to take over like you were never taught any manners."

I take another nut, look up at the screen with the game on it, and respond, "Sure you were. I could tell you were just salivating over it while you ordered."

"Maybe I'm allergic to mushrooms and hate the taste of fries," she retorts.

"Are you?" Taking my eyes from the screen, I quirk a brow at her.

She rubs her lips together, her eyes forming slits. "No."

"Good. Now let's focus on eating, then I will get to what I brought you here for."

"Oh, what, you didn't bring me here to proposition me for sex while manhandling me in the parking lot and picking my food like you're the founder of the damn patriarchy?"

Goddamn. She's not fucking submissive. That's for sure. Breaking her just might be the best part of this whole plan.

Ten

HANNA

I CAN FEEL HIS EYES ON ME, WATCHING ME. AND normally, I would say he is judging me, but instead, it's as if he's trying to memorize me, learn my habits and movements—understand all my tics.

I ate—but not all the food. I didn't want to come off as some slob who eats like she won't get another meal. Theo, however, cleared his plate. How is that fair? I work out—but not intensely. An afternoon walk a couple of times a week. I watch what I drink and basically starve myself to attempt to lose weight. And he can down a hearty, buttery, and calorie-filled meal and still look the way he does.

Science sucks or God has favorites. Either way, I was on the shitty receiving end of creation. We talked a little while eating. He asked me about work and settling into Cherry Hill, and a little about JD.

That is always a sore topic for me. Because the more people I meet and talk to, the more they ask questions about my grandfather that I don't know the answers to. In turn, this makes me feel even more out of my element and truly uncomfortable. Living in his house, knowing he knew of me and never tried to contact me except in the event of his death, still hurts.

Why wouldn't he have tried? Did he hate me for some reason, and his last F-you was giving me his home? That way I could feel this? The hurt. The embarrassment. The never ending what-if questions. I guess I'll never know, since he left me nothing but a giant home, an astronomical amount of money, and two dogs. The most important thing he could have left—answers—are nowhere to be found.

"You think you want to stay here?" Theo breaks the silence, pushing the plates aside for the waiter.

"I think so. I have nowhere else to go."

"No family back home?"

"I think you know that." Brenda is a gentle soul. She's fierce and loud, but I've noticed when it comes to others, especially people she considers friends, she is gentle. There is no way she didn't already tell Theo a little bit about me. Most likely, she would have done it in attempt to make him leave me alone.

"Fair," he responds.

"Theo..." I'm exhausted over all the cat-and-mouse, back-and-forth crap from tonight. "What do you want? Can you just say it so I can go home?" I came tonight, knowing I would turn him down. But I knew, until I heard him out fully, he wasn't going to back off.

"You sure? We can make some more small talk before I throw this at you."

"No. I don't want to make small talk. It's pointless. You and I both know that." I'm not an idiot. I've been made to play the poor fat girl all my life, the butt of every sick joke.

"Fine." Adjusting in his seat, he leans forward, and those honey-brown eyes pierce mine, paralyzing me. "I want you, Hanna. I want to fuck you so goddamn bad. I want you to be mine while I'm here for a job. I want to break you and do very fucked-up, dirty things to that perfect body of yours."

My breath shudders, my entire body erupting in goose bumps. Who talks like that? And why is he the only one who makes me want it?

"Theo—"

"I'm not fucking done, puppet. You speak when I let you."

I bite my tongue and clench my thighs, trying to soothe the dull ache, find relief. I nod slowly, shamefully hanging on to his words, standing on the edge of the cliff, begging to hear what he has to say next.

"You and I are strangers, but that doesn't have to mean anything when we're in the bedroom. I can't stop thinking of all things I want to do. You're consuming me, and I know I'm doing the same to you."

I lift a brow. He's cocky as hell but isn't wrong. I hate that, but a man like him has never shown me this kind of desire. I'm not a virgin, nor have I never had a boyfriend, but the one I did...he took it all from me. My heart. My love and my virtue. I hated him, not because he fell out of love with me. No, that's understandable; sometimes things don't work out. But because he *never* loved me. It was a cruel joke. Make the school loser, the fat girl, sleep with him, tell all his buddies, and then tell the whole school how desperate I was and how he pity-fucked me.

Those memories come back, and I'm suddenly a stone wall, his words not holding control over me like they were mere seconds ago.

"Hanna?" He must notice that my body language changed. Just as I open my mouth to tell him there is no deal, no chance I will agree to this, we're interrupted.

"Fitzgerald?" a man says to Theo, calling him by his last name.

We both turn our heads to the man standing there. He looks a bit out of place here, wearing khaki pants with a mint polo and some slip-on shoes. Way out of place. If frat houses had a stereotype, he'd check all the boxes. Theo has a look on his face—he looks annoyed. The man simply said hello. Maybe there's bad blood?

"Jerrick."

"Man, I haven't seen you since that grad party at Steener's house! Dude, that's gotta be what…twelve years?"

Yup, he was definitely in a fraternity.

"Yes, that's right." His tone is even, flat, and uninterested.

"Can't believe we're in our thirties now."

I never thought to ask how old he is. I know Brenda is year

older than me. I'm twenty-three, giving us at least a seven-year difference. Another small thing I've learned.

Another reason this could never work. I have to know more than just someone's body if I'm going to be that intimate with him. Hell, the way Theo says it—that animalistic.

"Yeah, big surprise, man," Theo mocks, and I wonder why he's being so callous with this man.

"Who's this? Family friend?"

"My date," he bites out, and I snap my eyes to him, seeing a fire brewing in his brown orbs. What is his problem?

"Theo?" I reach across the table, placing my hand on his forearm. It's on fire. His neck is growing red, the veins becoming more pronounced. This man must really be an enemy to elicit this reaction. I pull my hand back as if he scorched me.

"Your date? Yeah right. Theo, the town playboy, slumming it with a fat girl?" He throws his head back, and immediately, my insides turn. This is reality. I've been here before, and sadly...he is not wrong. Men like Theo don't normally exist, and they especially don't exist and are attracted to women like me. I stand up fast, hiding my tears and just focusing my blurred vision as best as I can to get out of here.

The trauma. The ridicule. The gut-shattering pain that comes with being treated like anything but a human. It eats me alive.

I hear it then. The sound of bones crunching. And it stops me in my tracks. Turning slowly, I see Theo towering over the man, who is now lying on the floor and holding his bloody nose while groaning. "You ever disrespect her again, I'll rearrange your entire fucking face."

"Dang it, Fitzgerald. Get out of this bar before I have to call the cops," someone hollers from the bar.

"Fucking gladly."

I watch as he throws down a wad of cash, and then he is on me. Taking my hand roughly, he pulls me toward the exit. I stumble a bit, unable to keep up. "Theo, please, stop. I can't...."

Finally outside, he throws me against the wall with just enough force I gasp and look up at him. He grabs my throat and drags the tip of his nose up my jaw to my cheek and ear.

"I will never let a man, or anyone for that matter, disrespect you, puppet." He brings his other hand up, the one with a bit of blood on the knuckles, and moves my hair. The blood streaks my cheek, and I shiver. "Now you wear the blood of the man who disrespected you."

"Theo." The idea would normally repulse me, but it's as if he's empowering me. Giving me the power back. Why does it feel like I defeated a monster?

"Tell me you don't want me to kiss you. Tell me you don't want this arrangement. Because if you *don't* tell me that, I'm going to fucking kiss you, and I'm going to make you beg for me to keep going."

In that moment, I let the adrenaline, the desire, the heavy weight of lust drowning me take over, and I nod softly. Then he does. Those full lips collide with mine, and the instant they do, he growls, and it goes straight to the spot between my legs. I trust him in this brief moment, believing there is no way he would have done that if he truly had the wrong intentions. Could it be he really does want to have this type of relationship with me?

A crass, sexual relationship that I hate to admit may keep me hungry and make me feel the most alive I will ever feel?

Maybe.

"You taste so fucking good, puppet. God, I bet that honey between your legs tastes like a delicacy." He bites my bottom lip, and a moan escapes me right before he takes the opportunity to bring our tongues together.

Holy hell. He taste good too. Like a stranger but someone I know all at the same time. It's exciting, invigorating, downright lethal the way it all makes sense but confuses me more. He tightens his hand on my throat, controlling the kiss, showing me how he wants it and just how I need it.

"I have to have this with you, Hanna. You and me and nothing but silk, ropes, and violence. You make me want to do it all. But you have to be willing. All of it. We will make rules." He says all this in between bites, licks, and suction along my lips, cheek, and jawline.

I peer up at the night sky, the stars drowned out by the bar's neon lights. It looks like a pit of blackness, and it's oddly similar to how I'm feeling inside. Lost and falling into the unknown, never knowing when my feet are going to find solid ground again.

"What are the rules then?" I get out the words the best I can, yet they still sound shaky.

"No love. No relationship. Just you, me, and sex. I will not sleep with other women, and you best believe you will not let another man touch you. You will be mine. You understand?"

"So you think you will own me?"

"No, I *know* I will, and once you let down this wall, you will see just how much you want this too, Hanna. You won't be able to want anything else. You will want this more than air." He tightens his grip on my neck, and I feel the restriction, making it harder to breathe.

"You can't hurt me," I choke out, and he loosens his grip.

"Oh, I plan to." He leans back, smirking sinisterly, taking his thumb and rubbing it up and down the column of my throat.

"I mean...we need to discuss that a little more, because I mean literally. I'm not saying you have to love me, but you can't hurt me after we end whatever this is. Don't make me feel like I was a joke."

He eyes me over, and he whispers, "I want you to draw me a map of all the places you've ever hated on your body."

I scoff. "No map needed. Just look at me, and you will see it everywhere." I feel naked in my vulnerability. But if he wants me to let him in enough to have me intimately, he needs to know what I can't handle.

"Oh, puppet. What a shame that this world ever made you afraid or ashamed to love yourself. What a shame they don't see what I see."

"And what is that, Theo?" My voice is harsh, not sure where

he's going with this.

"A woman so beautiful. Someone who craves and deserves the touch and desire of the man who is standing in front of her—wanting so badly to give it to her. A woman who was lied to by the whole world. A blind world. I see everything I wish you could."

"That will never happen." No one will ever be able to undo the damage that was done to me.

"You will choke on those words. Regret them. And I can't wait to watch them drain from you and be replaced with lust. Not just for me...but for yourself."

I laugh, my cheeks reddening. "How can one lust after their own self?"

He cups my face, leans in, and bites my earlobe. "Don't worry. I'll show you."

With that, he's gone, breaking all physical contact. "Now let's get you home and eat dessert. Our dinner was ruined before we could get to it, and we still need to go over rules."

I nod slowly, not sure what else to say. I'm all out of one-liners and smart-ass comments. I just want to...try it.

Eleven

THEO

THE ENTIRE DRIVE, I STILL TASTE HER ON MY LIPS—innocence, deprivation, and hunger. If I didn't have to lay down more rules, I would take her, fuck her right now. Make her climb on top of me as I drive and ride my cock as I drive us home.

But that won't happen. Besides, I really need her to understand this will be more about sex, pleasure, and me helping her learn to love her body in a way she needs to. That I need her to in order for this to work.

We pull up to her place, and she waits like a good girl for me to come get her out. It shouldn't be too hard to get her to submit if we take the small victories and turn them into big ones. I won't lie; guilt swarms to the surface, making my throat tight. There is a lot at stake here, and though she says she won't fall in love and can handle this for what it is, what if she can't? Then I'd feel like the worst of the worst when all is said and done.

Who cares? You don't care for people, I remind myself, shutting that shit down.

Getting to the door, the tension is thick. You can feel the desire, the pull and push, the kinetic energy between the two of us. The silence makes it that much more intense.

"I can make something real quick. I think I have ice cream," she speaks first, breaking the silence.

"Don't worry. I ordered something already." I wave my phone at her. Technology makes it so easy these days.

"Right. You assume you know what I like."

There it is.

Hanna may seem like a meek, timid woman, but really, she's the perfect balance, surprising me with her sassy little responses. Those will come in handy some nights. The pent-up nights. The moments where life drives me mad and I need to fuck the sass right out of her.

"Let's go over the rules. You have wine?"

She nods toward where it's sitting in the rack next to the pantry. I pick out a nice white, which will be perfect with the dessert I ordered. The dessert we should have eaten before that son of a bitch had to ruin it. I wanted to do more to his smug, disgusting face, but....

Manners. He needs to learn some fucking manners.

"Here." She hands me some long-stem glasses, and I pop the cork with the corkscrew she placed on the island. After I pour us some, I hand her one and nod to the sitting room.

She sits first, leaning and removing her boots. I watch with great attention, loving the curve of her calf. I want to bite it. In time, I will. When she's done, she puts her thighs to her stomach and looks at me over the rim of the glass she sips from.

"Are you a virgin?"

Hanna nearly spits out the wine. "What happened to 'hello, how are you'?"

I smirk. "We are far past pleasantries."

"I guess so."

Entertaining her, I adjust myself, placing my ankle atop my opposite knee, and lift a brow.

"Hello, Hanna. How are you?"

Rolling her eyes, she takes another sip before responding. "You are such a smartass. I just meant you shouldn't just ask a woman if she's a virgin like you're asking her what the weather is outside. It's crass." I shrug, and she asks, "You have no qualms with these types of questions, do you?"

"I'm qualm-less, baby."

"Clearly. It's a bit much." She tells me this, but it's written all over her that she's intrigued. She can try to push me away, but it won't work. I have my eyes set on the prize, and if I can keep her clinging to me like this, she won't be able to turn down my offer.

"What are the rules?"

"Now who's jumping right into it?"

"Theo...," she warns, and I nod.

"All right, it would be built purely around a sexual relationship. As I stated earlier, no emotions. No love. Nothing but sex. Can you do that?"

"Maybe."

"Maybe isn't the right answer. Something you need to know about me, puppet, is I like control, and if I can't have it...my reactions can be...a bit much—as you so eloquently put it. I *will* reclaim it, and I need to know you're ready for that. This isn't something for everyone. You have to be prepared, Hanna." My tone is serious, without any room for her to misunderstand what it is I'm wanting. This can get messy if the terms are not laid out just right.

"You know not every woman is going to fall in love with you because you're handsome and can fuck well."

Her words shock me, as they do her.

Slapping her hand over her mouth, she shakes her head. "I can't believe I just said that. That was so crude. I'm sorry."

"I like it. You being bold and brazen needs to happen more often."

"Why?"

"Because, it's all part of owning yourself, your sexuality, and you're giving yourself more confidence. Which...when are you going to tell me what that is all about?"

"I have to have a story, all because I'm not bold or brazen?" she asks, and I look her over, taking in each move she makes, whether that be just a lift of her brow or the twitch of her lip.

God, I'd like to suck on the plump flesh.

"No, let's just say I have a knack for reading people, and I can tell you have some things you've been through that have made you closed off and maybe afraid to be the real you."

This intrigues her, making her pause a moment. I can imagine she's trying to decide what or just how much to tell me.

"Listen, it's so easy for women like me—"

I interrupt her, "Women like you? What do you mean, Hanna?"

Rolling her eyes and tsking at me, she answers, "As if you don't know."

"No, Hanna, I don't. And I'm wishing you would stop skating around it. Just say it," I demand, and she rights herself.

Lifting her chin in defense, she answers, "Being a plus-sized woman. In today's world, it is so easy to pretend we love ourselves, voice it to the world with gusto. But inside, we are still hurting. It comes off weak and as more reason to lose weight or eat better, so we hide the pain. We aren't allowed to show when the world bites us."

I understand what she means, but with her, I don't see it. I see flaws, but they only add to her desirable features. I see curves, dips, and more, and it makes me want to explore. Why can't she believe, while she may not be for everyone, her body is exactly right for me?

"Well said, puppet, but can you trust when I say I find you arousing? That I have thought about exploring your body nonstop since the day I first saw you?"

She shakes her head, rolling the stem of her wine glass in her between her fingers.

"Why not?" I push, and I swear it's on the tip of her tongue and that I am on the cusp of getting it out.

"I've always been told I'm 'pretty for a big girl.' You don't have to tell me that," she responds, still avoiding whatever is under the surface.

"Those are two different things, Hanna. I'm not talking about your facial beauty. I'm referring to your body. If you want me to discuss what I think of your characteristics, I can, but I mean it's all appealing; *all* of you is desirable."

Her eyes widen as she slowly lifts her head to look at me.

Did it finally get through? That I want to make this woman fucking mine? Make her so damn mad over me that she craves me constantly? Needs me to come at all hours, to be raw and harsh with her? Do things she would never have imagined?

"When I was in high school, a guy like you, attractive…" She quirks a brow. "Don't let your head get too big. Anyway, he was attractive, fairly popular. I wouldn't say the most, but he was well known. Well, one day, he started showing interest in me. I was skeptical, as I wasn't the ideal type I had seen him with. But he was nice." She shakes her head. "God, why am I telling you this?"

"Because I asked you to, and you trust me enough to. Trust is important in these arrangements. Keep going."

"Fine. So after he asked me out, I of course was excited. I'd never been on a date or had anyone interested in me. Add the fact that I was in my third foster home that year, and it was refreshing. Even if it would only lead to friendship, which I assumed that was going to be the likely outcome."

She's interrupted when the doorbell rings.

"Hold that thought. Let me get us our sweets." I make quick work of grabbing the bag, plating the food, and setting it up in the living room.

"Did you just order dessert from the restaurant we left?" She laughs, looking at the spread.

"You're correct. I wanted their cake. And we need the extra fuel."

"I guess there's always room for dessert."

I watch in amazement as she cuts off a bite of the cake and moans around the chocolate now filling her mouth. My cock hardens instantly. I fork off a piece of my own and take a bite. Not surprisingly, it taste just like I remember. It's a hit or miss sometimes with Dean's when it comes to their food, but their desserts have been the same recipe since I was a kid.

"You can continue." I urge her to finish her story.

"Basically, he had an agenda. He took me out, said all the right things. Told me I was beautiful. Asked me to be his girlfriend. Some cliché, Cinderella-type stuff, and I was at his feet. And after a few more dates and him treating me like I was God's gift to green earth, I gave him all of me. I let him have my virginity. Hell, I even told him I loved him." She takes a sip of wine, but instead of picking the fork back up and eating more, she nervously starts running her palms up and down her jean-clad thighs.

"Hanna?" I stop and place my hand on her shoulder, bending my head just enough to see her face better. Her chest is red, her eyes wet, and I hear the small whimper.

"Theo. Can we please not do this tonight? Please go. I can't...listen to this." She stands, pacing the room and growing more nervous, her anxiety heightening. I see the pain so deeply embedded in her eyes that even I feel remorse, and I don't even know the whole story.

"No. I'm not leaving. You need to calm down; you are getting too worked up." I stand and move to her.

"No, please, just leave! Please."

Suddenly, my mind hones in, focusing on what needs to be done. Control. I have to gain it back, and I have to show her that she needs it. Grabbing her by the hips, I lift her and move us to the couch, and she yelps.

"Theo! What are you doing?" Sitting down first, I lay her across my lap, and before she can ask me again, I swat her round ass so hard she screams.

"Theo! What are you—"

Thwack! Another one.

"Please—"

Thwack!

"You need to calm down, and if this will get you to listen, then so be it," I tell her, slapping her once more, and this time, she moans. Not just a little noise—it's loud, erotic, and it takes everything in me not to remove her jeans and panties, to hit skin with skin, show her what pleasure really feels like. "Was that a moan, puppet?"

She hesitates, slowly lifting her head and turning it to the side to look at me. Swallowing thickly, she nods.

"Yes. Another...please?"

My chest swells with pleasure and pride. "I knew you were the perfect woman for this arrangement."

I pull my hand back and give her thick ass one more slap, the sound echoing in the room. I help sit her up, and she doesn't say anything. Instead, she keeps her head hung in shame.

"Come here, Hanna." I pull her to me and make her straddle my lap. Her body tries to put up a fight, and I'm assuming she thinks I can't handle her weight. Oh, but I can. When she's fully seated on my lap, I place my hand around her neck and kiss her cheeks, her jaw, the places on her neck that are exposed.

I move her hair from her face, and she looks me in the eyes, slowly leaning back. "This seems a lot like romance. Your tender touch? I thought whatever this is can't have romance attached?"

Smiling, I nod. "It's called aftercare. Do not mistake it for love, Hanna. When I'm rough with you, I know I need to take care of you and tend to you afterward. I need to make sure you feel safe in the environment. That it wasn't too much for you."

"Okay, so what now?" Her question is breathy, filled with wonder.

"Now, we pick a safe word. We won't always have sex like this. There will be times where I will need a release without the other things, and I fully expect you to voice when you need a release as well."

"I'm embarrassed to admit I liked that. Why did I like it, Theo?"

I shrug. "We will find out why as we start to explore, but what's for sure is you need to voice to me the things you like and don't, and if something you don't like happens when we are in the middle of fucking, you need to have a safe word."

"Like stop?"

"No." I chuckle. "That's something you may say when you actually want more. If the pleasure seems too much but you still want to keep going...that word may come out often." I run my hands over her thighs, loving the feel of her curves and the soft skin that isn't distracted from by bones. It's so god damn enticing. Moving around to her ass and massaging the skin that my hand surely left prints on. She squirms a bit but keeps her mind here and focused. I already know what the word is, but it will be interesting to see what she comes up with. I love a little game with my submissive toy.

"So what should it be?" I ask

I watch her rack her brain, not being able to think of anything and when she blushes and shrugs, I know she won't be able to pick one, so I tell her what I already know, what she actually already knows...

"Sirius."

She snorts. "Like...serious?"

"No, S-I-R-I-U-S."

She laughs harder, the sound fucking stunning. "You must really like Harry Potter. You put your number in my phone with that name too."

Smiling inwardly at her choice of words, I shake my head. "No, puppet. The star Sirius. It explains so well what will happen when we do this. It is the brightest and hottest star in the sky. If my touch starts to burn too much and you say that, I'll know." We have spent most of the night talking about this arrangement and other things, but she has not fully agreed.

"Yes."

"Yes?" I want to make sure what she means, double check with her.

"Yes. To the safe word. To everything. I trust you. But you better not be the one person who makes me regret everything again. I won't be a foolish woman twice, Theo. When this is over, end it the right way. I'm not a pawn. I'm not a joke. I'm a person. You will treat me as such, and that's *my* rule."

Nodding, my lips curve. Her answer shocks me. I was expecting she would ask me more questions or tell me she isn't sure yet, but just like that, she gives in. Maybe me slapping her ass and her enjoying it showed her a different side to this. "I can do that. You have so much to learn from a real man, Hanna. In time."

Nodding, she ends there, and we sit in comfortable silence for a bit, her eyes roaming over my covered torso. I can tell she's wondering what's underneath and is starving for just a glimpse. But this is only night one. In time.

"We need to finish eating, then I need to get going. I have work early, and you need rest."

This stuns her. Sitting back, she eyes me. "So we aren't doing anything tonight?"

Smiling, I shake my head in response. "No, not tonight. You need just a little bit more time with me. You think you're comfortable, but I need to make sure I feel you are too."

"I won't fall in love with you. Trust me." She stands, taking her seat next to me on the couch.

"I'm counting on that, greens."

Soon, we finish the food and share one more glass of wine, and then I'm gone. I'm ready for the next time we will meet, and I have just the fucking plan.

Twelve

HANNA

His touch was electrifying. I felt it from the top of my head to the tips of my toes. It ignited something in me that I didn't even know I needed—hell, that I wanted. But he was thrilling, and I was aching for more. In fact, I spent almost the entire night thinking about all of it. A knot in my stomach sat heavy, and I couldn't get it to leave. Until the exhaustion finally made it.

Waking up the next morning, I felt invigorated, even though I lost hours of sleep I should have gotten. Now, I'm working and stocking shelves, trying my hardest not to mess up the price tags, because all I can think about is what this thing is with Theo.

If last night was just a prelude, what will the main scene be?

"Hey? You in there?"

Shaking my head when I hear Brenda, I look to her and see her eyeing me worriedly.

"No, I'm great. Just got a lot on my mind. Sorry. Were you

standing here long?" I put down the pricing gun and turn my focus to her.

"I mean I said your name three times before you finally noticed me. I heard you and my brother were at Dean's last night." It's a statement, not a question.

"Yeah, I mean...is that okay? I'll totally understand if it's not."

She waves me off. "Please, as long as you're happy and okay with it, I have no say in what two adults want to do. But if it goes to hell in a hand basket, I will beat his ass, and you will have to choose me in the divorce."

I giggle, pushing her shoulder with a roll of my eyes.

"It's nothing. Just casual. That's all."

"Hmm. Casual. Sure. Anyway, I need help this weekend with payroll. Janice is out, and I am swamped. You think you could help me with some office stuff this week?"

"Of course! I'm good with numbers, so hopefully I'll be your saving grace."

We both share a laugh. "It's easy, but with all the other things I need to do, I could just use the extra help. You're the best! I'll update your schedule to reflect this, and if you see anything you need changed, let me know."

"Absolutely, thanks, Brenda."

Winking, she turns with a happy jaunt in her step. I'm ninety-nine percent sure she is seeing someone new. The way she's been this week, all giddy, checking her phone constantly...and I swear I caught her snapping some flirty pictures and sending them. But we are still fairly new as friends, and I don't want to overstep.

Tonight, I have plans to do some more research on my grandfather and my parents. There's been this hole, it feels like, inside my chest since the day I found out about him, and even more since I've been here. It's made it hard to truly settle into the space and get comfortable. I feel like a ghost roaming the halls—an unwanted ghost. Even though Jack and Brenda have both assured me that JD would never think that, I can't help it. Feeling unwanted is all I've ever known. Projecting that onto everyone and everything is sort of a habit for me now.

The most I know is he was well known around town, basically a celebrity. He was ridiculously wealthy, and he was my mother's father. I don't know who my grandmother was either. She died before Jack even got to meet her. Why not leave this all to my mother? Really.

Sure, they didn't talk, from what Jack has said, but neither did we. So why? There has to be a reason, and I don't think I'll be able to let it go until I truly know the real reason. Don't I deserve that? To know who I am? Where I came from? Why someone never helped me out of the world I grew up in? Can't I be afforded that, at least? Everyone deserves to know where they came from so they can find where they belong. Wandering aimlessly without any idea of who you are is isolating; it's lonely. It's heartbreaking, and I just want a moment for my heart to slowly heal, the cracks to bind together gently, so that I can start to find myself.

But now, Theo is in the mix. How did I get here? In less than a month, I've been left with a house, millions, got a new job, and now know a man who wants to have an intense sexual relationship. I would say friends with benefits, but that would indicate that we know each other personally on a deeper level, and we don't. This is going to be purely physical.

Is this part of me feeling lost? Am I doing this because I want to have this type of relationship to find myself, or am I trying to fill a void? Maybe both? All this thinking has my head hurting, bringing on a throbbing migraine. Good thing I only have a few hours left of work, and then I can get home and take it easy.

Thirteen

HANNA

"DID JACK GIVE YOU A KEY TO THIS DOOR?" BRENDA asks, standing at the opposite end of the hall from the master bedroom. She jiggles the handle, and I shake my head.

"Nope, he said he gave me everything that was left."

"What if there are dead bodies on the other side?" she questions, smiling.

"Ha-ha," I mock. "Can you take this seriously and come help me look through these boxes?"

Sighing, she walks to me. "Yeah, I guess. I just think it's weird that this door is locked and there is no key."

I thought this too, but I assume it's somewhere in this house. "It might be in these boxes. I pulled them out of the attic yesterday and wanted to take a look through them. Maybe there will be some useful things in here."

"Yeah, like the key to the morgue over there." She nods toward the locked door she was just at.

I giggle. "Seriously, you watch too much true crime television."

Lifting her shoulders, she shakes her head. "You say that now, but one day, I could save your life if you ever go missing. Laugh it up. Make fun of me—I'll remember it."

Her sense of humor is my favorite thing about her. I've never had a friend like Brenda, and that says a lot, since it's been less than a month.

"Bills. Paperwork and just useless stuff. I can't find anything about *me*. Not even one picture." I huff, growing angry by the third box.

"Maybe we should throw in the towel and do something else. You will find something, okay?" Placing her hand on my forearm, she rubs the skin reassuringly with her thumb.

"Yeah, you're right. Thanks. Sorry, I feel like any time we hang out, it's been nothing but pity stories and treasure hunting for said pity stories." Standing, I move the boxes and line them up in two different stacks—a completed one and what I still need to sift through.

"I don't mind. You are like a real-life unsolved mystery."

"Ugh, rude." I shove her shoulder, and we both laugh.

"I got you laughing. So how rude am I now?"

"Touché. Want to go see a movie or something? I could use a night of distraction." I pull out my phone and check to see if Theo has messaged me, but there is nothing. After he left last night, it's been silent. I'd been expecting him to at least tell me when we would see each other, but nothing. Work must be that busy. Or he realized he had a lapse in judgement and wants out of this whole thing.

Negative thoughts—shut them down, Hanna, I inwardly scold.

"Yes! There is a new horror movie. You like them?" Brenda claps her hands.

"I'm not the biggest fan, but I can try it out. Is it more slasher or psychological thriller?" I ask, slipping on my brown knee-high boots.

"Thriller, which is scary to me," she admits.

"Agreed. All right, let me feed the pups, then we can go."

● ● ●

"I WON'T BE SLEEPING TONIGHT. SO THAT'S FUN," I ADMIT as we step out of the small theater and onto the main street sidewalk. I like this small town at night, lots of people walking around, neon lights flashing. People sitting and sipping drinks while taking up benches. It's like New York, except you aren't shoulder-to-shoulder, and everyone knows everyone. It's not just people passing by without a care in the world or without worry of what the other passersby are doing.

"I knew it was him the entire time. I'm good at this stuff."

"What stuff?" I reach into my purse and pull out some gum for the both of us.

"Guessing the plot and knowing the ending. I used to narrate movies while we watched them as a family, and I swear it used to get under my brother's skin so bad." She laughs, and suddenly my mind is back on Theo.

I don't mind that he hasn't called. That's not what this is. But he did go radio-silent and then nothing. Am I anxious to start this thing with him? Yes, but I'm also ready despite my fears. The way I craved his harsh touch after he slapped my ass—it's all I've thought of since.

"Yeah, I'm terrible at guessing things. Most the time, I'm wrong about how the movie is going to go." I don't bring up Theo. I skirt so far around her mentioning him, because truth be told, I don't want to make her uncomfortable or worry we are going to take this to a point where she may have to get involved.

No strings attached.

"I'm a Libra, the most powerful sign," she says as explanation, and I snort. She nudges my shoulder. "What?"

"Nothing. That's just such a Libra thing to say."

"Oh really, and what are you? Oh, let me guess, a Pisces!"

"Not even close. I'm Scorpio."

"Fuck off. No way, that is impossible. You don't read like a Scorpio."

Brenda isn't wrong. I don't have one ounce of bravery in my bones. But maybe being here, that will change. I'm hoping it will. In fact, I've set out to make this a thing. I want this to work.

There was a life before Cherry Hill that I never want to remember. Reinventing myself sounds like the perfect thing to do. New friends, new job, new life, and a deviously handsome man who wants to please me in a way I will most likely never experience again when we grow tired of one another?

One would say I'm halfway to this reinvention.

"I'm too nice." I shrug.

"I mean, you're nice, but I wouldn't say *too* nice."

Scoffing, I climb into the car after she unlocks it. Once we are both inside, I respond, "I'm sure you could basically call me a pushover."

"No, see? I hate that shit. Women can be kind and still be bad-ass. People are always mistaking our kindness for weakness. You ever seen a kind person snap?" When she turns the key, the engine starts.

"No." I snap my seatbelt. "What's that like?"

"Lethal. Keep the kindness, but don't be ashamed of it. You will stick up for you when you need to."

"Ah, such a Libra, all about lifting others up." I sigh in a teasing manner.

"Yeah, but I'm also a fierce one. I have a little sassy streak. It gets me in trouble a lot."

"Oh, I bet. I wouldn't want to be caught in a brawl with you."

"Exactly." She winks.

We share a small conversation before she drops me off, and we call it a night. I have an early shift to go in and help her with payroll, so an early bedtime tonight is just the thing.

Stepping into the bathroom to shower, I then put on an oversized T-shirt and some panties. For some reason, I feel emotionally, mentally, and physically drained. I walk out of the bathroom, flip off the light, and stop.

I look around the room, and my eyes land on the bed. I haven't slept in it yet, too afraid it will be weird. But my hell does it look comfortable. There are guest rooms I've slept in, but the beds are as hard as a rock, making me favor the couch. Tiptoeing to the bed, I approach it as if it's not an inanimate object but more like some sort of animal that may get spooked if I step up to it too fast.

Slowly, I turn and sit, and instantly, my body sinks into the mattress as I moan. *God, that's nice.* I run my hands over the new bedding I bought. It seemed like the right thing to do, in case I ever got to this point. My palm glides over the soft fabric of the intricate floral bedding I found at this small shop in town.

"Nice," I whisper.

Is it weird sleeping in his bed? In his room?

Maybe. But I'm so tired of stiff beds, and I'm not made for sleeping on sofas. I want one night of comfortable rest. Maybe I'll try it out, and if I like it and it doesn't feel too wrong, I'll sleep in here every other night. Build up to the full commitment.

God, Hanna, it's a bed, not a marriage proposal.

Climbing all the way on, I lift my hips, move the blanket, and slide under it, getting comfortable. The second my head hits the pillow, I'm in bliss, too cozy to think about much, and I drift off fast. So fast I can't even remember anything past my head meeting the pillow.

I jolt up when I hear Dorothy and Clyde barking at the front door downstairs, hurriedly tossing my feet over the side of the bed.

My heart rate is beating like a jackhammer. I feel the anxiousness setting in, the unsettling feeling of being watched, being followed, being someone's prey, and it overwhelms me.

The barking gets more aggressive, and that's when I hear the clear sound of the door handle being violently pulled and turned, someone clearly attempting to get in. Panic overtakes me, and I do the only thing that comes to mind.

Call Theo.

Reaching over to the bedside table, I grab my phone, my shaky hands doing a terrible job of trying to scroll to his number. Once I'm on it, I click Dial.

"Puppet? What's going on? It's two in the morning." He doesn't sound groggy.

Was he even asleep?

"Someone is trying to break in! Theo, I'm scared. It's all happening again. I'm not crazy." He has no idea what I mean, but the fear has me at its mercy, and I can't help but word-vomit. I don't know what possesses me in that moment, but I stand and move to the doorway and down the hall until I'm at the end, taking a peek around the wall. I see a shadow pacing the front porch, looking in windows, and I feel sweat drip down my neck and back.

"Theo," I whisper.

"Hanna, listen to me. Go into the bathroom, lock yourself in there, and I will be there in less than two minutes."

I must have not heard him when he got in the truck while lost in my own thoughts. I can hear it roar to life and the tires screeching.

"I'm at the top of the stairs. I can see someone on the porch. They're looking into the windows. I'm scared they're going to—"

The sound of glass shattering stops me, and I scream, running back into the bedroom and then the bathroom.

"Hanna, talk to me! What was that?" Theo hollers. Locking the bathroom door and running into the closet, I cower into a corner as the tears stream down my face.

"They broke the window. Theo! Please hurry! Please!" I'm desperate. I can't be here again. This can't be real. There is no way in hell this is happening. It has to be a random break-in. It has to. No one in New York would know where I am. Not a single person.

"I'm almost there. Where are you? Did you lock yourself in the bathroom like I told you?"

"Y-Yes," I stutter.

"Good. I'm almost there. Do you hear anything?"

"No. The dogs are barking. Wait." I hear the sound of a loud engine starting. "Are you here?"

"Almost. What do you hear?"

"I think they're leaving. I'm going to check."

"The fuck you are. You don't move until I'm at the door. What's the safe word, baby? So you know it's me."

"It's um...shit." I wipe at my errant tears, overwhelmed.

"Breathe. You listen and do as I say, puppet. What is the safe word?" His voice is cool, collected—calm. And it works.

"Sirius."

"Good girl. I'm pulling up now, and I'm going to check around the house, then I'll be up. Stay put."

"Yeah. I mean, yes. Okay."

He stays on the phone, and I hear him walking around, boots hitting gravel then the wood of the porch.

"Fucker," he grits out, the sound of a lock unlatching and then glass cracking. I hear the dogs and footsteps padding up the stairs, and I anxiously await his voice. There is a rap on the door followed by his low timbre. "Sirius, puppet."

With that, I'm on my feet, running to the door and throwing it open. He's on me just as fast as I'm on him, and I cry into his chest, a full-on sob, unashamed and unrestrained.

Fourteen

HANNA

"LOOK AT ME, HANNA."

I lean back and wipe at the tears. He towers over me, and surprisingly, given the situation, it's comforting. I feel safe.

He grabs my neck, a tight grip like he so often does, a signature move of his that I've come to crave. "You are going to tell me what the fuck happened," he demands, using his thumb to lift my chin.

"Someone tried to get in."

"No, no. You said it's happening *again*, and you're going to tell me what is going on."

"It's complicated," I rasp out. What is there to say that won't make me sound like a madwoman? I couldn't get the cops to believe me. Why would he?

"I'm a smart man. I'll manage. Now," he bites out, and I wait a brief moment, trying to decide where I'm going with this. How to lead in a way he will follow yet not think I'm crazy.

"I know someone was stalking me in New York. I'm sure of it.

And I can't help but feel they followed me here." My voice is as calm as it can be.

"You were being stalked?"

"Yes. I always felt someone watching me. I know it sounds crazy, but I felt it, right in my bones. But then I confirmed it when every other night, if not *every* night, someone would come to my door and just rattle the handle. It's like they were trying to taunt me, build up to some grand finale. Get me good and ready and then come get me when I least expected it. Like some sick cat-and-mouse game."

He looks angry, like he wishes he could take my words and squeeze the life from them. "You didn't go to the cops?"

I nod. "I did, but I had no proof. Whoever it was, they were smart. They never left anything, never made themselves known other than the nightly visits. I looked like a crazy person. And I started to believe it."

"Is that why you came here? Running from a stalker? Did you have enemies, Hanna?"

My eyes widen, and I shake my head frantically. "Theo, I didn't know anyone. I didn't even have friends. I kept to myself, and anyone I came in contact with, I was more than nice to. I have no reason to be mean, and I especially have no reason to have any enemies."

"You aren't lying to me, are you?" He squeezes tighter, and I'm confused by his question.

"No. What's wrong? Why are you questioning me?" Then it

hits. "Oh God. You think I'm crazy too. You think it's all in my head."

"Puppet, I never said that. I'm just trying to figure this shit out."

"*You* are? What about me? I'm the one whose house got broken into. I'm the one who was ran out of New York because of some crazed person who for whatever reason is after me. I don't need another person to make me feel like I'm insane. If that's what you're thinking, then just leave." I step back, breaking the contact.

"No, I'm not fucking leaving." He sounds on edge.

I turn my back to him. "Theo, I've never had any reason to make up lies or hide anything. I'm telling the truth, and if you want to be another person who doesn't believe that or can't see me for who I am, then you and I can't have this. Us. Whatever this thing is."

He's on me, his hard front to my back, his large hands cupping my waist and squeezing. "I never said that. I'm still trying to feel you out and get to know you. You have to give me a second to work this all out in my head." There is something more there that he isn't telling me. I can feel it. How? I don't know, but I can.

"What's this really about?"

"What do you mean? I just told you," he tells me, and I turn to face him.

"No, two can play this game. I'm trying to figure *you* out. You're all broody and hot and cold. One minute, you're telling me you want this and want to do all these things, but then you don't call or text me at all. Then you show up and start questioning me as if I made up whatever happened tonight. So what is this really about, Theo?" I raise my voice, irritated now.

"Fuck this." His lips land on mine hard, claiming me, possessing me, hungry and eager for more.

"What—" I try to get words out, but he has a mission, and I'm not going to survive it. I give in and kiss back, our hands exploring each other, fighting for dominance.

He reaches down and in one swift motion grabs the side of my panties and pulls, ripping them from me. The shredded material falls to ground, and he moves us backward toward the bathroom, our tongues and lips still dueling.

"You are so infuriating. You ruined everything. You got in my head, and now all I want to do is fuck you senseless. Punish you for making me crave you," he growls, stepping back a couple of feet when we're in the bathroom. He eyes me over, and I'm suddenly fully aware of myself and my body. Without his closeness, it's a stark reminder of my blaring insecurities.

"Shirt off," he demands.

I jump at the harshness, and I scramble to do so. He has to see it all, to know if this is really what he wants. If in all my nakedness—covered in flaws, imperfections—he can still desire me, lust for me, then maybe I can start to embody that confidence I've been praying to one day have...and have so boldly. I lift it slowly, each inch of fabric like a suit of armor that is protecting me from the war all around me. The war with myself and the war I have with the world that made me anything and everything opposite of brave.

I feel it all, each inch of fabric like the loss of my last piece of protection. Once it's off, I'm bared. All of me and every part of me, especially the parts I dread to ever call beautiful.

He rubs his hands together, licking his bottom lip. "I'm going to have so much fun with your body, puppet."

I gulp at the hunger so evident on his face that even my loudest insecurities can't doubt it.

"Where now?" I don't know what to say or do. I'm at his will.

"Good girl, asking me what to do. I love the idea of controlling you tonight."

"Then...then do it," I whisper.

"In the shower, rinse under the water. Take your body wash and clean yourself for me."

I hesitate for just a moment. But that pause is short-lived, my desire so loud my ears burn from it. My toes curl, and the hair on my head feels hot.

I step in, never breaking eye contact with him. I leave the glass door open, and he starts to take his shirt off. And the image in front of me is better than the fantasy I had in my head all this time. His skin is so golden he must spend a lot of time out in the East Coast sun. His abs are defined, each side meeting at the deep line down his stomach. His pecs are thick, his collarbone contoured in a masculine way, and that's the best way to describe *him*. Male and flawless.

We are the flawed and flawless, standing in front of one another.

He shuts the bathroom door so the shower can create steam as he closes me in, pulling the shower door closed as well. Why is he adding the barrier? I reach for the honeysuckle-scented body wash, and I put just a little on my hands and begin to run the soap over my arms first. He watches, not breaking eye contact as his hands work at removing his belt. Biting my lip, I move my hands over my collarbone and neck.

"Breasts, Hanna. Pinch your nipples for me."

My eyes widen. I've never heard a man make crass language and crude actions sound so desirable. I'm teetering on the line of wanting to do this without pause all while hesitating to give into it. No matter the arousal, I still have insecurities.

Slowly, I do as he ordered. My nipples are peaked, and my body thrums to life. Hungry with desire for his touch, for the pleasure I pray he is going to finally give me.

"Just like that, baby girl. So fucking good. Stroke between your legs." He has this raw look in his eyes, like a rabid animal loose from his confines. It's hard to look away and even harder to say no when he traps me with that look. It's like he's tethered to me, controlling each move.

Slowly, slipping my hand down my curves, each indent, jagged edge, and all, I reach between my legs and rub my clit, immediately crying out. And right as I do this, he releases his cock from his pants. It's large, curved, and nearly hitting his navel. And God is he thick. I can feel the sting of him entering me already, but that sting can't overshadow how pleasurable it will feel. I just know it.

"Eyes on me. Work your clit until you come. You break eye contact with me and I will make you do it again before I give you my cock. I mean it."

I nod and start circling faster, the pleasure intensifying. I'm overcome with all the sensations. The small part of me with a million nerves igniting is too much, and when he bites his lip and squeezes his cock, I orgasm, throwing my head back. It lasts forever, dragging on and on until I can't take it anymore and it becomes overly sensitive. I roll my head forward when I hear him speak.

"Tsk, tsk, you didn't look at me. Again," he commands.

"Wh-What?" I stutter through my heavy breaths. He places one palm on the fogged glass, and his other works his cock, and all I can think about—all I crave—is him putting it inside me. I've never wanted anything more.

"You didn't look me in the eye. I want to see that look."

"What look?"

"The one where reality slips away and euphoria numbs you."

Dear God.

"But I...I can't. It's too sensitive."

His lips lift in the corner, his honey eyes turning a much darker shade. A man turning into a beast. A hungry beast who wants to devour and will not let anything stop him.

"You have no idea. You will come again. And then I'll take that sore pussy and make you come all over me. Now do it again." He tilts his head and dares me to say no.

I don't want to. I want to say yes a million times, and I fear I just might. Bend and break at his demands.

I start to rub my clit again, my body shivering and my upper body jolting forward a bit from the hypersensitivity.

"Chase that. Don't lose pressure. When it hurts like that, push harder, rub faster. Match my pace." He picks up speed, jacking his cock, and the image if I were a fly on the wall—two hungry people, ready to devour and do whatever is necessary to touch, consume, and claim one another—is intense. I've heard of passion, but I never knew it could feel like this.

"I feel it. It hurts, Theo."

"Good, circle it harder."

I do just that, and I orgasm. This time, I keep my eyes on him and hold myself up with my free hand against the glass, right against where his is on the other side. He doesn't come yet, and I can't help but wonder if it's me. If the image of me naked and pleasing myself wasn't what he thought he'd see.

"Self-sabotage. I see it the moment you do it. Enough, Hanna." Throwing the door open, he steps in and up to me, gaining on me as I back up against the shower wall. He cages me in, one hand on the wall next to my head and the other at my throat. "You're going to take my cock like a good puppet, aren't you?"

I can't move my head when he has his fingers around my neck like a vice, so I whimper out a yes. "But please don't hurt me."

"Not yet. You have to get used to me. You on the pill?"

"No. I'm not."

"Fuck."

"I just finished my period. I won't be ovulating. Besides…I have a condition that makes it really hard to get pregnant." I hope he doesn't ask about that. He has no reason to, since this is purely sexual.

"The idea of you taking my cum, every drop, bare, is more than enough to make me mad with anticipation. I'm not waiting."

"Good."

He kisses me, and God does he kiss me. Our tongues dual, trying to steal each other's taste. "Fuck, you taste so damn good. Let's see what you taste like elsewhere, baby." He sinks to his knees, and my shoulders stiffen.

I've never had a man go down on me. When he touches the plush, soft skin of my stomach, I look down. And then he's kissing me…right there, my most insecure place. The place I wish I could cut a thousand and one times with a knife or scissors. And he kisses it…so sensually. Like the skin there, the fat, is just there, nothing to be bothered by or in the way. It's almost like it doesn't exist. I fight back the tears, watching a man kiss me in my most despised place. This is the most vulnerable I've ever been.

"You want this?" he asks, obviously sensing my hesitation.

"Yes. Please." I want to give in to it for once, lean in to the fall. Turn my back on my insecurities and just feel. Be numb in the euphoria like he said. I deserve it. Every woman, no matter her shape or size, deserves to feel what desire is like and not spend her entire time afraid of it.

For just this moment, I want to act as if I'm the girl I always wanted to be.

Without another word, he lifts my leg and places my foot on his shoulder, biting, sucking, and licking up my calf and thigh. And when his mouth meets my center and the warmth and feel of him floods me, I'm gone. I'm in the pleasure, enthralled by it, more lost in it than I can explain. But he's an expert with his tongue. He massages my thighs as he strokes up and down my center, from my opening to my clit.

"Theo...that's so good," I moan, gripping his hair.

"You can fuck my face, puppet. Don't be ashamed. Take your pleasure first."

I do exactly as he says. I start to roll my hips in tandem with his licks, and it matches perfectly, hitting all the right spots that I need it to. I'm on the edge, so close I'm about to fall off the cliff, and just as I'm about to, he stops.

"Fuck. I need you on my cock. Now." He gets more aggressive with his touch, standing and walking me to the seated part of the shower. "You are going to ride me. It will be easier to adjust from this position."

Suddenly, that bold vixen from just moments ago goes back into hiding. "Theo, I can't do that."

"You can, and you will." He sits, his cock large and erect, and our difference in weight is highly apparent in this moment. "Hanna. I'm not going to change all the sinful ways I'm going to take you just because you think I can't handle it. I want your body. I want your cunt, and I need it now. So be a good girl and come sit on this cock." My eyes widen, my legs rubbing together.

"Dirty talk. Is that the trick? Does my puppet like that?"

I nod, blushing.

"Good to know. Now, here." He uses his middle and index finger to signal me to him, and I walk on shaky legs, uneven steps and all, but I do it. I place one hand on his shoulder, the taut muscle warm and thick. He places his hand on my hip and the other on my opposite leg to help me straddle him.

"Slowly. You need to go slow," Theo instructs.

"I can do that." I've only ever had sex once, and it wasn't an experience worth remembering. Not only did it hold zero pleasure, but it also held the most malicious of pain.

Using one hand, he aligns his cock with my center and lowers me with his hand on my hip. When the first inch enters, we both let out a breath. My eyes peer at him beneath hooded lids, and he is watching me, not taking his gaze from me. I match that look; it's the only thing helping me keep up this façade that I'm not wildly intimidated by his perfection and my flaws meeting face to face.

"You feel so damn good, puppet. Take some more. You're taking me so well."

"You feel really big," I admit.

"I am. You'll appreciate that when you get used to it." He winks.

"Cocky."

He grins. "Exactly."

I roll my eyes and let him help me take a few more inches. The stretch and the pull, it's like mania. You are caught in the high, unable to come down.

"Good girl. Almost all the way. You have the tightest cunt."

I have always heard that word and associated it with all the things you should never use it for. Never did I think about how good it would sound coming from his deep timbre. He rubs and squeezes at the fat on my hip and stomach. I feel a brief moment of insecurity, but then he moans, kneading it deeper. And suddenly, that skin I usually find repulsive is being used as a sexual and desirable thing. And I can't help but, dare I say...feel absolutely beautiful.

"I don't know how to do what's next," I tell him when he is fully inside. Trying not to read too much more into his touch. I can't go there.

"First, you're going to adjust, giving it a minute, then you will let me control your hips."

"Okay."

"Tell me what you feel. I need words too."

"You feel good. I want more. I want it all," I admit.

"You look so fucking sexy on top of me. I'm going to need this view in my everyday routine."

I shake my head. "You don't know if I'll be any good at it," I counter.

"That's the best part. Nothing better than teaching you how to take cock like a good puppet."

"You call me puppet a lot. And greens," I point out.

"Get used to it. Ready?"

I nod. Both his hands are on my hips, and he does what he said he would. Controls them, pulling me forward and lifting me up, then down.

"Now, I want you to roll your hips back and forth when I bring you down."

"Okay." I nod, putting all my trust into him. He lifts me up the length of him, and I swear I feel every outline, vein, and inch. And when he pulls me back down, I do as he says, and the sound he releases has my core tightening. I have never felt more powerful over not only my body but a man's.

"That's what a man needs. That's what I like. You have power here. You see that, don't you?"

I nod, too drunk on the pleasure to speak.

"Words."

"Yes, I feel it."

"But make no mistake, puppet—you have power, but I have control."

"Isn't power bigger than control?" I moan when he pulls my hips forward.

Leaning in, he bites my nipple, and I yelp. "Power can't thrive if it isn't controlled, if someone can't harness it. That someone is me."

"Theo, it feels so good," I moan, the combination of his words and more becoming too much.

"Yeah, it does. You can't deny that I was right about this, can you?"

"No." After that, we fall silent for a moment. Instead, we are lost in one another—with me feeling pleasure that seems like it will forever be unmatched. This is what I will envision for the rest of my life. True lust, raw carnality.

He grips my hip tighter, reaching up with the other to grab my neck and keep my eyes on him. He keeps our pace steady and without fail.

"You take my cock so well. If only you could see what I see," he groans. This time, his head rolls back, and I watch the Adam's apple bob with his male appreciation.

"I think I'm going to come," I cry.

"Reach down and pinch your clit when I say. You come when I'm coming. I need you squeezing the cum from me with your tight cunt."

"Oh God, yes! Please!" I yell out.

"Right there. I'm there. Pinch it, puppet." Reaching between us, I pinch my clit, and I detonate around him, my core clenching tightly, and that's when I feel it. Hot spurts of his cum filling me as he keeps me riding out my orgasm, and I do until my body jolts and twitches from oversensitivity.

"Good girl." He leans in and kisses my neck, and I focus on breathing, trying to come down from the high. Except when I do, I regret it. Those pesky insecurities come washing over me again, drowning me in their depths. Coupled with me just having sex with Theo, a man I've barely known for a week, who I'm *only* having a sexual relationship with.

What do we do? Shake hands and say good day?

"What's going through your head, Hanna?" he asks me, the water behind us starting to turn lukewarm as it hits my back.

"Nothing. The water's getting cold, and we should probably shower?" I phrase it as a question. For what reason? I don't know. I'm nervous as hell if I'm being totally transparent.

"Yes, let's shower before I leave for the night."

There it is. Why do I suddenly feel dirty?

"Yeah, yes. Sure." I stand, and he slips from me, and I make sure I don't make a noise or look at him directly. This could be awkward for all parties involved. Yet, he seems so cool and collected. And it has me spiraling. "How many women have you been with?" I turn, the water cascading down my shoulders and back.

"Is that why you look like you just sinned in the middle of a church? Because you want to know how many women I've had this type of relationship with?"

Crossing my arms, I tilt my head up. I don't want to seem meek. "You know more about me than I do about you. And I think you and I should know a little bit about each other. Is this a fuck-and-bye type of thing, or are we at least going to attempt to enjoy each other's company?"

"That would imply dating, Hanna," he tells me, reaching for the shampoo. "Turn. I'm going to wash your hair."

I lift my hand before he does. "Enjoying each other's company is too serious, like dating, but washing my hair isn't?"

That has him stunned for a minute, his eyes searching mine

back and forth. "Touché. Now, turn. We can talk more about it."

Rolling my eyes, I do so, and the second my back is to him, he slaps my ass. I turn my head and look over my shoulder, the movement not only surprising me, but it jarred me just enough to where the water hit my face.

"Ouch," I scold.

"Get used to it. We will get there soon."

I turn back slowly, making sure he sees my annoyance in my eyes before I do. He starts to put the shampoo in my hair, and the second his long, thick fingers work at massages it in, I curse myself inwardly that it feels nice. Some moments go by before I ask him my question again. "So...how many women do I need to live up to?"

"None. I don't think about past flings."

"Ouch, that's harsh." I'll be one of those one day, but hey, I agreed to this.

"It's the truth."

"Can I just get the number?" I ask, exasperated.

"Forty-six."

I nearly choke on my damn breath. "Forty-six. You've been with forty-six women?"

"Yes." Collected. Unfazed. Unbothered. And any other word that could describe being completely careless.

"And we didn't use a condom." My stomach turns.

"Don't worry, Hanna. I've been checked since my last partner. I may not be into relationships, but I'm not a tool bag who is going to risk someone's health," he reassures me, and I release a deep breath.

Thank heavens. I wait a minute, processing what he just told me and what my next question should be.

"Rinse," he orders, buying me more time. I let the water rush over me, noticing how much cooler it is getting by the minute.

Completely rinsed, I turn. "You should go next. The water's getting cold."

He nods, and we switch places, but I don't stay in. Climbing out, I can feel his eyes on me, watching me, assessing my mood.

Stepping into the closet, I pull out a big, loose tee, one I bought in the men's section. I slip it on and step back into the bathroom. Brenda got me started on all these hair care and skin routines, so I start on those. Every few seconds, I look over at Theo, and he is alternating between looking at me and focusing on cleaning himself. Once my hair has all its leave-in products, I put on my night cream and step out into the bedroom, needing a minute to collect my thoughts.

I know I agreed to this, and I'm more than okay with it, but I think I deserve some wiggle room to adjust to this new development in my life.

My phone dings next to the bed, and I grab it, taking a seat on the edge of the bed and opening the message.

Brenda: Hey, I just got home and saw my brother's truck at your place. You okay?

I look at the time. It's nearing two in the morning.

Me: I'm fine. And it's awful late to be coming home...

Brenda: Deflecting much? I was out with a friend.

Me: Of the male or female category? lol

Brenda: It's 2am, and my brother is at your house. Glass houses—that's how the saying starts out, right?

Me: Fine. Listen, I know you said it was all right as long as I was okay with it, but I really don't want to make this weird. Is this weird?

Brenda: As hell, but I'm more than fine with it. You're adults. Just spare me any details. :D

Me: Gladly.

Brenda: Anyway. I was thinking we could go to the lake this weekend? Me and some of the girls are dying to get out while it's still not too busy. You in?

Me: Um, yeah sure.

Bathing suits. I hate bathing suits.

Brenda: We will get you a suit you are comfortable with.

I have not shied away from Brenda and basically wear my insecurities on my sleeve. I'm not surprised she read my mind.

Me: Perfect.

"It's getting late, and I have work in the morning. You do too. I was going to leave, but with a busted window and someone trying to break in, I'll stay here tonight," Theo says, coming out of the bathroom.

I wave him off. "You don't have to do that. I'll be fine."

"Not up for discussion." He's only in his briefs, and my tongue gets caught, because I can't stop looking at his lean and defined muscular physique.

"Control. Right," I finally say.

"Power and control. A good combination. Now, in bed, puppet." He goes to leave the room, and I let him, assuming he's going to sleep on the couch. I have nothing more to say. I'm tired. Stressed. Beyond overwhelmed with what happened tonight between him and me.

I feel used yet pleased. Confused...yet it makes perfect sense. This is going to take some adjusting, and we have less than a month left of this. I doubt I'll make it that far anyway. Guess I better buckle up, enjoy the ride that won't last long, but it's one I'll never forgot.

Nor do I want to.

Fifteen

THEO

I LIE ON THE COUCH, STARING UP AT THE CEILING, knowing she's above me and wearing nothing but a T-shirt. I still feel her around me, clinging to me. Her moans, her pleasure, the brief moment when she let go of the insecurities and gave in to her desires.

Less than a month. That's not enough time. Now that I've tasted her, had a glimpse of having her body at my mercy...less than a month isn't enough time to have my fill. I'll have to think something up, prolong my job here. Whatever it takes to get more of what I had tonight. What's more is I know this is just the beginning. This was just a prelude to the best sex we could ever have.

I didn't want to take her tonight, especially in such a savage adrenaline rush. But when I saw that glass on the floor, then the fear in her eyes, I needed it. I had to immerse myself in it, be inside her, let go of the anger that someone tried to break in and hurt her.

And if I would have been a minute behind, they just may have.

Making note that I need to come fix the window next to her front door, I focus on that. If I continue to fixate on my desire for her, I will march my ass back up there, pin her to the bed, and bury myself between her thick thighs.

I force my body to shut down. I have a lot to do tomorrow and can't focus on anything else. It's a busy day; that's where the focus needs to be.

Until the next time I get to have her.

※ ※ ※

I LOOK OVER THE FILES THAT WERE SENT OVER TO ME from my client, and I type up a new report. A report I'm sure they won't be happy with, as it will indicate needing more information, and it's not going in the direction they were hoping. I'm buying the time needed.

I click Send.

Now, I need to go to Hanna's and work on the window before she gets home. Brenda let me know she's working late to help her with payroll. Which is needed. I have dinner tonight with one of my old friends from high school, and if I'm being honest, if she were home or came home while I'm there, I wouldn't be going anywhere but the nearest flat surface—to fuck her on it.

Grabbing items needed at the hardware store, I'm almost out the door when I see her. Fuck me.

"Theo! Hey, I heard you were back in town."

Holly, my first girlfriend and last one I ever had. She hasn't changed much. She's wearing heavier makeup, but besides that, she still looks like the same girl I broke up with. She's the woman who made me realize I can't do monogamy. Do I feel bad? No. But she didn't do anything when we were together or today to cause me to be a total dick in this moment.

"Hey, Holly. Yep, in town for work."

She steps closer, now a little too close for my liking. Sensing her intentions the minute she looks me up and down with siren-like eyes, I know I need to end the conversation as fast as possible. There isn't an ounce of me interested in whatever she is trying to do here.

"That's great! For how long?"

"Long enough."

She tries to play off the sting of my obvious indication that I don't want to talk to her for much longer. A simple hi and bye would have sufficed.

"Oh, well, we should get dinner before you head back. I'd love to hear what it's like in New York!"

"Not this time, Holly. It was good seeing you." I walk around her, and she calls after me.

"If you change your mind, Brenda has my number."

I don't give her a look over my shoulder, a wave goodbye, nothing.

If Hanna wasn't in the picture, she would have done for a quick fuck, because I'm only here for a short time.

I finish up the window just in time. Hanna had texted me her response when I asked her what her plans for the upcoming weekend were. She said she was on her way home now to get into some normal clothes and then shopping for a swimsuit. A suit for the lake. The thought of her looking for a suit is the only thing on replay in my mind now. Brenda is dragging her out, and I told Hanna it's my time after that.

Heading back to my place, I shower and get ready to hang out with one of my old buddies from high school for a casual poker night in. Win for me—it gets a bit old going to the same old place like Dean's.

I get dressed and leave the house, but knowing that Hanna is out buying some swimsuit for the weekend right now is all I can think about. What will she pick? I should be there helping her choose, as I won't be at the lake this weekend. Some shit Brenda said about it being a girls-only thing.

Before I start the truck and head off, I text her.

Me: I want you to send me pictures.

Hanna: Of?

Me: Whatever you try on. Each item. Got it?

Hanna: Not gonna happen.

Theo: What was that?

Hanna: You heard me. I'm not sending you pictures of me in swimsuits. I don't need those landing in someone else's hands.

Theo: Okay.

Hanna: That was easy. I expected a full-on power trip.

Theo: Nope. Have fun.

I leave the text and go to my contacts. Clicking Dial on a name, I wait as it rings.

"Hey, Fitz. You on your way?" my buddy, James, asks.

"No. Change of plans. I have something I need to do. Raincheck."

"Man, that sucks. But I get it. Besides, I'm feeling lucky tonight. Don't want to clean your wallet out." He laughs, and I back up the truck.

"Bullshit. I always win. But I'll let you have this one. Catch ya later."

"Yeah, later."

My destination is about an hour away, but the drive will be worth the reward.

Pulling up in front of the mall, I enter and head toward the swim shop the nice concierge lady pointed me to. When I walk in, I scan the store and don't see them…but then I hear Brenda toward the back.

"I need to run to the bathroom. I'll be right back!" I see her stand from the seats by the fitting rooms, and I turn and face the wall, watching her over my shoulder. Her face is buried thankfully in her cell, so she doesn't see me. The minute she clears the store's entry, I'm moving. All the fitting room doors are open but one, and that tells me all I need to know.

"Hello, sir, is there something I can help you find?"

I think up something quick. "No, I'm good. Just meeting back up with my wife. She's in the fitting room."

She eyes me over, about to question me, but when she sees I'm not even sweating it, she buys it. "Okay, let me know if there's anything she may need."

"Will do, thank you." I move to the back and tap on the closed door.

"That was fast. Listen, I don't like—" She stops as the door opens and she sees me towering over her. "Theo? What are you doing here?" She tries to cover her body. She's wearing some two piece, and it's high-waisted. In my opinion, it doesn't show enough of her beautiful curves. As I step in, she backs up, and I close the door, locking it.

"You didn't want to send me pictures, so I came for something better—a live reel."

Her jaw drops. "You're insane, you know that? You need to leave so I can change."

I sit on the bench and cross my arms over my chest. "No, I'm good. Go on." I nudge my chin up and down at her, indicating for her to continue.

"Theo, no. I'm not letting you see me naked."

I chuckle. "Baby, I saw that bare pink pussy taking this cock so good while soaking-wet last night."

"Theo," she breathes out, arousal evident in her voice.

"Yes, Hanna?"

She rubs her thighs together, her chest turning red. How fucking beautiful is that? "You can't say things like that."

"And why is that? You afraid of how much you like it?"

"No. I just..." She stops, biting her lip, then soothes it with a lick.

I should be doing that.

"Exactly. You like the control. Now put on a show for me." Telling her this so brazenly is exactly what I know she wants.

She hesitates at first, looking me over. Then, without enough time to try to think of any way to say no even against her own desires, she reaches behind her and removes the string of the two-piece's top. And when it falls, those beautiful, full breasts expose themselves to me, and I instantly grow hard.

"I'm going to fuck you there one day...come on your beautiful tits."

She gasps but keeps going, removing her bottoms. Now, with her naked in front of me, I debate telling her to put the next one on, but what I really want is far darker and more dangerous. I have only a few minutes to do it before my sister is back.

With my middle and index finger, I signal her to come to me. She takes timid steps, like she always does, and I'm cruel to say I like it—her shyness, her blaring insecurities—because they belong to me now. They are mine to change and make her see what I see. Pure fucking beauty and raw sex appeal.

"You make a noise and we will be caught. You want that?" I ask her once she's up against the bench, between my legs. Shaking her head, she keeps her hands knotted in front of her stomach, trying to hide herself from me. Angry at this, I grab those hands and rip them apart before putting them behind her back, holding them together with one hand.

"Spread your legs a little for me. Don't make a sound. Eyes on me."

"Yes." So responsive. Prompt.

"Good girl."

She does as I say, and I reach between her legs, spreading her swollen, aroused lips to find her clit that's slick with her arousal, begging for a touch. "Wet in public. So dirty. You like me here. You like when I take what I want from you. Because it's what you want. Isn't it?" She nods, and I rub slow, such slow circles on her clit, that she bucks and gasps.

I remove my finger. "I said no noise, or I will open this door, bend you over, and fuck you in front of everyone."

"You wouldn't," she challenges.

"Oh, puppet. I would." My eyes don't waver, and that drives it home. "No more noise. I need you to come fast, or my sister is going to catch you getting finger-fucked by me. You want that?"

"No."

"Then hush." With that, I rub at her clit in strong circular motions, alternating between stroking and pinching. Her eyes don't leave mine. She's learning. I bite my lip.

"Can you do it?" she asks, a rosy hue highlighting her cheeks.

"Do what? Make you come?"

"No…the words. Those words," she whispers.

"Dirty girl. So dirty. You like to be fucked and told all the things I want to do to this body?"

"God, yes," she breathes.

"No god could touch you like this. You call me by my name. It's Theo. Now, I want you to come on my fingers, then I want you on your knees, sucking me off as if I paid you for it. You want that?"

She nods eagerly. It's amazing how she goes from wildly insecure to completely free of inhibitions when I get her to the point of pleasure that overtakes her.

"Come." A simple demand with the pinch of my fingers, and she does. That's all it takes.

I'm going to break her to fit every fantasy and desire I have. And in turn, they will become hers too.

There is a tap on the door. "Is…um…everything all right in there?"

I smirk, and Hanna covers her face, mortified.

"Yes, we found one she really, *really* likes. We will be out in a minute," I call to the saleswoman, then murmur against Hanna's ear, "Guess we will have to save you getting on your knees for next time." It makes her shiver.

"Okay. Let me know if there is anything you need," the woman replies, and I know she knows what just happened.

"You're bad for me," Hanna finally says, putting on her clothes.

"Precisely. That's why we're perfect. I'm bad for you, and you're exactly right for me."

Slipping the jeans up her hips, she pays no mind to my perusal of her curves.

"I'm back!" my sister announces, and instant panic settles on Hanna's face. Me? I'm not worried. Brenda can't tell me who I can and can't sleep with.

"You think you're so funny," the beauty in front of me scolds when I chuckle.

"Oh my God. Theo! Are you in there? You better march your ass out here with your tail between your legs."

Hanna shakes her head, grabbing a suit and opening the door. I follow behind her, and I'm met with my sister's much shorter frame, where she glares up at me with her arms folded across her chest.

"You are incorrigible."

"No. I'm determined. Big difference, right, Hanna?" I wink at her.

"You smug ass. Brenda, I'm sorry. I had no idea he was going to show up."

"Oh, I know. This is all him. This is why the lake is a girls' thing. I don't need your horny self showing up and watching Hanna like she belongs to you."

I smirk. "She does."

"Theo!" Hanna squawks, her face now red. She looks like she's both mortified and could slap me senseless. I like a little feistiness in her.

"Next time, don't deny me what I want." I shrug, walking past them both.

"You're a jerk," Hanna hollers after me.

"Really? Moments ago, you were calling me a god." And just like that, I'm gone as quickly as I arrived.

I came to show her what exactly this arrangement means. We always have access to each other's body. Whenever and wherever. Maybe now, she'll see I mean business.

Sixteen

HANNA

"Brenda, I'm so embarrassed. Please forget any of that happened," I beg for the fifth time on the ride back to Cherry Hill.

"Woman, it's fine, really. Stop apologizing. I'm just worried about you; that's all."

"What do you mean?" I turn toward her a little, adjusting in my seat.

Shaking her head, she spits it out, "Listen. My brother cares about no one. I think I'm the only one who owns a soft spot in his stone heart. I would hate to see you fall for him and then him break your heart when he leaves."

I look out at the road ahead, processing her words. "I won't fall in love with him. I don't think I ever could, even if he wanted to," I say out loud, which I did not mean to.

"What?" Brenda questions.

"I've been alone all my life. I don't get attached to things.

Getting attached always broke my heart. Foster care will do that. No family will do that."

"Oh, Hanna. I'm sorry. I didn't mean to bring this up. Let's change the subject."

"Yeah, let's." I don't want to always have to tell the sob story of my upbringing. It's done and over with. I'm an adult and on my own. And maybe one day soon I'll find out the last piece of what seems to be missing.

Why did my grandfather never contact me? He's the last person I know of to find answers out from. But he's dead. How do you get answers from a dead man? I don't know, but I plan to keep digging. Sift through every part of that house to see if there is any evidence of other family members or friends who would know him well enough to have the answers to my questions.

"Hanna?" Brenda pulls me from my wayward thoughts.

"Yeah, sorry. Just super tired. So the lake. How many people are coming?" I shift the conversation and silently give thanks that she buys it.

We talk mainly about the weekend and some work stuff, and by the time we're done, we're pulling up in my driveway. I'm dragging my feet after I feed the pups, let them run around the front yard to go to the bathroom, and cook dinner. Work was long. Shopping was…interesting, to say the least. I just want to close my eyes and get lost in slumber.

The rest of the week is pretty mundane, a bit more routine. I work, come home, read, sleep, and repeat. Theo hasn't said much to me at all. In fact, I have gotten only one text from him, and it was asking me if I've had anymore weird activity happening at night.

Other than that, radio silence. So is this just a him thing? Only comes when he has time to fuck and leave? God, he's cold and hot. Like Antarctica melting into the Sahara Desert.

But that's the arrangement. Sex. He owes me nothing, as I owe him nothing. I'm not going to ponder on it. Not at all. Or so I hope.

※ ※ ※

"THIS IS BEAUTIFUL, BRENDA." I LOOK AROUND AT THE crystal lake; it's almost completely see-through, clear enough you can see your feet. It's surrounded by tall pine trees. And between the sun and just the right amount of breeze, I would say this is as close to paradise as I've ever been.

"Yeah, it's my favorite. We came here all the time growing up. Over the years, it's become overrun by the younger crowd, fewer families coming now. We come here a lot during the summer months," she tells me, setting up her lounge chair.

"I get it. I would be here every day if I could."

"We will come here as often as possible." Brenda nudges my shoulder. "Also, love the suit you picked." I look down at the simple black one piece and black semi-sheer cover-up that is wrapped around my hips and knotted at the side. The top of the suit drops into a deep V with three straps to help give some cleavage. Not that I need it. My naturally large breasts already give me enough of that.

"Thanks. Still feels weird. I haven't worn a swimsuit since high school," I admit.

"Not many places in the city to wear one?" she asks, filling the cooler with the ice and drinks we brought. I start taking the beers and waters out of their boxes to help.

"No, I mean there are places to go, but I wasn't a fan. You know me. Indoors. Books. And all that. It's more my thing."

"Well, we will make you a swimsuit-wearing, sun-loving, South Carolinian in no time!"

I appreciate Brenda for never making me feel like being an introvert is a bother. We are polar opposites, but she makes it work. In fact, I don't think I've ever met an extrovert who is as kind to an introvert as she is. Those two can coexist, but usually it takes a lot of work. But she and I, it's somehow effortless.

Soon, all the girls show up. Semra, who is the sweetest—but I feel like she's the badass of the group. Takes-no-shit type. Then Vanessa, I call her the giver, always asking what we need and being the first to show up. And last, Heather, she's the ride-or-die type. First in line to back you up. I've not spent much time with these ladies, but the times I have, this is what I've gathered.

I also take notice that this group of girls so far seems to lack any cattiness. Every group usually has at least one, but so far, nothing. They all seem genuine.

"So you and Theo?" Semra asks, taking up her spot next to me.

I shake my head. "No, we're just friends. Who said something?"

"Word spreads fast here, babes, and when he knocked out Jerrick for you, people started talking," Vanessa adds.

That's new, something I knew about small towns but never experienced before, since news doesn't spread like that in New York. "No, we were just hanging out. He's a nice guy."

"Psh, nice? Hanna, everyone here knows Theo is anything but nice. Someone must be taking a liking to you," Semra says, leaning in and nudging my shoulder.

"You guys, stop. The poor girl already has to deal with my brother," Brenda inserts, and I mouth a thank-you when they agree and say their "fine" and "you're right."

"So since you're just friends, have you thought of maybe going on a date with anyone?" Heather finally joins the conversation after putting on her sunscreen. She lays out on a towel in front of our chairs.

"No, not really. I've never been the dating type."

"Dating type? Isn't that part of how you find a boyfriend?" She giggles, and when I just look down at my hands in my lap, the entire peanut gallery gasps.

"You've never had a boyfriend?" Semra exclaims.

"No, I've had one, but he kind of ruined it all for me if I'm being honest."

"What did he do?" Heather's eyebrows draw in, concern etched on her face.

"It's a long story and a really woe-is-me kind. It's totally in the past."

"Clearly not if it's ruined you for dating still," Vanessa speaks softly. I can tell there is no judgement or ridicule coming from them, nor is there any pity.

"You don't have to talk about it, Hanna." Brenda jumps to my defense as always, but there is no defense needed. One thing about coming to Cherry Hill is I want to be more open, give myself the chance to have friends, be social, open up, and find a place that I never had. A home.

Little by little, I'm peeling back layers of myself, some parts more painful than others, but in time, I hope that I blossom into the version of me that makes me the happiest. The one I can feel safe in, comfortable in, content in.

"It's fine. I was dating this guy; he was way out of my league. We were in high school. I was convinced when he started talking to me that it was a joke." Tilting my head, I breathe out. "Turns out, I was right. We dated for a little over two weeks. He complimented me left and right, spoiled me with time and affection, and the minute after I gave my everything to him…" They know what I mean when I say this. I can see it in their eyes. There's the pity. I don't need it. I have enough self-loathing-like pity. "The next day, everyone at school knew, and he and his buddies were laughing about it, saying that the poor chubby girl was desperate, and it turned out I was the punchline to the worst joke of my life."

"What a fucking asshole! What's his name, and I swear I'll tackle his bitch ass to the ground," Heather expresses.

"Seriously. We can all show up at his house and punch him in the nut sac." Semra looks out at the water, shaking her head.

"I love you girls. Thank you, but I'm good now. I've gone through a lot worse." I lie. I lie through my teeth as if I'm so good at hiding it, because I am. I'm deeply wounded. Hurt by my past. It haunts me most days, but I'm also tired of being the sad girl at every new gathering I'm at. Some scars are closed and only outwardly show for a reason, to remind you to be careful and to never open the skin again.

"Well, you know what? I fucking applaud you for going through all the shit you did and still being a kickass, bad bitch." Brenda holds up her beer in cheers, and I tap my Smirnoff against hers.

"Agreed!" The three other girls join in, and for the first time in a long time, it feels different. I feel a little bit bolder and little bit more like me. Whoever I am.

The day is going nicely, the sun, the water, the company. It's all perfect. Surprisingly, I didn't burn, but a nice tan is coming in.

"Ladies, you all look lovely. Want some company?" A group of men approach us, and I instantly get the creeps from all of them.

You know that moment in every college movie when they step into a frat party, and instantly everything seems like it's going to end badly? Yeah, that's what these guys bring. I keep my head down in the book I brought. Brenda is out on the water in a tube, leaving Semra, Vanessa, and Heather to do the talking. They seem to know some of the guys, so handling them should be something they can do on their own.

"Hey, you must be JD's granddaughter," the one with shaggy sandy-blonde hair says, coming to sit in the empty chair Brenda was sitting in earlier.

"Oh yeah, I'm Hanna." I stick out my hand to shake his, and he takes it.

"I'm Ryland. I'm—"

"Fucking leaving," a low grumble sounds from behind us, and I know that voice all too well already.

Turning, I see Theo, his fists balled at his sides, the veins in his neck protruding. He looks murderous.

"Theo, what are you doing here? This was a girls' day!" Brenda yells from her tube in the water.

"Clearly not, since these townies are here where they don't belong," he seethes, and I shake my head.

"Ryland, I'm sorry. I don't know what his problem is. You don't have to leave," I tell him, fuming when he stands to leave anyway.

"No, really, I should. I have something I've got to get to anyway." He looks to Theo, and I see the fear he holds.

"Hanna. Come with me. Now," Theo growls.

"Not a fat chance. You were so rude," I scold him.

"Hanna. I will claim you in front of all of these people if you don't listen. You have a few seconds to get up before I lose my composure."

"This is composed to you? You are such an ass." I stand, and before Ryland and the other guys scurry off, Theo hollers after them.

"Touch her again, and I'll detach your fucking hands from your arms."

"Theo!" I yell as he takes my hand and pulls me away from everyone. I try to keep up, but his long, determined strides are making it impossible, and I start stumbling as we head down a dirt path surrounded by trees. "Theo! You're hurting my arm, and I'm going to face-plant!"

He stops abruptly, making me collide with his back. He whips around, his honey eyes that black-color they turn whenever he is aroused. I swallow thickly when I see that lust pointed right at me, but what's more dangerous is the anger that accompanies it.

"What in God's name is your problem? And why are you here?" I tug my arm free, and he stays perfectly still, his chest heaving up and down. "Theo?" I ask again when he doesn't respond.

"You let another man touch you."

Lightly jerking my head back, confused, I respond, "What? Shaking his hand?"

"Yes, shaking your hand," he rumbles, so low you would almost miss it.

"Theo, I'm not your girlfriend, and we aren't a couple, and even if we were, shaking hands doesn't mean anything. That's a bit crazy, don't you think?"

He's on me then, grabbing my hip and my throat, moving me back and against a tree.

"We may not be a couple, but I made it very clear when my cock was in you that you're mine and mine only. I won't share, and

I wasn't fucking playing, puppet. If a man touches you again, I will detach his fucking hands from his body."

Our eyes search each other, and something about his possessiveness combined with the lust in his eyes...I cave. I give in to it. His lips are on me and mine on his, our tongues tasting and captivating one another.

"You're driving me fucking crazy. I can't stop thinking about this cunt and how fucking good you taste, Hanna," he says between licks and bites on my neck. Throwing my head back, I moan, and he goes to cover my mouth.

"Shh, they will hear you." I realize that if anyone walks maybe a hundred feet, they would see us, and Brenda is here. I don't want her to hear this either.

"Reach down like a good girl, move your bathing suit to the side, and offer your beautiful cunt to me, baby. My cock is hungry. I need it."

I nod, wanting him just as badly. I shouldn't after what he just did, but maybe the madness is where I thrive too. The desire and the obsession for each other's passion.

I do as he says, and he unbuckles his belt and messes with his zipper and button, freeing his hard cock.

"So pretty. Such a pretty pussy," he praises me, my head lulling back as he slowly enters me.

"Don't get too comfortable, puppet. I'm going to fuck you hard. Show you what happens when you let other hands touch what I own."

"Oh God!" I cry out when he slams all the way in and starts to relentlessly fuck me. No compassion, no mercy. He fucks me. Thrust after thrust without pause, and the bark of the tree scratches my skin, adding both a touch of pain, but a bite of pleasure.

"I came here because I wanted to take you to my house, cuff you to my bed, and fuck you out of my system," he groans in my ear, still thrusting into me without missing a beat.

"Then do it. Please," I beg him. I want to see him unhinged. I want to know these promises of pleasure he keeps telling me. So far, it's been absolute pleasure, but he hasn't shown me the darker side of what he says he plans to do, and our time is limited. When I look back on this, on my time with him, I want to remember every detail. Recall all the wild things I did that I will never be able to do again. I want. It. All.

"Oh, I plan on it, but first...you come. I want you to soak me, and then I want you on your knees, saying you're sorry with those pretty lips. God, you have the sexiest lips." He bites them for emphasis.

"I've never—oh God," I whimper, he cock hitting me so deep and in that one place I swear he has a map to. "I've never done that before. You have to teach me."

"Fuck! You just make me crazier."

"How?" I moan as he keeps hitting that spot, and I'm seconds away from orgasming. The bite of the tree bark hardly even registers in my mind.

"You need me. You thrive under my hands. I get to mold you

into whatever I want."

"You're crazy," I tell him.

"Say it again. I like the sound of it."

"I said you're—oh God! You're fucking crazy!"

Reaching between us, he flicks my clit, and I detonate around him.

"Fuck it." He keeps at it, thrusting into me.

"I thought you wanted—oooh..." I trail off when he keeps rubbing my sensitive clit.

"I want you to be filled with my cum when you go back out there. I want you marked so they understand who you belong to." With that, he comes, filling me with hot spurts, and I can't help the scream that comes out when he pinches my clit so hard that I come again.

"That'll show them." He laughs sinisterly. "I'll teach you how to suck my cock the way I like tonight. I'm not even close to being done with you." Once the adrenaline settles, I start to feel the pain in my back from the scratches the bark left. "I'll take care of those when we get home. Let's get your stuff and go. I've had a hell of a day, and I need to get lost in you."

That statement gives me butterflies. And I don't like it. Butterflies are different than arousal. No strings attached. This is supposed to be purely physical.

"The marks on my back...I'm mortified they may have heard me, but I don't want them to see the marks."

He rights himself in his jeans and nods. "I'll go grab your

towel."

He leaves me then, and I'm left there to think about what he and I just did. Why is it that, whenever he is around, I lose all my inhibitions? It's as if I had this confidence all along. This person I am with him is bold; she knows what she wants. She revels in the crazy.

This isn't me. I've never been one to be like this, yet here I am.

"Here, put this around you. Then we can say goodbye to the girls." I hesitate for a minute. "What's wrong?" He seems concerned—genuinely.

"Did they hear me? I'm so embarrassed."

"They were all in the water and didn't seem to notice at all. You're good." Releasing a deep breath, I follow him, hoping his assumption is correct. When we get back, they are all in the water, catching the last bit of sun that is setting behind the trees.

"Theo, I see you've come to take away our favorite girl," Semra teases.

"Yes. I gave you all day with her. My turn."

I gasp. I told them we were nothing, and here he is making it sound like we're something.

"Interesting. Isn't that interesting, girls?" Semra prompts, looking at Vanessa, Brenda, and Heather, and my cheeks flush, going red, I'm sure.

"Sure is! Have fun, you two, but not too much!" Vanessa hollers, and they all join in, whistling and catcalling, and now I am indeed mortified.

"You owe me. I told them we weren't anything but friends," I hiss at him when we're on the way back to his place.

"We aren't anything."

That stings, I hate to admit. I let this man do things to me that no one has before, and to hear him say we aren't anything—yeah, that hurts. Even if I knew what the cards were.

"Can you not make it sound like I'm a whore?" It comes out before I can stop it. I told him I wouldn't get attached, and I'm not, but the least he could do is label it something a little more kind than being nothing.

He looks over at me. I feel it and can see it in my peripheral vision.

"I don't think you're a whore, Hanna, but it is what it is. We are purely in this for the mutual pleasure," he tells me, and this just amps me up more.

"I get that, Theo, but maybe I would like to be at least considered a friend or something. I've let you do and will be letting you do things to me that no one has. I would like some respect to be given to me." I cross my arms and hide my angry tears.

He pulls the truck over on the side of the road then. It's abrupt, and he slams on the brakes, making me jolt forward and brace my hands on the dash.

"Jesus. You could have eased into that."

"I respect you, Hanna. More than a lot of people. In fact, more than anyone. I shouldn't have come off so crass, but I don't want wires getting crossed here. You agreed this wouldn't turn into anything. Is that happening?"

Is he serious?

I turn and glare him down. "You are so arrogant. Just because I don't want to be referred to just as the girl you fuck doesn't mean I'm falling in love with you. You know what? I don't want to do this tonight. Take me home." I turn away and face the window, crossing my arms in defense.

I'm not falling in love...am I?

No, no, I'm not, but what I am doing is making sure he understands that even though he has control over my body when we are skin-to-skin, it doesn't mean I have no self-respect.

If he wants unlimited access to me, he has to respect me and treat me like more than just something to fuck. When the truck doesn't move, I glance over at him, and he's looking out the window, his knuckles gripping the steering wheel.

"Theo." I remind him that I want to go with my strict tone, and he slams his hand on the steering wheel.

"Damn it!" he barks, and I jump. "You make me crazy. I just want to get inside you. Get lost in you. And you thinking I don't respect you is the furthest thing from the truth. I always respect the women I go into these arrangements with, but I don't show up at every place they're at so I can take them back home with me. Yet here we are. Don't say I don't respect you, Hanna. That's anything but the truth."

Shaking my head, I look out the window. "I wish I could believe that, Theo, but I don't even know you. So how do I know you're being sincere?" Honestly.

"You do know me."

"No! All I know is that you like to have control, you are good in bed, and that you are borderline psychotic."

He cracks up then, laughing. It pisses me off, but I can't help but smile begrudgingly when he won't stop.

"What? It's not funny. It's true."

"You think I'm good in bed, huh?"

"You're so glib. And annoying." I tighten my arms across my chest. Seriously irritated with him.

"Fine. I'm sorry. You're right. It's fair to get to know one another. What do you want to know then?" He puts the car in drive and slowly merges back onto the highway. I'm stunned. Here I am saying I want to get to know him, and yet I'm stumped on what to ask.

"Why do I want to ask you your favorite color? That is so stupid." I chuckle, and he smiles.

"It's a good start. Green."

"Hmm. I would have thought blue."

"Why is that?" he questions.

"You are always wearing it."

"You always wear black. Is that your favorite color?" he counters.

"No, but it makes my body look somewhat thinner."

"I'll address that comment later," he grumbles. "This is for you. What else?"

I hope he forgets what I said. I don't like to talk about my insecurities. I wear them loud enough as it is. "Brenda seems close with you guys' parents. Are you as close?"

"Not as close but not estranged. I've never been one who's overly affectionate or clings to any type of relationship."

I snort. "Sorry." I cover my mouth. How rude can I be? Asking him to open up, then laughing when he does.

"What's so funny?" he asks me.

"Nothing. It's obvious you don't like to have any relationship. I mean, look at us. Is there a reason?" Understanding that this could be too personal and I'm likely to be shut down, I still go for it.

"Nope. I just never felt the need or desire to have close relationships." He shrugs.

"It must be lonely. I would know," I whisper.

"Not at all. At least for me it's not. There is peace in silence and being comfortable alone."

That comment isn't meant to be offensive, but for me, it is.

"I grew up alone and found no peace at all. It was the loneliest, darkest part of my life." I bare my vulnerability almost too freely now. Maybe it's because I have nothing to hide from anymore. I'm making friends, creating the life I wished for, so baring the wounds seems inevitable. I feel safe for the first time in my life.

What does that say about the life I led up to this? My most confusing time, in a new place I don't know, making friends, and having an intense sexual relationship with a man I thought would never give me one glance, let alone two. Amidst all that, I feel... safe.

"Your circumstances were different, and for that, Hanna, I am truly sorry." He reaches over and grabs my hand. "I always knew if I needed someone to lean on, I had it, so being alone wasn't as scary. You didn't. I'm sorry. Really. The people who hurt you, they didn't deserve you."

The tears start coming, and I want to suck them back up. But for someone to show me care, to show empathy for a past I had no control over, it's hard to not feel the emotions, and truthfully, I don't want to.

"Can we not do this...please? Can we focus on you?"

He doesn't hesitate. Respecting my boundaries, he changes the subject. "What else do you want to know, baby?"

"How about your friends? Do you have a lot back in New York?" He turns down the road I haven't seen before, and it dawns on me he said he is taking me to his house.

"A few, mostly guys from work."

"I seriously can't peg you for an IT guy. Seems way off," I point out.

"How is that? I didn't know IT guys had a profile."

I laugh. "They don't, but you seem like the type of guy who would be in some type of public service. A cop, firefighter, maybe even own your own gym."

His brow quirks. "How so?"

I hesitate. How do I phrase this without sounding like a total bitch? "Well, you have a kick-rocks type of attitude."

This makes him laugh. "Maybe that's why I like IT. I don't have to socialize or put up with people."

Tilting my head from side to side, I agree. "That makes sense, actually."

"You like books. You would think judging a book by its cover would be in the literal sense. Especially for you."

"You got me. Do you like to read?"

"Sure. The newspaper."

"That's not reading. That's just staying up on current events. Don't you like escapism?" I lean in, enthralled in this conversation.

"Not really, I have enough in my life to keep me entertained."

"Oh yeah, like what?"

"You. God, you. I could read each part of you like a goddamn book. Get lost in you. That is my escapism, Hanna." The tension in the truck thickens, near the point of stealing the very air out of this small space.

"Theo. Why do you do this? Why do you say things like that to me?" I basically choke this out.

"Why do you ask that? You enjoy it, don't you? This is the type of thing you read, isn't it? In those books?"

I swallow. "How do you know what I read?"

He tilts his head down to my bag, and right at the top is my book he must have looked at when packing up my things at the lake. The man on the front is shirtless, the cover anything but discreet.

"You like men like that? Does that turn you on? The things they do in those books?" He asks me that just as we pull up to his house. I would take it in, but I'm hanging on the edge of my seat, gripped tightly by his words.

"Maybe," I murmur.

"Why? What do you like about it, Hanna? The romance, or the fact that they fuck—and they fuck in ways you want to be fucked? Because I can fuck you so much better than that, puppet. I can make those men look like they're beginners."

Feeling bold, I challenge him, "Prove it. Make me believe you even stand a chance to be in that elite group."

Clicking his tongue, I see the control brewing in his eyes. He's losing a bit of it, and that angers him. I'm learning Theo will never back down from a challenge, especially one that questions his power and control. Call it payback for making me feel like nothing but a whore just moments ago. The new Hanna isn't just finding a home here in Cherry Hill. I'm finding my voice, my backbone—my courage. Something I never had before.

Power is starting to feel good.

"You pushed, puppet. Way too far. I'm going to make you choke on those words." His voice is low, the storm raging madly in his eyes, and I suddenly worry he may just be right. I won't admit this, but the two times we've had sex had my books paling in comparison to what we did. But pushing him to new limits could do two things—please me or ruin me—both things equally as dangerous.

"What are you going to do?" I gulp.

"Grab the book."

"What? Why would I grab the book?"

"Because I said grab the book, Hanna. Challenge accepted."

"Oh God." He's really going to do it.

What, exactly? I don't know, but he's going to do something to compete with the men I'm reading about.

There is no comparison. This is it. He's going to show me that side of him he's been holding back. The tree episode was a prelude to what he really has planned. I know it.

"I'm nervous. Maybe we should take a second." I start to choke, that bout of confidence shivering in her regret.

His eyes are cold. "You awoke me. Now, you're going to satisfy my needs, even more so…your needs. Book. Now."

Reaching down, I grab it with shaky hands. What did I just ask for?

Seventeen

THEO

HANNA IS GETTING UNDER MY SKIN. POSSESSING MY thoughts. First, I showed up at the store, because she refused to send me photos. Then, I showed up at the lake so I could take her home like a goddamn caveman. Now, she's daring to say I need to prove I can do things to her that the men in her romance novels can.

I would scoff and brush off any other woman. Not even bother to prove anything. But with her, it's an impulse. A need that has to happen or I will lose my mind.

Her taking her own pleasure and making me insane for more of her is a dangerous game. A very dangerous game that I'm so fucking determined to win. I'm not falling in love…no. Never. But I'm obsessed. She's like a siren, a goddess, a woman who could pull me in and make me do whatever she wants if it means I get her taste on my tongue and my cock buried in her at every moment.

This is going to end badly. If she only knew the truth about me.

She would break, and I know that, and I should walk away, but I can't. She has me by the fucking throat.

Rounding the truck, I meet her at the door, and the second her feet hit the ground, I bend and toss her over my shoulder.

"Oh my God, Theo! Put me down. You're going to get hurt!" She squirms, and I slap her ass hard, causing a yelp to come from her lips. I can handle her. She's weightless. I'm in the peak of my strength, and real men can handle real women.

"You worry about what's going to happen to your body when we get inside. Don't worry about me." That makes her quiet, and her squirming ceases. I unlock and open the door with one hand, and my feet lead us straight to my bedroom at the back of the house. She can get a tour later. I have plans, and that isn't included in them.

Kicking my slightly ajar bedroom door open, I feel her body jolt against me. That made her jumpy? Wait until she sees what's about to happen when we're in the thick of my plans tonight. She will jolt, squirm, bend, beg, and scream. All of it.

When I toss her on the bed, she looks up at me with fear. *Good girl. Fear me.* The fear will take her pleasure to new levels. That fear will mold into desire, into everything she has imagined and lusted after in the shadows of her wildest dreams.

"Theo—"

"Safe word," I interrupt her, walking over to my drawer.

"Theo," she says again, this time more hesitation in her voice.

"Safe word and I will stop. If not, let go, and let me take over.

Give me the control and trust that I know what you need and what you want." I look over my shoulder at her, giving her a chance to take the out. There is quite the pause, one that makes me think she just may say the word and not want this, and just as I'm about to turn to walk back to her and put a halt to my plans, she shakes her head.

"I want it. I—I trust you."

"Good, puppet. What is the safe word in case it gets to be too much?"

"Sirius."

"You use it if it's more than you can take."

She nods softly, sitting up on her knees now. The image is art. Her in the center of my bed, her eyes round and inquisitive in all the right ways. Curiosity is flowing through her veins, lacing with the desire that's pumping inside her.

Removing my shirt, I move back to the drawer and open it, pulling out my ankle cuffs attached by a long nylon strap. Turning back, she tilts her head and looks at it, her eyes widening when I step up closer. The cuffs at the ends is all she needs to understand there will be some sort of restraint.

"Up."

She scurries to her feet. Eager. There it is, the fear being drowned out by desire.

"Strip for me, lie on the bed, and open the book to your favorite scene." Knowing what I mean, she does just that, removing the sheer fabric from her waist. It slides to the floor, and then she's left in the one piece. It gives her the best fucking cleavage.

"Keep going," I guide her. She removes one strap and hisses. The elastic hit the little scratches from our rough fucking against the tree. "I will take care of those after we're done. Be careful."

She nods, removing the rest of the fabric. Once she's naked, I slowly take a few steps back and look her over, my thumb grazing back and forth over my bottom lip.

"I want to bite and bruise those beautiful thighs," I tell her.

"Why?"

"Because they look like they need my mark. All of you needs my mark."

"Is that what you're going to do? Mark me so everyone knows about us?" Hanna's voice is low, a slight tremble to it.

"Baby, if I weren't a jealous man, I would fuck you in the open, in front of crowds, so they'd know who owns you."

"Oh."

"Yeah, now, on the bed. Open the book." Turning, she climbs on all fours, and I get a glimpse of her cunt. A delicacy, like a dessert. "Stop." She pauses, still on all fours, and I walk up to her. My hard cock hits her ass, and she moans. I slap her ass hard, and she moans louder.

"Another?" she whispers.

"I decide what to give you." Stepping back, I bend and lick her lips, ending on her clit and giving it a gentle suck.

She jerks forward. "Theo!" The sound of my name from those lips in any moment of passion is sinful. Should be criminal.

"Be good, and I will do that again tonight."

"Yes, Theo."

"Oh, puppet, you make this so thrilling." I watch her get into position, and she looks up at me.

"You do things that make me lose all sense. I'm not this woman," Hanna admits.

"But you are. You just needed the right person to set her free. Find the scene, and let go of your body. It's mine now." She lies flat, being careful with her scratches, and begins to go through the page. I take the item I'm excited to use and cuff one foot. I see her pause her search and look at what I'm doing in my peripherals. "Hanna," I warn.

Quickly, she looks back in the book. I tighten the cuff, then take the strap, slide it under the bedframe, and up to her other ankle, restraining her, her cunt bared to me.

"I think I got it. What is this?" She nods down to her feet.

"A little something to help me control your legs."

"Why would you want to control my legs?"

My next words come out dark and sinister. "This allows me to keep your legs from closing when your orgasm is too intense. I control your pleasure. All of it."

"I know you do," she admits, and my cock jerks at her submission.

"Start reading."

She blushes. "I don't know if I can—"

"If this makes you blush, you're going to be fire-engine-red when we do the things we do tonight."

"Promise you won't laugh?"

I unbuckle my belt and free my cock. Biting her lip, she peruses my body, admiring me. I've never been much for vanity, but the idea that my body is something she thoroughly enjoys? You could say my chest is swelling with male pride.

"Read the scene. I'm growing impatient."

"Um...okay. 'He touches me, my center growing wet with heavy need.'" Losing my pants, I get on my knees just beside her, using the knuckle of my middle finger to graze over her clit. "Oh, fuck," she moans. "'I feel like he's controlling my body with such simple touches that I could lose my mind. I crave his tongue between my legs, pleasing me and teasing me.'" Leaning down, I lightly spread her swollen lips and lick her softly, alternating between up and down and circles. "'I wait eagerly for it, but he takes his time with his fingers, leaving me craving both. His tongue, his fingers, his...'" She stops, and I glance up at her, licking her clit but stopping at the same time she does.

"Say it." I smirk cockily, craving to hear her say the word.

"'...his...his cock. I'm waiting for it, and with each passing second, my anticipation grows.'" The way her full lips read erotic words, it's like jumping off a cliff with no restraints. It's wild.

I go back to rubbing her clit with my thumb, but this time, I do what her character is begging for. I use my tongue and lick her tight hole, circling it first, then plunging it inside her. Her back leaves the bed, and her legs spread farther.

"That's what you wanted, right?" She looks curious yet nervous.

"Yes, try closing your legs." I keep rubbing her clit, soft and steady.

Attempting to do as I say, she fails. "Theo, I can't close them."

"Exactly, like I said. Now, what does he do next, puppet?"

"Um...'Finally, he gives me what I'm craving. Moving down between my legs, he circles my clit, slowly but with the right pressure, and I buck forward, jolted by the feeling.'"

Taking two fingers as I continue licking her clit, I insert them in her snug heat. Fuck me, she's tight. So damn tight.

"Oh yes, please!" she screams out.

Looking up, I tilt my head. "Was that in the book, puppet?"

"God, no, it's you, all you. You win. Okay. You're better than these men. I need more."

"Hmm. I want to give you that, but remember I told you that you would choke on those words, Hanna?" She nods, biting her lip and squirming, wanting my touch, which I break all connection of. "Good."

Leaving the bed, I grab the pillows and places them under her head, she eyes me quizzically but doesn't say anything, and when I have her head high enough and at an angle perfect for my plans, I get back on my knees, this time right beside her face.

"Open your mouth." She does as she's told, and without warning, I grab the back of her head, gripping her hair and shoving my cock into her mouth. She gags when I go as deep as I can, but I don't let up. I start to control her head, making her take me in and out, hitting the back of her throat each time.

"No man can ever do the things I do to you. You will be fucking ruined. When I'm gone, you're going to search for this with someone else and will never find it. Because I'll own that part of you forever," I tell her, and her eyes water, tears leaking, spit dripping from the corner of her mouth. It's violent-looking but exquisite. "Tap my arm if you want me to stop. If not, you're going to take every drop."

She doesn't tap; instead, she locks those wet green eyes on me, and we don't break contact. My abs flex, and I groan at the image of her right now.

"You look so beautiful choking on my cock." What little mascara she was wearing begins to run down her cheeks, and I fuck into her mouth harder. She moans, and I look to see her fingers between her legs, rubbing at her clit just as vigorously as I am fucking her mouth. "It turns you on when I do this to you... doesn't it?"

She moans an inaudible agreement, and suddenly, I'm coming, pushing my cock to the back of her mouth and holding her head tightly in place as I drain my cum down her throat.

"Fuck, puppet. Dammit." I throw my head back and make her take every drop. My orgasm seems never-ending, but she keeps taking it, even as it drips out the side of her lips. It's wet, so wet between her saliva and my cum. Her running mascara. It's a sight to behold, one I will lock inside for the rest of my life and revisit frequently.

When I finally finish and she's taken all of me, I slowly pull her by her hair, moving her off my cock. Seeing me still on her lips, I use my thumb and rub it in, spreading it over her lips.

"Now you see what happens when you challenge me."

She is a vision, covered in my cum, running mascara, and red skin. No artist could paint a better work of art. It's cruel, crude, but makes perfect sense. Hanna was molded to be exactly what I need her to be. Shy yet thriving under a lustful touch. Needing me to need her in a possessive way, all while having her independence. I've never met a woman more unique or powerful.

Hanna holds the control too. And that is something I fear. So much so, I need to fuck it out of my system, regain it, reclaim it as mine. She can't have both power and control. Standing, I pace at the foot of the bed, watching her watch me, anticipating my next move.

"Why aren't you touching me? Did I do something wrong?" Her insecurity turns me on, because she couldn't be more wrong, but her insecurity means she needs me to remind her what her worth is. Does a woman like her need me? No, but will I happily be at her mercy to remind her? Yes.

"You took my cock perfectly, puppet. But you need a breather, because I'm nowhere near done."

"Then touch me. I want more like that," she admits, lying restrained and at my mercy.

"You like me to use you. Like a slut? Like a naughty little slut?" I watch her gulp. She's debating if she liked that or not, but

I already know the answer when she tries so hard to rub her thighs together, but the bar keeps her from being able to do so.

"Do you really think I'm a slut?" she whimpers.

"In the bedroom. You are my toy. You're *my* slut. My puppet. Whatever I want you to be. But remember, you have what, Hanna?" I break our scene for a moment.

"Power," she recalls.

"Exactly. What we do in our intimate moments is without borders. We are here to unleash the wildest. The dirtiest. The deepest fantasies."

"Then do it. Use me. Take whatever you want. Remind me what I can't seem to remember."

This stumps me. What does she mean? "And what is that?"

"That a man like you can desire a woman like me."

Instantly, my cock is hard again. My rage is at a ten, and my skin turns red. When I grab the flogger once more, she looks panicked yet thrilled. What an exquisite combination.

"No, no. Theo. Not—"

"What? *No* isn't the word." I take the flogger, and I bring it down hard on her thigh and then again on her clit. She screams out. "You have the word. Say it if you want this to stop." I bring the flogger down on her hip, then her slit again.

"I can't!" she yells, her head rolling back into the pillows.

"And why is that, baby?"

"Damn you, because I want it. You make me want this. I hate you for ruining me!" she cries, and I throw the flogger to the side of the bed. Then it happens. I yank the Velcro of the cuffs free, grab her hips, and flip her over. She lands on her stomach, her feet crossing, letting me know her pussy will be so tight that I'll risk coming the minute I'm inside her. Lining her up with my cock, without warning, I slam into her.

"Yes!" we both gasp in unison.

"You are so damn maddening. I've never had it this fucking good with anyone, Hanna. You are a curse." I pound into her, my movements never faltering.

"You're the devil," she retorts, looking over her shoulder.

"Oh yeah?" Wrapping her hair around my fist, I pull her up and bring her back to my chest. The position she's in can't be comfortable, especially with her skin all raw from the tree, and that's my point exactly. There can be no pleasure without lustful pain.

"You ever let another man touch you like you did today, and I will fuck you like this in front of him. I will make him watch, and then I will take out his eyes. You want the devil? You got him, Hanna. Here I fucking am." Pushing her back down, I start pounding into her harder.

This all stemmed from another man merely talking to her and shaking her hand.

I would never care before. Never have. But with her, I can't stand the idea of anyone having her, even after this is over. I hope I destroy her for any other man so that she never finds anyone again. Because that's exactly what this siren has done to me.

"Theo, please. I need you. Make me come. Take what's yours."

"Yes, what's mine. You're mine. All mine, puppet." Reaching around, I flick her clit, and she comes, squeezing me so tight and releasing erotic noises so arousing that I come seconds later, our orgasms melting into one.

Now, we're left in the heavy breathing and lingering confessions that show us both that this isn't safe. It has danger written all over it, but who will be the first to walk away? I declare now that it won't be me, and if she ever tries to…I will follow her, find her, and keep her consumed with me. I may never love her, but I won't ever let someone get the chance to love her at all. That's the scariest part of all this.

I'm fucked.

Eighteen

HANNA

It's been thirty minutes since he put away the cuffs and flogger. He went in the shower and cleaned off, and now he enters the room in nothing but boxer briefs. His body is out of this world. He is out of my league. I will revel in him wanting me until he realizes what I already know. We are of two different worlds, ones that will eventually collide, and all of this will end. An ending that will most likely destroy me.

"Baby, come here." His voice is caring and soft. It throws me a little. I slowly sit up and move to the edge of the bed to stand. I stumble a bit, and he moves to me, picking me up. "Wrap your legs around me."

I do as he says, clinging to him. Something overtakes me, and I do something I don't know if he will be okay with, as it seems so intimate, but I lean in and kiss his shoulder, neck, and then jaw ever so softly, as if it's a whisper against his skin. He doesn't seem to mind, so I repeat it until we're in the bathroom, and he sets me on the counter.

Leaving me there, he moves to his large jacuzzi tub. I take this time to look around the bathroom, which has dark wood flooring in a gray color, white cabinets, and granite countertops. It's really modern and nice. He pores in some bath salts, and instantly the scent of lavender fills the bathroom, and I groan. God, that smells heavenly.

He removes his underwear and holds out his hand to me. "Can you stand, baby?"

He keeps calling me baby, and it's so foreign. It's more intimate than sex almost.

"Yes. Didn't you already shower?"

"Yes, but I need to take care of you now." Oh, right. Aftercare. That's why he is being so kind to me. Standing, I take slow steps, taking his hand as he helps me in, then he follows suit. When he sits down, he puts his back against the tub and spreads his legs. "Sit, beautiful."

I do as he says, but the second the water hits the scratches on my back, I hiss. "Ow!" I cry.

"I know it hurts, but this lavender will help, and I have ointment I will put on it."

I nod, and he takes a loofa and begins to wash me, starting with my arms, then my neck, and around to my chest. Once he gets to my back, he loses the sponge and uses his hands to cup water and pour it over my skin. Once he does that, he leans in and kisses each one.

Something happens inside me. My stomach feels heavy, but it's not the kind that comes with the way he turns me on. It's something else. It's...no...I can't be. It's not love. It's affection. I've never had it, and this is the first time. That's all it is. A first time sign of affection. I shut it down right there. We agreed this was nothing, and I can't let it be anything but sex.

"Today and tonight were intense, baby. Are you okay?"

I nod. "I think so. Thank you for checking."

"Always, I need to make sure you're always in the right head space and physical space after we get like that." He kisses my shoulder, and that feeling in my stomach comes back.

My heart even skips a fucking beat, and I get so angry with myself. *No. Please, no.* I almost want to cry, pissed that I'm even thinking like this right now. If he knew I was even thinking about having feelings outside the sexual nature for him, he would run and never talk to me again.

"What are you thinking?" he interrupts my thoughts, thank God. Except he asks me about those damn thoughts. I try to come up with something quick.

"Were you always into sex like this? Darker stuff?"

"At first, no, but as I got older, my tastes changed."

"I feel like there is always a reason people are the way they are, why they crave darker sides of things."

I can feel him smiling behind me. "People can have particular tastes without having to go through things. I like control, and I like to use it to fuck. It's just who I am." He may be the simplest man, yet it makes him so much more complicated. It feels like there are secrets he's drowning in and doesn't want to share. There has to be more to him than he is leading on. Maybe there is a wall so high that I need to find out how to climb over it.

What happens if I do? Would this make him capable of feeling more for someone? Could it make him love? Or is he really just simply programed this way, and I'm projecting my own life struggles and the way they made me the way I am?

Most likely the latter.

"Hanna, you didn't have enemies back home, did you?" His question is so left field.

"Why are you asking me this? I told you no. I had no one and nothing. This is the most social I've been in my life." Really, why is he asking this again?

"Turn and face me."

I do as he asks, and now face to face, he cups mine, and I lean into it, pretending his aftercare is genuine affection.

"You seem too kind to have someone find you and follow you here. Was there ever someone who had it out for you for any reason?"

Now, I'm really confused. "Theo, why does this matter?"

He rubs his hand over his lips and jaw, looking out the window next to his bathtub.

"Ever since the break-in and all you told me, I can't help but think that someone is after you, and I want to keep you safe."

He cares. He does. That is care. That's respect. He may not

admit it, but that is him opening up and letting me in just a little.

"Enemies is a word I would never be able to associate with any experience in my life. I never hurt anyone, would never want to, emotionally or physically. Even though the world hurt me, I would never bite back. I would never want someone to feel what I did. Pain like that isn't something I would wish on anyone, even if I had an enemy," I admit.

"Your parents? You think they were trying to find you?" Dropping my eyes, I shake my head. I can't go there. My wounds from my parents will never close. I'm convinced.

"They would never want to find me. Ever. If they could leave me as a child, why would they ever want to know or be in my life as an adult? If you could abandon your child, you could never love them as an adult. Those things could not exist." These words burn my throat. They stab my chest, right in my heart. I should hate my parents. Their choices should not hurt me anymore, but they do.

Some wounds can dry and close. But they don't always mend. The skin may remain tender to the touch. And when I think of my parents, or talk about them, their lack of love is a tender-to-touch pain I will never forget. I will never mend fully. An ache will always linger. Always.

"Hey, we don't have to talk about it. I just wanted to cross all my T's. I don't want anything to happen to you, and if we can keep you safe, that's all I want."

I shake my head. "Sounds a lot like you care for me. Careful, you might just fall in love, Theo, and then who will eat their words?"

I'm only teasing, but when he doesn't respond, I look up, and he is looking at me intensely.

"What?"

"Nothing. If I ever fall in love, you can make me eat my words. Just like I made you eat yours. You can feed me your beautiful cunt." The look that was there just moments ago fades, and it's replaced with a playful Theo. Maybe we are both forgetting this is just aftercare and respect.

Or maybe not?

Nineteen

HANNA

I jolt up, a nightmare overtaking me, and for a moment, I forget where I am and how I got here.

"Hey, Hanna, it's okay. I'm here."

In the darkness, I make out the shadow of Theo next to me, his voice bringing me back down to earth and reminding me of what happened tonight.

"Sorry. It's just the nightmares." My heart is beating heavily, rising and falling in sync with the rapid panic consuming my body.

"Come here. I got you." He pulls me into him, laying us back onto the pillows and covering us with the sheet. He grabs my thigh and lifts it to drape over his lower stomach. He begins to stroke it, massaging the skin. "What was the nightmare about?"

I shiver. "Nothing." Abruptly, I put a stop to his question. Some things I talk about with him, but there are other times I want to keep them close. He doesn't say anything, just keeps soothing me with his dominant touch. I didn't think it was possible to feel so small and feminine in a man's arms, especially at my size. But somehow, he makes me feel this way.

"Have you found out anything about your grandfather?"

"No. No one knows anything. I feel like I'm just chasing a dead end. I know it's only been a month, but how can no one know about why he never came to look for me?" I pause, absentmindedly drawing shapes on his chest.

"He was well known here, so this surprises me too," he adds.

"Exactly. He had so many people that claimed to be so close to him, and yet none of them knew of me or why he never tried to find me."

I nod slowly. "Is that why you aren't comfortable in his home?"

"Yes," he admits.

"It feels weird being there. Being in his house and trying to live in it as if it wasn't his. I get that he left it to me. But that makes it even more infuriating."

Pulling me in tighter, he locks his hands in my hair now, massaging my scalp. God, that feels good, so good I nuzzle in closer. "There has to be a reason he didn't find you. I really believe that. I knew him, not as well, since I moved a long time ago, but I know he would have come to you if he could. There was some roadblock there."

I nod. "I keep clinging to that and trying to believe it. I've been attempting to find a key to this one room. Jack told me it's his office. But no luck."

"Greens, I can open the door. Why didn't you tell me?"

"I mean, I know I could call a locksmith, but it seems wrong. He kept it locked and didn't give me a key for a reason."

His chest shakes with laughter. "You seriously just spend most of your day worried about others. Doesn't it get exhausting?"

"No. People matter. They deserve kindness and respect. Doesn't it get exhausting not caring for anyone but yourself?" I counter, jabbing his side lightly.

"Nope, it's freeing. You should try it sometime."

"No, if I did that, I would be like my parents. I'll take a hard pass." Even I hear the slight painful sting in my voice.

"Listen, you need answers, and they could be behind that door. We will open it tomorrow, and you can see what's in there."

Rolling my eyes, I don't bother to argue with him. Last time I didn't do what he wanted, he showed up and trapped me in a fitting room with him. "Fine. But if there are a bunch of dead bodies, you are picking up that mess."

His entire body then rattles and shakes with his deep laughter. Even that sound is sexy.

"What?" he chokes out between breaths.

"Your sister said she thinks it's a whole *Dexter* situation and that my grandfather could have been a low-key killer. She could be right."

He keeps laughing. "Fuck me, you two are crazy." Suddenly, he flips me over and maneuvers himself between my legs, his hard cock nudging my entrance. "Enough talking. Let me take your mind off the dream. Let me fuck you to sleep, baby," he growls, sliding inside me without warning, and my back bows off the bed, my head rolling back into the pillows.

"You feel so fucking good, baby. Goddamn, I could do this for hours."

"I won't...oh, right there." He pivots his hips and hits that spot. "I won't complain. You're so good at this."

"Yeah, I am. You like that, Hanna? You like this big cock in your snug pussy?" His crass words turn me on further. "Yeah, you do. You just soaked my cock. Beautiful."

"Theo." I cup his face, and he drops his forehead to mine. Our eyes lock in on each other, and something passes in his. Those honey eyes look like there is more than just lust or a man lost in pleasure. It's gentle-looking, vulnerable, a side of him he's never shown.

"What is it, puppet?" He keeps a steady pace, his hips rolling, up and down, around, and rolling again.

"Will it ever be like this with anyone else?"

That softness leaves him. "When this is done, you will never find a man to do this to you. I hope you always picture me. In fact, I know you will. I will haunt your dreams, invade your fantasies, and every face above or under you will be me. You will always belong to me, puppet, even after I'm gone." He thrusts up hard into me, and I cry out. "I take pleasure in knowing I ruined you."

I hate him for this, because it's true. No matter what happens, Theo will be the one I compare anyone I ever let touch me again to. Yet, at the same time, I will never regret being ruined by him.

"You're my mess," I whisper.

"No, I'm your demise. A mess can be cleaned up. A demise, you can't come back from." With that, he takes my pleasure, claiming it. Making me orgasm, his coming soon after mine. And I hate to admit it, but this was a little different. There was a connection, and I think we both felt it.

And not only did we both feel it, but we also both feared it and didn't talk about it after. Sleep took us, and we let whatever happened back there hang in the air with our passion, lust, and heavy breathing.

Twenty

THEO

LAST NIGHT, SOMETHING HAPPENED, AND I DON'T know what to do. When I looked in her eyes, those green irises that remind me of how much she can crawl beneath my skin, I felt this ache. Yes, a goddamn ache, in my chest. Like she was in there, clawing away at my barriers that I worked hard to build up.

I can't feel this. The lines we would be crossing are complicated for so many reasons. Hanna has to stay an arrangement, not a complication, not a wrench in my plans. If falling for her happens, I will have to end it. She can never mean more to me than a woman I find sexual pleasure in. She just can't.

Fuck. Pulling up to my sister's place, I see her on the porch waiting, but she's on the phone, a wide smile splaying across her face. She holds up a finger when I honk, and I assess her, watching her closely. That smile turns into a blush and some giddy jump happens after she ends the call. When she runs to the car, I'm on her the second she opens the door.

"Are you talking to him again?" I scowl.

"What?" She climbs in, putting her seatbelt on.

"Are you talking to that motherfucker again?"

"Oh my hell, Theo. No, I'm not talking to him, and please don't bring him up and spoil my good mood." She looks at me like I'm not going to let up.

"Promise?" I don't want to invade her privacy if this is someone new. We have a strong relationship, and if it's someone new, she will tell me in time when she's ready.

"Theo, I wouldn't lie to you. You're the only one I will always be a hundred percent open with. Okay?" She reaches over and rubs my arm, and I back out, giving her a quick nod.

"Good. Hanna said she will be home soon. She got held up at work."

"Yeah, we are short staffed, and I had my appointments today. So she helped by staying a little later. She's heaven sent. When my assistant manager moves, I think I'm going to promote her."

"That will be nice." Driving just a mile and a half up the road, we pull up to Hanna's place. Climbing up the porch steps, we sit in the rocking chairs, waiting for her to get home, and I check a few emails.

"The month is almost up. You ready to leave again?" Brenda asks, looking out over the afternoon sights. It's a nice temperature out, and the crickets have started making their noises. There is something peaceful about it. That may be the one and only thing I like about living in a small town.

"I actually have to stay a couple more weeks. There was a hold-up with the job."

"Oh really? A 'hold up'?" She air quotes.

"What does that mean, smartass?"

"You know exactly what I mean, Theo. Don't play dumb." She finally looks at me, giving me an "it's obvious" type of expression.

"It's not about her. Shut that shit down. I don't need you talking to her and making her think it's anything but the job keeping me here. We have a deal, and it's going just fine," I lie. I lie so easily, because truth is, there is something happening. I can't deny that. And it angers me. Hanna isn't just a sight to behold and fuck when I want. I catch myself enthralled in learning more about her life. Comforting her when she has hard times, like the nightmares.

When we aren't together, I have to fight the urge to text her just to ask her how her day is going. The way she laughs, the way she drops her head when I give her any type of compliment, all these little things shouldn't do a single thing to me, yet they seem to do the opposite. They pull me in, like she's the damn puppeteer, and I'm the desperate man hanging from the strings.

I'm drawn to her like people are tethered to earth by gravity, and with each moment we are together, that pull grows stronger, making me angrier and more determined to fuck her harder, as if she means nothing more than a quick fling. But I made a mistake by letting her see me vulnerable last night. I have to rein it in. Stop myself from whatever messed up thing is happening in my mind.

I chalk this up to being without a woman for a while. Even

before I came here, I hadn't had an arrangement in some time. That's it. Yep. That's all it is.

"Listen, you don't have to be afraid to admit you like someone. People can change their ways, bud."

Rolling my eyes, I grumble, "Come on, B. You know that's not me."

"Why can't it be? You think I don't see it? The way you look at her when you think none of us are looking? And don't get me started on both the shopping and lake incidents. What the hell was that then?"

"What?"

She scoffs. "You about ripped off his arms, and then you tore her away like a caveman. You could have waited for her to get home to do whatever it is you two are doing, but you came and stole her away. And if she means nothing to you, then why does the idea of another man showing interest in her bother you so damn much, macho man?" As she points out all the exact things I've been ruminating over, I realize we are more similar than I like to admit.

I cling most to the idea of any other man eventually coming around after I end it. I want to end *them*. Literally cut off their hands that will touch her. Remove their eyes from their skulls for even looking at her. I am territorial and possessive when it comes to her, and that isn't something I've hidden very well.

I think up something quick. "Because part of our agreement is she and I are exclusive. I don't have to love her, to not want another man trying to take her from me."

"Who said anything about love? I just said like."

Hanna pulls into the driveway, and Brenda is up, heading to meet her, but I'm stunned silent in my chair. She's right. She never said anything about love.

What am I going to do? What's going to happen when the truth comes out? Because it has to.

It *has* to.

The lines just blurred, and I'm not sure what to do now.

Brenda and Hanna come walking up the steps, and even in just jeans and a tank top that I'm sure she wore under her work shirt, she looks gorgeous. Her long hair is in a ponytail curled at the ends, and some loose hairs fall and frame her face. Her makeup is light, showing a little of the freckles that came from the tan she got at the lake.

I want her then, tempted to send Brenda away. Imagining myself lapping at her slit, biting her thick thighs, kissing her soft stomach, sucking her neck, all of it, it's all I want to do. It's been less than twelve hours since I've seen her, and it's like days have passed.

"Theo?" she prompts.

"Huh, yeah?"

"I said hi, and you were zoned out. You all right?" Hanna steps up to me, rubbing my arm. Her touch sends an electric bolt through me, and I ignite.

"Hand Brenda the key. Go inside, B, and give us a minute." I don't take my hungry eyes off Hanna.

Worry overtakes her face, and she hands her keys to Brenda.

"Whatever you say, Captain."

Once she's inside and out of view, I pin Hanna to wall beside her front door.

She gasps. "Theo, what—"

Cutting her off, I take her mouth viciously. She moans against my tongue, finally giving in and matching me. We sync up, and she puts her hands on my hips. Violently, I grab her breast in one hand and her neck with the other. Finally moving from her lips, I want to taste the rest of her. I move to her cheek, then her jaw and to her ear, sucking and groaning, rubbing my erection against her.

"Theo. What's wrong? Are you okay?"

"I just want you so goddamn bad. You look so beautiful, so sexy. All I can think about is being inside you."

She giggles when I kiss her neck, my three-day stubble tickling her. "Baby." She throws her head back.

Her calling me that stops me, and I lean back, searching her eyes.

"Sorry, I don't know where that came from. I—I just…You have pet names for me, so I just tried it out. I won't do it again. Sorry."

"No, say it again. Now."

She looks worried, not standing so tall in this moment, like if she says it again, I just might rage. But it's the opposite. There was ownership with it. The way she said, it came out so fucking good. "Baby?"

"Good girl. From now on, when I'm taking you, you call me

that. Understood?"

"Yes." She nods, her fingers slowly moving under the hem of my shirt on my hips. Her nails graze my bare skin, and I shiver.

"You're horny, aren't you, puppet?"

Biting her lip, she nods. "Yes. I want you. Really bad. I'm hurting," she whispers.

Fuck me. I didn't think I could get any harder than I already was. "Tell me why you hurt." I smirk.

"I feel so empty it hurts when you're not there. I thought about you all day, wished you were inside me again." She blushes.

"Your body is being molded to take only me, isn't it?" She nods, and I lean in and kiss the top of both of her breasts. I'm fucking these beautiful tits tonight. It's my life's fucking mission to do so and to come all over her neck and face. What a beautiful image to see.

"Tonight, I will take care of you. I'll soothe that ache, puppet. Be a good girl for me now, and let's get this done so I can get you alone."

"Okay," she agrees.

"Promise me something first."

Nodding, she leans in, gripping my hips tighter. "Anything."

"I need you to need me. I need you to cling to me and act as if you can't fucking breathe without me. I want you to fawn over me. Got it?"

"I already do," she admits, and my chest swells with pride.

"Let's go inside, but make sure you remember that tonight

you're mine. I want you badly, and the second we can, I want my sister gone." I don't care that I sound like an absolute prick.

"Wait," she stops me.

"What's up?"

She looks at me with doe eyes. "What if there is something in that room that breaks me more?" Her admission of fear is devastating to hear.

"Then we will work through it. I will be here; Brenda will be here. We will hold your hand through it, Hanna." I pause, gripping her neck like I so frequently do. Lifting her chin, I put my forehead to hers. "You aren't alone here anymore. You have people in your life who will lift you up when you are falling apart." Tears well in her green eyes, turning them a shade lighter, and it tugs at my heart.

Hanna is inside me. She is there. I made a mistake, but I refuse to leave her. It's not even refusal. It's not an option; my entire being won't let it.

"I wish you wouldn't say that. You're leaving in less than a week. You're making me miss you already." She hurries and follows that up. "I mean, as a friend. It's been nice having people in my life."

My ego is stroked. I know what she meant. She wants me too. She needs me. We fucked up. We both fucked up, and now I can't back out. "Don't worry. The job just got complicated, and I have more time."

Those sad eyes light up, then her smile reappears. "Really? So we get to do this a little bit longer?" She drops her head shyly, and I'm reminded how those little things she does make me more obsessed with her. Those mindless, small acts become so much more. They're the things that make me want to taste her. Lay her down. Own her. Consume her.

"Yeah, we still get to do this, greens. I knew you would miss me," I tease.

"Now you're being cocky. I changed my mind." She winks and slides under my other arm outstretched beside her. And I hurry and slap her ass as she enters the house.

"It's about time, horn dogs. We need to get this going. I have plans," Brenda says, her arms crossed as she eyes us like two troublemakers.

"As do we." I give Hanna's ass a tight squeeze, and she slaps my chest.

"We agreed. Not in front of your sister."

"I second that. Boundaries, Theo."

When I toss my hands up in mock surrender, we all three laugh, enjoying the lightheartedness. Putting my hands down, I reach into my back pocket and take out my lockpicking tools.

"Where's the room?" I ask.

"Upstairs. Follow me."

"Gladly."

Hanna goes first, and I don't even try to hide it as I check her out, not caring one damn bit. She's mine, and I can take in the view of what's mine all I want. Soon, I'll fuck that tight, thick ass. Fuck me, society is blind to ever see a woman built like this and think she's anything less than a motherfucking delicacy.

Hanna calls herself fat. *No, sweet little puppet. You are built for real men, men who need more of something deemed perfection.* The more of her, the better.

"Obvious much?" Brenda taunts, watching me check out Hanna's backside.

Hanna turns, now at the top of the stairs. "What?" she asks, looking between the both of us.

"Nothi—" Brenda goes to say, but I cut her off.

"She was watching me check out your ass."

Hanna blushes, and Brenda gasps behind me. "I knew you were crude, but my hell, Theo. Mom would clutch her pearls. Hanna, blink twice if you're in danger and need an out."

"She does need an out, but good luck getting her out of my fucking hands."

"I'm gonna be sick. You two need therapy. Seriously." Brenda nudges my back to keep going, and Hanna's blush never fades as she turns and heads down the hall opposite her bedroom.

"This is it," she says, gesturing to the door.

"Yes, the room of a thousand corpses. Let us pray the town's golden boy wasn't also the town's serial killer," Brenda says, and I look at her.

"And you think we need therapy? You're twisted, sis. Stop with all the true crime podcasts."

"Listen, it's always the ones who are loved the most." She shrugs, and Hanna giggles.

That cute damn giggle.

Focus! I tell myself.

Lowering on my haunches, I start to pick at the lock on the door. A few twists and turns, some little tweaks, and the doorknob clicks, letting me know I'm in. I stand and turn the brass handle and look to Hanna. "You ready, greens?"

She plays with her hands anxiously and gnaws at her bottom lip. I take my thumb, bring it to her lips, and tug that sweet skin free.

"Look at me, Hanna. Are you ready? Are you sure you want to do this?" When she looks at me, I see her debate it, but I give her the best surge of psychological strength I can, letting her draw it from me.

"Yes. Let's go."

We step in, Hanna first, then Brenda and me. It is, in fact, his office.

"Good news! No bodies. That's one point for Gramps."

"Say something about dead bodies one more time, sis, and I will have you institutionalized. Seriously, I'm worried for you," I tell her as my eyes focus on Hanna. She moves around the room slowly, touching the mahogany furniture, the bookcase first.

Looking at the books, she quietly says, "Classics. He has Brante in here. He liked to read." She looks to us, but we both stay silent.

This is a moment for her. She needs this. There is a need to find answers or a place to belong, and some part of her believes it's going to be in this room. And I actually feel that too. I think we all do.

She pulls out one book and opens it, her fingers delicately touching the pages. From here, they seem frayed a bit.

"Wow, this is a first edition. This must have cost him a fortune. I would have loved to own a book like this—a first edition." Tucking the loose hair that falls from her ponytail behind her ear, she keeps looking through the book. The sun coming from the window frames her, casting a glow around her entire body. Her profile is perfect. Just as stunning as she is head-on. She is studying a book she claims to be a classic work of art, when I'm in fact looking at the most beautiful masterpiece ever to be cast in an aura of light.

I catch myself staring, stumbling on the thoughts I'm having, knowing damn well they aren't something I should be feeling. They begin to suffocate me and give me the urge to push away instead of pull her in. My head is a mess, making me feel like my feet are cemented to the ground when all I want to do is run.

"I'm going to look in the drawers over there," Brenda says, moving across the room.

"Yeah, I'll check his desk too." Hanna finally closes the book and moves to the large desk sitting in front of the huge window. She opens the top drawer, sifts through it, and closes it when she finds nothing. Moving to the next one, to the side, the bigger drawer, she pulls, but it doesn't open.

"Theo, this one is locked. Can you pick it?"

I move, my feet feeling heavy, still stuck in my own thoughts. "Yeah." I get down and unlock the drawer. Pulling it open, we see it is nearly filled to the brim with envelopes. We both look at each other, and I see it in her eyes. That fear she had coming to life—the answers will be within these envelopes.

All stamped with Return to Sender.

"That's my mother's name," she chokes out.

"What is it?" Brenda walks over to us.

"Letters. Or something. But they have my mother's name on them."

"Shit," Brenda breathes out.

"Yeah. Do we just read them?" Hanna looks to each of us.

"That's up to you, babe," Brenda tells her, and I nod in agreement.

"Fuck. I hate this. Why is it this way? Why did this have to be my life?" She stands and pushes the drawer shut.

We stay silent, letting her say and feel whatever it is she needs to in order to process this. Brenda and I could never begin to relate, and we shouldn't pretend like we do. All we can do is help her through whatever is inside those letters. Which could be nothing, or they could be everything.

"We don't have to do this if you aren't ready." Brenda goes to her, but I keep my distance, watching her. I will let her have her space until she needs me. I'm learning her. Learning when she needs support and when she needs time to decompress and figure it out on her own.

"I know that, but if I don't, I will be driven to madness. And if I do, I just might end up more broken than I already am."

"Puppet." My voice is sharp and demanding, and she looks at me.

"Yes?" She aligns with me, feeling me.

"What did I say outside?" She nods. "Come here to me. Brenda. Leave." This is one of the rare times I'm short with my sister. Hearing the undeniable command in my voice, she moves fast, leaving the room. Hanna and I now stand alone in the middle of JD's office.

"You need me. I told you to lean on me and depend on me, and you're not doing it. Are you?"

She shakes her head. Hanna thrives under control. "I do need you. But to what extent? What if I need you too much? What if it scares you, and then you assume I'm falling in love with you?"

I don't admit my internal thoughts. Since that would mean I'd have to tell her that she's starting to make me feel things. Not love. It can't be love. We are still learning, getting to know each other, and we spend most of our time together fucking or in the presence of other people. Slowly, we're opening up, but this right here, her finding what could be her release or her rabbit hole, this is the most intimate we've been.

"I trust you to not cross that line. Needing me obsessively will only match what I feel. Let me be your release. Take your fear, pain, and everything else out on me. Lay it on me; take it out on me in the bedroom. That doesn't have to blur the lines. That's what the whole point of us is." What a great liar and deflector I am. To let this go as far as it has and to feel certain things, just to tell her to not cross lines. I'm such a fucking hypocrite.

"Okay. I'm ready. I want to read whatever is in there." When she buys my lines, not seeing through me, I hide the sigh of relief so well. Turning, she heads back to the desk and pulls out a stack of the envelopes.

Here we go...

Twenty-One

HANNA

THE ENVELOPE IS HEAVY IN MY HANDS. IT'S DAUNTING, and for what reason? I don't know, seeing as I've been too chicken shit to open it yet. Theo stands beside me where I sit, towering over me. Usually, that would intimidate me and make me nervous, but in this situation, it does the opposite. It makes me feel comforted, and I don't feel so alone for the first time in a long time. Releasing a deep breath and closing my eyes, I lift the tab of the first letter with my mother's name on it.

> Lizbeth,
> Please, just let me talk to her. Let me have time with Hanna. I've tried now multiple times, and you've cast me out. We haven't always seen eye to eye, and we may have had our fair share of hardships, but I love you, and I love my granddaughter. Denying me time with her will only cause more damage to her.
> What can I do? Saying sorry isn't enough, and I know that, but

I need you to tell me what I can do to just see her. I have a right to see her. You know this. Don't punish her because of our history. Please. I beg you a thousand times, please, give me a chance to have a relationship. I don't know what else to say but please.

I still love you. I love you and my granddaughter, and I know you don't believe it, but it's true. Hear me. Please.

Love you, Dad

The tears fall, hitting the ink on the paper and causing it to thin out to the point that it would rip if I'm not careful. I don't say anything. I instead drop the paper on the desk and reach for the next one, opening it quickly.

> JD,
> Hanna doesn't want to know you, and we don't want you knowing her either. You kicked me out and left me to fend for myself. Please stop. Just stop. We have nothing to say. Hanna, her father, and I are happy finally after what you did to us.

I keep going, confused by what I read each time, because they're not in any kind of order.

> JD,
> I read Hanna the letters. She doesn't want to know you either. You need to live with the consequences of what you did. LEAVE ME ALONE.

Lizbeth,

Sweetie, I miss you. I know I shouldn't have kicked you out after I found out what Joe did. Money is nothing compared to family. I shouldn't have kicked you out. If you would have told me that you were pregnant, I would have forgiven it all.

I was angry. I didn't want you to be with a dishonest man who would steal, cheat, and lie. He stole a lot of our money, sweetheart, and I know he hits you. I see the marks. Please come home so I can keep you safe. You and the baby...is it a girl a boy? I love you, Lizbeth. Please know that.

JD,

You kicked me out. You kicked me to the curb, but that doesn't matter. What matters is that you did it when I was pregnant. I thought you should know I'm having a baby, and I will never let you meet this child.

Lizbeth,

The drugs. Did you stop them at least? Now that you're pregnant? Please tell me you stopped. Keep my grandchild safe. If you won't do it for yourself, then do it for her. I can't believe it's a girl. Please come home, and I will take care of you.

JD,

I hate you. You ruined my life. After mom died, you left the burden on me. You locked yourself away and left me alone to suffer. My life ended up the way it did because of you. I was left to suffer alone, because you couldn't even get out of bed. You never cared to ask me how this was hurting me. I hate you. So much!

Dearest Hanna,

I'm writing this in hopes that it may let you have some insight on why your mother and I are estranged. If I'm honest, it's my fault. It wasn't right of me to mourn your grandmother, her mother, so deeply that I let Lizbeth suffer alone. It was my job to protect her, to keep her safe, to be the parent she needed when she lost her mom- her best friend. But I can't take that back.

I won't blame her for anything. Because I want her to know I am to blame. We all have faults, but at the end of the day, I was her parent and should have taken care of her and taken the blame.

When she left, I didn't know she was pregnant with you. I just knew about the bad things happening between your father, her, and me, and I felt I had no choice. I see now that I was so very wrong for that. But please, let me be in your life. Give me the chance to be. We are family, and I want to bring my girls home.

You should be eighteen now. Old enough to make your own choices. And I hope that somewhere in those choices, you can find it in you to forgive me and give me a chance.

I understand you may need time, but please consider. I have letters for you, stored away for every birthday I missed, every special occasion. Because I didn't know if you would want to read them. I held on to them, because I felt you were too young to be put in the middle, to make a choice on whether or not to forgive me and get to know me.

I'm here, waiting. My door is always open. There is love here. I'm waiting. I love you. No matter what, know that I love you. I don't know who you are or what you're like, and I bet you're thinking "how could he love someone he's never met." But I do. I've loved you since the minute your mother told me she was pregnant with you.

I want to see if you look like her. Or like me. Did you get my genes or your grandmother's, or even your father's? I want to know what you like. Music? Books? Movies? I love books; they are my escape. Do you read? If not, what do you like to do?

God, there is so much I want to know about you. But most of all, I want to be a family. Maybe we can start now?

Write back when you are ready. Only when you're ready. The ball is in your court, my sweet grandchild.

I love you.

Love, Grandpa

> JD
> I read your letter. But it's too late. What you did to my parents is unforgivable. My mother turned to drugs and stealing, a life of danger and darkness, because of you. I don't want to know you. I want to protect my mom and dad. I choose my parents. In fact, I will act as if you never existed. You are dead to us. You left my parents broke, without a penny to their name, and now I suffer for it too. The least you could do is send them money to help them.
> Do not contact me again. Now you can know what it's like for family to abandon you when you want and need them most.
> Hanna

"They lied." I cover my mouth and weep. The last letter. They gave me up when I was just a child. They lied to him and created a fake world where I never even existed.

I wipe at my tears and stand, running and leaving the room. I pass Brenda in the hall and ignore her calling after me. Slamming my bedroom door, I lock it and run to the closet, sinking to the floor and letting my heart just fall to pieces.

Those were just a few of the letters. What else will be in them? Do I want to know? They lied. Made him believe I was with them and wanted nothing to do with my grandfather. They could have left me with him the moment she gave birth. Clearly, I was someone he wanted in his life. Did he send them money after they lied and sent them the letter posing as me?

All my life, I thought my parents were lost souls who just didn't know what to do when they had me. I even made scenarios in my head where they thought I would have a better life, where I could be cared for, loved in more ways than they ever could. All of that was wrong. They never wanted me. And in a disgusting attempt to get money, they used me. They talked about me with so much conviction, as if I existed to them and they knew me.

They didn't know me at all, and these letters, their actions, may be crueler than the day they left me at that damn police station and took off.

"Sweetie?" There is a knock followed by Brenda's soft voice coming from the bedroom.

I don't answer; I don't want to face them. On top of my overwhelming heartbreak, the pain of betrayal, loneliness, and lack of love, I'm embarrassed. I can faintly hear the sound of them mumbling. But I don't care. I'm locked away and alone. Like I've always been.

To know that his love was there, that he not only tried for eighteen years to contact me, but he also still never gave up on me, *especially* after that cruel letter written under my name...

He gave me everything left to his name. He wrote me letters on days he knew would be important. There has to be more to the story in the rest of those letters, and I know I could piece them together like a puzzle. But I don't think my fragile heart can handle it. I was a mistake, and my parents' selfish act was the worst thing to ever happen to me. And it was the one thing that would affect me the rest of my life.

While my heart breaks for *me*, I also hurt for my grandfather. How painful would those words be to hear while still mourning the loss of his daughter? How lonely did he feel? Did he feel lonely like me? Looks like we were both handed a similar fate. He had friends and a world with people who loved him by design, but he lost all the family he ever had, and just like me, it was in the cruelest way.

Suddenly, now knowing the story, I feel a deep pit in my chest and stomach, the feeling of mourning the death of a man who wanted so badly to love me.

I lost the only family who loved me, and I'm surrounded by him. In his home, in his town and his life, but I'm without *him*, the most important thing I wish I could have. I would trade all of this to just talk to him, meet him, at least get a hello before suffering through a goodbye.

A scream leaves me, the sound so piercing it numbs my eardrums. If they could bleed from it, they would. Over the ringing, I hear the sound of shattering wood and thumps. In seconds, while wailing and crying through my devastation, I'm lifted and engulfed in strong arms.

Arms that have held me in every way but this. They have held me in lust and passion, but never in solace.

"Baby, I have you. You can breathe. I'm here." He carries me to the bed and lays me down, my screams dying down to sobs so deep in my gut my entire body feels it.

"I hate them. I hate them." I slam my fist hard against the bed repeatedly.

"Hanna, stop, baby. Stop," Theo speaks softly, but I don't listen. "Hanna. Enough. Calm down and listen to me," he barks, and my body stills, his authority the one thing that always breaks me from whatever it is I'm going through.

"Brenda, go grab me some ice water please," he asks her, and in a fog of tears, I see a worried Brenda nod, then rush out the room. I'm aware of what a mess I am and how crazy I look right now, but my life just fell into alignment, but it wasn't in an easy way or the way that I thought would bring closure and peace. Instead, it brought rage and heartache, bitterness stronger than ever before.

Theo rubs my hair, wiping at my tears, pulling me in second by second. Soon, I hear Brenda enter the room, and he helps sits me up. "Take a sip for me."

Nodding, I want to oblige, because the screaming hurt my throat, and I could use something to soothe it. I take small sips, a few at a time, then Theo takes it and hands it to Brenda. I wipe at my eyes, clearing the tears from them as best as I can.

"You here with us?" Theo finally speaks, and my breathing starts to settle, evening out a bit. I nod. "Good. I'm sorry, Hanna. I read the last letter." I look to him, then Brenda, and back to my hands.

"How could they lie to me? Hurt not only me but my grandfather?"

"People are cruel, baby. This is why you have to let go and let people find their own way."

My eyes shoot to him. "If I stopped giving a shit about people, that would make me like my parents. I want to be nothing like them, the complete opposite." My statement isn't rude; it's honest.

"I know, but you also let yourself be the punching bag for so much pain. You need to set that free, or it's going to hurt you more, babe," Brenda says, dropping to her knees in front of me at the edge of the bed. Placing her hands on mine, she rubs her thumb softly over mine.

"I see him. Reading that letter. I feel it almost. Like I can feel his pain," I choke out, moving my hand to my chest where my heart pounds, and I claw at it, as if it will dull out the ache.

"Then to sit here in his home, knowing he forgave me, loved me enough to leave me everything I needed...I want to be him. Like that. The type who forgives. Because right now, I hate my parents. I wish I could find them and tell them I hate them. Tell them what pain and misery they caused me. The havoc and mess they left in my life." Tears fall. "But then I think of him. How he never once stopped loving me. And I bet those letters would show that he never stopped loving my mother."

Theo runs circles on my back with the softest touch. "What do you think he felt like? Dying without knowing the truth? With thinking I hated him?"

"I will tell you this. You grandfather never hated anyone. He was the first to help and the first to forgive. See the best in people. He had to know that one day you would learn the truth, and he had to know you would find the letters when he left you everything," Brenda tells me.

I smile a bit, hearing her sing his high praise, but it dies out fast. "But he didn't know the truth. He was buried with lies and secrets. I hate lies, and I hate secrets."

Theo stiffens next to me, and I look to him. His eyes are on the wall adjacent to the bed. His jaw tics and tightens. "What's wrong, Theo?" I ask.

"Nothing. Just keep talking. Open up to us." He must be trying to hide his anger the best he can.

"I really have nothing more to say. My parents have become bigger monsters. I never got to meet the man who could have shown me love and drastically changed my life. And now I have what I needed to know. He didn't refuse to find me; he just respected 'my' wishes." I air quote.

"What can we do to help you? We want to be here for you. Tell us what you need," Brenda prompts.

I think about this, hard, taking a long pause and wracking my brain. Theo looks so upset next to me, and suddenly I remember what he said on the porch, how he needs me to need him, and right now, I need that too. I need him to make me forget for a moment. Make this all fade to the back for a little bit.

"I need you," I whisper to him

That's all he needs to hear. I do what I told him I would when I need him most, and it works.

"Sis, you need to go. I will call you later." He doesn't look at her; instead, his eyes stay on me. I finally break eye contact with great effort and look to Brenda.

"You sure?" she asks, her brows drawn in.

"Yes, I'm sure. I promise. Thank you. I will call you when the dust settles, okay?" I stand, but Theo keeps a physical touch at all times, his hand on my hip, tethering me to him. The pang in my chest alerts me then, the same thing that's happened every time he shows a sign of need for me outside the bedroom. When he gives me small glimpses into him and what he needs, that's when I get that feeling I know I shouldn't. But I bury it down. My heart is broken over the letters, and that's all I need to focus on at the moment.

"Okay, I love you, Hanna. I'm here. Call me as soon as you can." We embrace; she wraps me up tight. It's the kind of hug you get when you experience a loss. And today, I was finally able to mourn my grandfather and the bed of lies my parents sold him.

Separating after some time, she leaves us. I watch her go, and once she's out of sight, Theo turns me and pulls me in with his hands on my hips.

"Talk to me." He guides me to straddle him, and once settled, I drop my forehead to his, cupping his face.

"I hurt, deeply. But not as much for me as I do for my grandfather. They sold him so many lies. He died thinking I hated him, Theo," I sob, those tears returning, blurring my vision.

"I know. That's the cruelest thing they could have ever done, second to leaving you behind. You see now though that clearly you were never the problem." He rubs my thighs.

"I do."

"How does that feel?" he asks.

"Foreign, it makes the guilt stronger. When you spend your whole life thinking you were so unlovable that even the ones programmed to love you couldn't, it seems like it still belongs to you. The blame, the pain. It's so hard to explain. It's too heavy to explain."

"You know when I was growing up, I had a friend. He was amazing. Hilarious and smart as hell. He always knew how to make me laugh. I swear I don't laugh that often, but he could always make me do that."

I wonder where he's going with this, but I don't interrupt.

"Our senior year, we were supposed to ditch school on the last day. We were going to get wasted, and I almost went, but Brenda found out and was so disappointed." He smiles. "I could never stand letting her down. She always had a way of making me feel like absolute garbage when I acted out or broke the rules. She's the only person I care enough for to let that matter."

A slight sting hits. I would like to think that just maybe I could mean something to him, and though we have talked about it and made it clear it will never go past sex, it sure seems like this could be something. This is a glimpse inside him he hasn't shown, and he asked me to call him baby, to need him and lean on him.

Lovers do those things. Not friends with benefits. That's what *lovers* do. But I could never be his. And I have to keep reminding myself of that, or I will fall head-first into it and won't be able to be pulled out.

"So I told him I wasn't going. He called me an ass and that I let him down. Told me he would go get fucked up while I stayed in class like a little bitch." We shared a laugh, and then he went, and I stayed. Two hours later, he was gone. He was hit head-on by a drunk driver." He scoffs. "He wasn't even drunk himself. He was on his way to get wasted, and his life was taken by a drunk driver."

He looks over at the floor-to-ceiling windows to the left. "I lost my best friend, and I lived with the guilt for so many years. Still do sometimes. So I know that guilt, puppet. You know it's not your fault, but it somehow feels better to take on the guilt. The idea of never feeling the blame or feeling guilty makes me feel worse. But at the end of the day, we both know it's not our fault."

I don't realize how emotional I was over his story until a tear lands on his hand on my leg.

"That's exactly how I feel. If I say it all makes sense and my parents were the ones who made these bad choices, I feel like I'm a selfish person. Guilt sometimes makes you feel better. It makes you believe they are worth forgiving, that they could love you. That's all we want is to be loved."

He looks back to me, and I stare deep into his honey eyes, and it's too much. For him and me.

For me, it's too much, because I know what I'm feeling and wouldn't be afraid to chase that and give it a chance. But for him, it's too much, because he wants to run so damn far. And just like that, he starts to let me in, but when he sees a side of himself that could change the person he has always been, he pushes me out again.

"Listen. I think we need a night out. I won't tell you what we are doing, but I want you to get dressed in your favorite outfit. Do your hair your favorite way and your makeup, whatever you like. I'm going to go grab some things and change." He stands, placing me on my feet.

Looking at his watch, he suddenly rushes. Grabbing my throat, he kisses me and hurries out. "You only have an hour though or we will miss it. Hurry up, greens! I'll be back in one hour!" he hollers as he runs down the hall and descends the stairs.

Left stunned and slightly disappointed, I stay in a standstill for a moment.

"You can't love him. He isn't capable of it. And your heart can't take another blow," I say into the nothing. The empty room. Me, my heartbreak, and the realization that I crossed a line. I fell in love with a man who was supposed to be nothing but a fling. I fucked up.

Twenty-Two

THEO

I PUT ON JEANS, BROWN BOOTS, A BLACK LONG-SLEEVED shirt, and a flat-bill hat. Grabbing my jacket, I hurry out the door with a cooler in my hand and my keys and phone in the other. I lock up the house and rush to the truck, the sun almost completely gone.

Starting the truck and heading to the store, I think about Hanna then. I can't believe I told her that story. No one knows that side of the story. Not Brenda, not my parents, no one. They know I lost a friend, and that's it. Not that I feel guilty and live with it daily.

But Hanna does something to me. She makes me feel like I have a safe place to talk, and I hate that. I'm not a man who needs safe places or confidants who I can lean on. But with Hanna, I saw pain, and I needed her to know she wasn't alone. I had to take on her pain and share mine so she didn't feel lost.

The constant pull in my head and that damn thing in my chest is exhausting. Love is a strong word, and that's all it's ever been to me—a word. I couldn't know it as anything else, because I never felt a romantic type of love. So I can't say that's what's happening here. That's something I cling to, my last bit of sanity and little piece of hope left that I didn't fuck up.

Hanna happened, and she happened fast. I couldn't put an end to it. And now I wish I could draw up a wall so high neither she nor I could climb it or break through it. This is a dangerous game, and at first, when I started it, I didn't think it would get to this place, but the moving pieces made all the wrong moves, and now I'm fighting what I'm feeling.

I have to stop thinking about this. I pull up to the store and run in to grab the items I need. Wine, cheese, strawberries, some chocolate syrup, candles, and a lighter. I grabbed a blanket and some pillows back at the house but forgot the lighter and candles.

The clerk at the cashier stand gives me a look that tells me she knows that tonight is going to be eventful. She isn't wrong, but it isn't just going to be mind-blowing sex. I have plans to be a softer man tonight. Hanna had the worst day, and I feel the need to give her something other than mind-numbing orgasms. Though those will definitely help.

"Have fun," she says as a send-off, and I have to hide my shock. She really has no shame. Hurrying to the truck, I climb in, put the items in the back seat, and get to Hanna's house in less than five minutes. When I pull up, I park the truck but leave it running. It's a summer night, so it's hot out. I want to keep the truck cool.

I get to the door and knock. I would walk in, but I locked the knob before I left. A minute later, the door opens, and I'm nearly knocked on my ass. Her hair is curled and falling all around her, and she has her makeup done in some smoky eye thing, and it makes her green eyes pop.

She looks dangerous. The best kind. But the red dress she wears and the shoes are what get me. I can't explain it, but the fabric on her body is hanging on her shoulders by thin straps and drops into a deep V, showing me her cleavage. Tonight, is the night I will slide my cock in between those exquisite globes. The dress tightens with some strap under her breasts, then it flows to just below her knees, except the front is higher than the back, showing me her freshly tanned legs. The wedge shoes with red matching lace wrap around her ankles and up her legs a couple of inches. Even with them, she is still so much shorter than me.

Feminine and desire-inducing. That's what she embodies in front of me. And the floral scent she wears hits me, and I have to resist pushing her back in and saying fuck it. "Baby, you look stunning. So damn beautiful." I step up to her until we're only about an inch or two apart. "Are you wearing panties, puppet?"

Scandalized, she blushes but nods. "Yes."

Looking around and making sure no cars are coming, I drop to my haunches and run my hands up and down her smooth, sexy legs. I kiss up each one and lift her dress.

"Theo...what are you— oooh." She stops when I wrap my index finger around the crotch of her panties and tug. They start to come down, and she helps me, slowly wiggling her hips.

"Such a good fucking girl." She didn't tell me to stop or get all embarrassed. No, she leans into the trust. When they fall to her ankles, I lift one leg at a time, kissing each knee as the panties fall off her foot. Collecting them, I lift her dress and plant a kiss on her pussy lips, and she cries out.

"Oh God!"

"Name's Theo, puppet. Don't give credit to anyone else. Only me," I growl, standing and putting her panties in my pocket.

"So I guess I don't need underwear for this event?" She lightens the mood, locking up the house.

"Correct. You'll see why soon."

She gulps, but an excited joy crosses her eyes. Taking her hand, I walk her to the truck. "You know, taking a woman's panties right before a date is very scandalous."

I laugh, buckling her in before I respond. "You won't be complaining when you see what I do. But yes, you will in fact feel scandalized."

Her eyes widen, and she captures her lips between her teeth. She doesn't reply, and I shut the door. The second we're on the road, I put on a song, the exact song I need for this moment—"I Wanna Be Your Slave" by Maneskin. I tell her to scoot in close to me, and she looks at me suspiciously for a moment. I warn her to do as I say, and when she scoots across the cab so she's sitting up against me, I turn the radio up louder. The bass of the music can be felt in our chests and throughout our entire bodies.

"What are you doing, Theo?" She looks terrified but at the same time thrilled. What a deadly combination for what I'm about to do.

"Puppet, you're going to spread your legs. I'm going to take two fingers, put them inside you, and then I want you to fuck them." The damn whimper that leaves her goes straight to my cock, and I'm instantly hard as the song picks up. She spreads her legs, and I can smell her arousal from here. I would wear that scent if I could so I could be reminded every single moment of every single day how sweet her cunt is.

The intensity of the moment paired with the song is overwhelming. Her legs now fully open, I keep one hand on the wheel and take my middle and pointer fingers and put them between her legs. Sliding them along her slit, I collect her juices as lube, then stiffen them. Moving them to her entrance, I insert them just a little, and now it's her turn to do the work.

"Slide your hips back and forth, and get your sweet cunt off on my fingers. Scandalize yourself." I use her words against her, and every part of her body that I can see from her breasts up turns red. But like she always does when lust consumes her, she does what I tell her. She starts rolling her hips, then slides them back and forth.

"Oh yes. That feels so good," she hisses, starting to move her hips to the rhythm of the song. Her cunt get so wet it soaks my hand. That's how I like it. Fucked up, dirty, and raw. I glance at her and watch her throw her head back in euphoria. Picking up speed, I know she's close by the repeated tightening, loosening, then tightening again of her walls.

"Theo, I need it," she cries out.

"You have to say it."

"Degrade me. Make me feel...dirty."

Look at her now, reveling in her kinks.

"Be my good little slut and come on my fingers. Good sluts do what their told."

And doing just as I demanded, she screams out my name. It overpowers the song, and she jitters, jolts, and shakes, coming hard. I pull my fingers from her and lick her taste off of them. But I don't give her time to come down from her high before I'm making her do what I want.

"Pull my cock out and choke on it, puppet." She's so eager from her orgasm that she doesn't hesitate. Rushing to her knees, she frees my cock, and before she takes it in her mouth, I stop her. "Spit on it." Her eyes widen, and I let her meet the eyes of the devil. "And look up at me while you do it." I glance at the road really quick, then look back to her, and she does it.

She spits and then deep-throats me, taking me to the back with a gag. I use my free hand and push her down, keeping her there, and she moans.

I fucking come.

So fast.

She didn't even have to do the work. Just the image of her and the sound of her choking on my cock was enough.

"Dirty slut, taking me so good. Stealing it. Fuck," I moan,

trying to keep my eyes open and on the road. Once she's taken every drop of me, I let up on her hair, and she sits up, wiping at the corners of her lips as she gives me a shy smile. And I praise her the way she deserves. "You're such a good girl. I'm proud of you."

She takes my praise, flourishing under it. Every time with her is more thrilling than the last. New kinks, new limits, new boundaries are pushed, and we both live for the next high. The next thrill.

"You...you came without me doing any work," she speaks softly.

"Yeah, that's because you're fucking deadly. You have no idea how sexy you are, Hanna."

"When you do that, that makes me feel powerful."

"You are power, and I'm control. What a force we are," I tell her, and now we're at the location I had planned.

"The lake? I didn't dress right for the lake." She laughs.

"You dressed perfectly. We aren't getting in the water," I tell her, climbing out.

"Then what are we doing?" she hollers when I shut the door to go help her out. Opening hers, I hold out my hand.

"Just trust me, greens. You're going to like this." When she climbs out, I help her to not stumble. It's dark, and the only light is the moon in the sky and the headlights on my truck. I walk us around to the truck bed, and I drop the tailgate.

Grabbing her hips, I lift her, making her squeak, and place her on the end. Every time I pick her up, it's effortless. I keep in shape, and it pays off. The shock it brings her every time makes me swell with pride that I can do that to her.

"Wait here," I tell her.

"I can do that. This view is stunning."

I backed the truck in, so we're just a few feet from the water's edge, and she's right. The view is breathtaking, especially when she's the main attraction.

Going to the back seat of the cab, I grab everything I brought and take it to where she's sitting. Not bothering to look at what I have, she keeps taking in the surroundings when I hop up in the truck bed behind her. I glance at my watch and see we only have maybe a few minutes before the main event starts.

"Hey, puppet, can you stand up for me so I can make us a bed real quick?" This finally draws her away from the view.

"You're setting us up a bed?" Her face lights up when she looks at all the things I brought.

"Yes, I am. And I have some snacks, and I need to set it up. There's something I want to show you, and I don't have a lot of time."

"Want me to light the candles?" she asks.

"Not yet. In fact, turn around, baby." I grab her hips, turn her, and bring her back flat against my chest.

"Theo, oh my God! This is...beautiful." Thousands of lights start to take up the entire space above the body of water.

"I knew you would love this."

"Fireflies. I've always wanted to see them in person." The lights not only fill the air but reflect on the water, and her face lights up along with them. I lean and place my chin on her shoulder, reaching one hand up to circle her throat. I sway us a bit, and she just melts, mesmerized.

"So we love fireflies, baby?" I whisper, kissing her shoulder.

"We do. This is really special. I didn't think you had this in you. And you thought you couldn't be a romantic." She grabs my wrist of the hand around her neck and squeezes, turning to give me her lips. I take them, sucking her bottom lip in and nipping it.

"I'm not romantic. I'm in the business of keeping Hanna happy. Two different things. But don't you go telling my sister I did this for you. I'll never hear the end of it." I tighten my grip on her neck and kiss her again.

"I won't. It will be our secret."

"Oh yeah? Can what I have planned to do to you tonight be our little secret too?"

She bites her lip. "Depends. What do you want to do to me?" The way she asks this, the control I feel run through me...it comes off as if she is so innocent, when really I know what happens when the lust takes over. The real Hanna was just waiting in the shadows, waiting for someone to free her and show her the power in not only herself but in her sexuality.

"I want to lay you down. Feed you. Pour chocolate all over you. Lick you from head to toe until you're clean, and then I want to mark your skin with bites, cum, and anything else I can. Every time I'm with you, I want to fucking destroy you." I tighten my grip on her throat to bring attention to my dominance.

"You already did. I tell you this all the time. I would let you do anything to me. I trust you. I crave you. I need all you have to give, and it's all I can think about. When you're gone, I'm going to be left to suffer the loss."

"Good. I hope you always feel misery when you're with others. Because I will own you forever. No matter where or when. No lover will ever get all of you back. You're my token, and I'll keep parts of you that others will never get to have."

"That's crazy," she pants.

"Exactly. I never claimed to be anything else. I thought you knew me better by now." I bite her shoulder and scoot back. I want to eat first and let her enjoy the view before I devour her body like it's my personal dessert. "Let's have some wine and some strawberries. I also bought that fancy cheese I heard you like," I tell her, and we crawl to the back of the bed, on the blanket and pillows. Somehow, she did it so gracefully.

"How many times a day do you call your sister to ask her things about me instead of just asking me?"

I pop the cork of the wine and pour us some, a little more in hers, as I'll be driving us home. "If I called and asked you, then you would know what sorts of things I have planned. I want it to be a surprise."

"Fair. This really is amazing. Thank you. I needed something to distract me," she says, taking the wine glass I hand to her. I lean on the pillows against the back window of my truck, and we stay silent for a little bit. I feed her some strawberries, watching her lips as she takes bites, and a simple act like that shouldn't be so erotic, but it is.

"Want to talk about what happened today?" I finally ask.

Dropping her head, she shakes it. "No. There isn't much to say. I still need to read all the letters, but the why is known now, and I just have to learn how to move forward." She shrugs, looking up at the moon. "What about you? Want to talk more about your friend? I'm sorry that happened to you," she adds, and I shut down.

I realized later how personal I got with her, and that scared me. I don't want to feel that right now. Tonight is about forgetting the world and just focusing on us. "It was a long time ago. No need to talk more on it." I come off short, and she immediately answers me back.

"Sorry." It's just as short, and I internally scold myself.

"I didn't mean to snap like that. I just think we need to take our minds off everything. I want to focus on us. Can we do that and not let the outside world in?" I plead with her, running my thumb along her jaw and chin.

"Yes. I agree."

"Good. How about we really close off our minds?" My voice lowers.

"What does that mean exactly?"

I click my tongue. "I told you what I wanted to do to you tonight. You ready for that?"

"Yes."

"Safe word?"

"Sirius."

The moment the word leaves her lips, I'm on her, taking her mouth, the sweet wine and strawberries lingering there. My hell. "I need to mark you."

"With what?"

"My cum. I want you to be a good girl and let me fuck your tits, and I'm going to come all over your neck. You think you're ready for that?" When I claim her lips, she nods against me, removing the straps of her dress and bra, the fabric falling and exposing her beautiful, large breasts. Her pink nipples look delicious. "You have the most beautiful tits I've ever seen, puppet."

"Then fuck them."

I wish she could see that. The moment she goes from insecure to knowing what she needs. It's a switch, a snap of fingers. Who knew a woman drowning in insecurities could be so unashamed and vocal with her sexual needs?

"You couldn't have been made more perfect for me. Beauty. Brains. And such a dirty little slut in the bedroom," I tell her, lying down on my back. I place my hands behind my head and get ready to enjoy the show. "Get to it."

She needs no further instruction. She makes works of my pants and belt, freeing my cock. I keep all my clothes on and just leave my cock out.

"What do I do next?" She bites her lip, her hand playing with my erection.

I groan, my head lulling back in my hands for a minute. "Goddamn, princess. Shit. Okay. Get on your knees and lean over me. Take my cock between your breasts, and use your hands to squeeze them as tight around me as you can, then bounce up and down. But put on a show. I want to see you enjoying pleasing me. Don't let me down, okay, puppet?" I take one hand and move her hair out of her face and behind her ear when she gets in position.

"I do enjoy it. There is something so hot about you watching me with that hungry look. Still dressed from your hat to your shoes. Only your big cock out."

I quirk a brow. I know I'm big, but hearing her say it never gets old.

"Every time you open that sweet mouth, you say things dirtier than the last. You like driving me mad," I tell her, and she giggles.

"I sure do. I like that power you keep telling me about."

"Less talking, more showing me how you plan to use it." Keeping my hands behind my head, I watch the masterpiece unfold as she does what I told her to. Once my cock is nestled deep in her chest, she starts to move up and down, and I let her know I like it. "Yeah, just like that, baby. You're doing so good. Fuck."

She picks up speed, watching my face as it warps and twists into pleasure. I've never done this before. I've never been with a woman as gifted as Hanna. All the ones I've been with have been average size but usually a lot less full. But Hanna? God…Hanna—she is perfect. I told her this, but there is no other woman who could ever compare.

She has it all. The body. The brains. The sex appeal. The same lust and hunger that matches mine.

Fuck.

"Am I doing it okay, Theo?"

I bite my lip, nodding, my cock twitching when she goes all the way down and licks the tip. "What the fuck, baby? Where did you learn that?" Jealousy starts to seep in. I know she's had sex, but she told me it was standard first-time, basic shit. Did she lie to me?

She shakes her head. "Nowhere, just couldn't help it." She starts blushing.

"Holy fuck." I connect the dots. "You like oral sex, don't you?"

She nods again, still working my cock without pause, and this nearly sends me over the edge.

"I bet you do. I'm about to fucking ruin you. Lift your head back so I can come on your neck and tits."

Hurrying, she does, and with a few more pumps and me watching my own fantasy play out in front of me, I come. So hard. And I watch the hot spurts shoot out and cover her throat and slide down that beautiful column to her heavy breasts.

"Fuck. Fuck. Fuck, baby!" My orgasm overtakes me. I could do this for hours. Be lost with her, spend any time I can between her legs, touched by her, and pleasing her.

"Wear that while I take you." I grab her, choking her enough to keep her in place, while I own her mouth. My cum spreads between my fingers, and she cries out when I lift her dress and slam into her so fucking hard. I need her to feel my possession, my obsession with her. The fact that I would rather keep her in my hands than breathe.

"I need your skin. Please."

I don't want to stop fucking her, but I have to give my woman what she wants. Not removing my cock from her, I sit up on my knees and take off my shirt. She eyes my abs, and her fingers trail down the center and end on my Adonis V.

"How can a man like you exist? Your body makes me feel so small and feminine. Like...you see me and treat me like I'm perfect and like all the other women. The normal, beautiful women."

My rage seeps in. I look her dead in her eyes, and I know my pupils dilate with fury. "Whoever told you that you aren't beautiful and quote, a fucking normal, beautiful woman...I will fucking end them. I see you as perfection. You're above any woman. Fight me on that. Seriously. Do it."

She gulps, and I lazily start stroking in and out of her. I stay on my knees and lift her hips to the angle I need.

"You should see how beautiful you look taking this cock. Your pussy lips are clinging to me. You're so tight." Reaching next to me, I grab my phone and open the camera. Turning it to Video, I start recording us.

"Are you filming this?" she moans, eagerly rocking her hips to get me to keep moving inside her.

"Yeah, and later, I'm gonna fuck you again while we watch it."

"Oh God!" she cries out, and I start pounding into her, using my strength to keep her suspended in the air with one hand on her hip and the other filming the sight of my thick cock taking her.

"Louder, baby. Moan louder. Say my name," I tell her, then

growl out when she tightens down on me.

"Theo. Please, harder. I need it harder."

"Yeah, you do, my beautiful puppet." I pick up the pace, and each time I slam back into her, she tightens, letting me know she's close to coming.

"Scream for me when you come. Let everyone know you're mine." No one may be out here, and honestly, I would call my own bluff, because I could never share her with anyone. Even sharing her moans would make me mad with possessiveness.

"You're so good at this, Theo. Oh...baby!" She screams the last word, and my balls draw up and tighten. I'm ready to let go again already, so I do, but not before, I move the camera up to her face, her breasts bouncing with each thrust, and she's lost in the throes of passion.

"Come for me, baby. Come on my cock." And she does just that as I record her sexy face.

Then, I toss the phone and lean back down, giving her a soft, gentle kiss. "Was that too much, baby?"

She shakes her head, dragging her nails lazily and softly up my exposed back. My body feels that from the top of my head to my toes. We don't need aftercare for this, but I still want to check in on her.

"No, it was perfect. Promise you won't show that video to anyone." Her face draws in concern.

"Fuck no. You're mine, Hanna. I won't share you. In any form." Finally, I end my lazy strokes and roll to the side.

She watches me, turns in, and wraps around me. I play with her hair, and we look up at the moon, the bright but shadowed orb enough to comfortably fill the void.

I want to say more, something I know I shouldn't, so I don't. Instead, I bite my tongue and swallow thickly. We can never go past what we are. Once again, that reminder plays devil's advocate, and a back and forth battle goes on inside me while she lies next to me, totally enthralled in the settling aftermath of our unhinged pleasure.

Twenty-Three

HANNA

THE NIGHT WENT ON, MOSTLY ONE-LINE COMMENTS, some nodding, but for the most part, we sat in silence. Surprisingly, it was a comfortable silence.

But the night is getting late, and I need to sleep, because I work in the morning. Standing, I start to right my dress. Theo watches me, not saying a word, and it's intimidating. Once the passion dies down and the adrenaline settles, that's when those insecurities speak so much louder than any other thing could.

"I need to get home. I work early again." I break the silence, hoping to also tear down the blatant self-loathing I'm feeling.

"You could skip work. Stay in the bed of this truck with me. Let me have my wicked way with you." He sits up on his elbows, looking me over.

"You already did that. And believe me—it was wicked." I laugh.

"You thrive when you are in those moments. You know that, right?"

He tells me this, and I stop what I'm doing to look at him. "What do you mean?" I sit on the edge of the tailgate, and he sits up, placing his back against the truck. His pants are still unbuttoned, but he has righted himself, his cock back in the confines of his boxer briefs. Each dent, defined muscle, and everything on his exposed upper half was handcrafted by the gods themselves. I think I've only ever seen men like him in movies and magazines.

"I watch you hate your body, ridicule yourself even in the silence. In fact, it's loudest then."

I hate this. I hate that he sees what I used to never have to share with the world. I've walked alone for so long that I didn't need to be afraid of people seeing the weaker parts of me, the vulnerable sides.

"You don't know that." I come off aggressive. It's the only defense I have.

"You turn into someone who isn't afraid of her pleasure, of her body, of her beauty, but the second the dust settles, you turn back in on yourself. Why?" he questions me, watching me like I'm a mystery. I don't want to be anyone's mystery. Why am I having to share all of me when he seems to have nothing to hide nor share?

"Why do you fear love?"

"I told you." He shrugs. "It doesn't appeal to me. I have no desire for it."

"Bullshit. That's a copout. There is something there that has you afraid that someone could get inside and maybe make you vulnerable. You can call my bluff and deflect all day long, but there is a story with you too, Theo." I'm not afraid to challenge him.

"Maybe it's because, when you depend on someone so much, they have the power to fucking crush you. Make you lose any sense of yourself. The identity of yourself is stolen."

"Or it can be heightened. Highlighted, celebrated. You can't speak on things you aren't willing to even try."

His eyes change, his face showing his deepening anger. "Hanna." It's a warning.

"What, Theo?"

"You said you could do this. You are crossing a line."

I roll my eyes and grab my phone. "No, Theo. I'm just trying to get to know you. You say I thrive and become the person I want to be when we are deep in the throes of passion. But I think you're the real you when you are deep in the aftercare. I saw a side of you that I think you could possibly enjoy. That doesn't mean it would be with me." Inside, I'm screaming, scolding myself. I don't believe I'm falling in love, but I do care for him.

How could any sane person do the things we have done and not at least have some sort of deep care for each other? Why does it always boil down to love? Why can't they be separate? Why can't care be care and love be love?

"I'm taking you home." He climbs out of the truck.

"No thanks. You got what you needed here, and clearly we can only seem to fuck, and conversation is off the table. I will walk home." And I hit the ground running, my feet moving fast. I hear him hollering after me, but I ignore him. I don't need his shit tonight.

I tried not once but twice to simply get to know him, but all it comes back to is sex and the rules that we can't be anything more. He gave me one moment into his past, and it was heartbreaking but deep and beautiful. How can he give me that and then nothing more?

"Hanna!" he yells after me as I head down the first road to get to the main one. Making it there, I pull out my phone and enter my address, since I have no idea where I am.

"Hanna, get your ass back here."

I flip him the bird over my shoulder. I don't bother looking back, but I know there is no way he was able to get dressed that fast. I hear the roar of his truck, and I pick up speed as if that will do me any good. I can't outrun a truck, but hell if I won't try.

Within less than a minute, his truck pulls up next to me, and he slams it into park. When he gets out and grabs me, I see he's still in his unbuttoned jeans and boots, his shirt and hat nowhere on him. Shirtless and all, he grabs me and tosses me over his shoulder.

"You egomaniac!" I scream as he does this.

"You stubborn pain in my ass. Why do you keep starting fights with me whenever it gets to be too much?" He slaps my ass and rounds the truck, throwing me in the cab. "You try and get out of this truck, Hanna, and I swear..." he warns, and when I right myself, I look at him to tell him to piss off, but his eyes—they're dark, his face filled with rage. Red with veins protruding from his forehead and neck.

I gulp. He looks murderous, and I'm on the receiving end. I bite back my words and stay put. When he sees I don't plan on going anywhere, he slams the door, and I watch him stalk back around to the driver seat.

Climbing in, he yanks the door closed and then brings his fist down hard on the steering wheel. The slam makes not only me jump but the truck move.

"You make me so frustrated. You get under my skin, and I don't want you there," he tells me.

"Then why the hell am I in this truck? Why did you chase me down like a psychopath?" I match his rage. I'm not going to let him hold all the cards here.

"You tell me, Hanna. You fucking tell me. Because I don't seem to know what the hell you're doing to me."

"I'm just existing here. I showed up to run away from literally nothing and no one, and then you come in and screw it all up!" I cross my arms over my chest, and I feel the tears coming. So much for standing my ground and not letting him see he is doing the same thing to me.

"Tell me now. Are you falling in love with me, Hanna?" He keeps his gaze focused on the steering wheel, and I gulp.

I don't want to answer this for two reasons. One, I don't know if this is becoming love. I've never had love or been in love, so how would I know? And two, if I am falling in love with Theo, could admitting it end it all and take away what we have? Both things, I'm unsure of. Both things, I'm terrified of.

"Hanna, are you falling in love with me?"

I look down at my hands, and I try not to cry, but it happens. I have to do what I know best. Run. Hide. And accept that I'm better off alone. Always have been and always will be.

"Take me home." It's all I say, and he doesn't argue. He watches me for a few moments while I avoid all contact. Staring out the window, I let the tears fall. How do we go from passionate sex to me being ready to say one word that has me breaking as I prepare to say it?

We don't speak the entire way home, and the second we pull into the driveway, I open the door, and he still says nothing. I shut the door, then turn and face him. He doesn't give me his eyes, and this makes it harder to do, but it's all I can think. My fight-or-flight instinct has kicked in.

"I'm sorry, Theo. This can't happen anymore." I shut the door, and the tears fall, unhindered. I just let them break free from my eyes, like the pain breaks free from the confines of my heart. I haven't known him long, but somehow, I felt something. A beat in my heart that was for someone else and not just for the sole purpose of living.

Almost a month here and he is giving me feelings I hate to admit. But it's better to end it now anyway. Before my heart aches and yearns for him more. His job will be done soon, and we'd have to be done anyway. It just makes sense. It's all we have. I get to the door, my ears ringing, the tears falling hard and fast. I tremble, my hands shaking as I struggle to unlock the door.

Suddenly, arms encase me, and his closeness warms me.

"I hate you for making me *love you*," he growls in my ear, moving my hair to the side and kissing my neck. I grip the door and drop my forehead, my chest shaking as I cry harder at his words. "Baby." He runs his nose against my neck.

"You don't love me. You just want to make me feel better. You pity the life I lived, alone and unloved. You can't love someone like me."

He reaches around me and grabs my stomach, squeezing, damn near clawing at me. "I love you. I hate it. Every fucking second. But it's not pity. I love you, because you made me love you. It's your fault." He kisses up the column of my neck.

"You won't let me in. You use me. Then you shut me out. How can you call that love?" I turn then and face him, showing him the heartbreak he's caused. The havoc he's rained down on my life in such a short amount of time.

"Because if I didn't love you, I wouldn't fear you. I wouldn't be crazy and mad and obsessed and in rage because I want to consume you and make you feel the misery I do."

My heart weeps. "Loving me causes you misery?"

"Yes, because it means I can't let you go. I can't walk away anymore."

"Why does that have to be misery? That knowledge that we love each other brings me peace. You are the only person who has seen me for me," I admit, hoping he'll let down barriers, ones I have let down so many times for him. I flourished unashamedly under his touch and told him my darkest desires. I told him my past and let him be there when I needed someone to collect the pieces after I read those letters.

He asked me today to need him. To cling to him. And I know that is love. He craves love, but he does it in a way that he feels he can still control the situation. He tries to make love seem scary, but really, it's freeing. I've never been in love, so this first time should scare me, especially when it's with a man like him. But Theo doesn't scare me. He frees me.

"You understand what happens now, Hanna?" he asks, but honestly I don't.

"No. What happens?" I ask, cupping his face and looking up into his vulnerable, honey eyes. I've craved so long to see the full Theo. The one with no bars, no walls, no arrangements, but the man who can show what he deems weakness and that I declare as strength. It's only been one month. It felt a lifetime, but it really wasn't. We are in love. I finally found love, and it's with the most complicated man. A complication I am so thankful to be lost in.

"It means you have to teach me. *You* have the control," he admits, dropping to his knees and wrapping his arms around me, kissing the rolls of my stomach. That makes me insecure, but I don't want to ruin his admission with my discomfort. "You have control now. I've never rendered control. But to you, I crave for you to have it."

My eyes water. "You have the power now." I lay it down in exchange for the control. Because I have a fragile heart, one that's been abandoned and bruised. He has the power to completely turn it to ashes in his hands if he hurts me.

What an exchange for two people who never should have ended up here.

"Theo."

He doesn't answer me. He keeps kissing me everywhere he can, lifting my dress to kiss my thighs, my hips, my stomach, and more.

"Baby," I call to him, and he looks up at me, his eyes so worn and filled with fear. "I will take care of you. I won't let you be afraid." I test out my newfound control.

"You're already doing it to me," he admits.

Reaching down, I have him stand, and when he towers over me, I kiss the spot over his heart. "Take me upstairs; take what we both need. Please?" I ask him, and he doesn't hesitate. He pulls me up, and I wrap my legs around his waist. He finishes opening the door by kicking it open.

I grab his face and kiss him, tasting his lips, and there is something different behind this one. There is love, and I never knew it could have a taste, but it does. We keep at it as he takes me up the stairs, never once letting our lips separate. Making it to my bedroom, he lays me down and hovers over me.

"You're beautiful. You know that?"

"No. But I believe you will show me I am."

He smiles, tucking my hair behind my ear. "Yeah, Hanna. I'm going to do that." Standing from the bed, he takes my hand and brings me to my feet once again. We don't speak with words, but when he starts to remove his boots, socks, and pants, I know what I need to do. Taking my dress at the hem, I remove it, left in just my bra. He removes his last item of clothing and watches me remove mine. The lace fabric hits the floor, and we stand in our nakedness. A man who was made of perfection and the woman believed to be built in flaws.

He moves first, sitting at the edge of the bed. I watch him, fighting the urge to cover my body as he peruses and worships it like it's a temple. Now isn't the time to ruin that we both just fell in love for the first time.

"Come here," he says, bringing me to stand between his legs. His hands start at my calves, moving them over all the cellulite and dents, the fat I thought about removing with sharp tools at least once a day.

But he doesn't treat me like that. If there is disgust like that in him, he wouldn't love me, right? He gets to my stomach and kisses the flap of skin I hate most, biting it, leaving his mark. Each stretch mark he sees, he kisses, lines it with his fingers, and praises me. Words like "beautiful," "handmade for him," and "exquisite." Words I would never believe a man would call me, especially one so in shape, handsome, and every word related to flawless. I almost feel guilty for not being on his level. He deserves perfection; he deserves the best. Though he is broken and programmed to not know how to love, he still deserves the type of woman worth challenging that for.

"I want you to ride me, sweet puppet."

I nod, planting my hands on his shoulder and climbing on top of him. We stay sitting, and he lines me up with him. We lock eyes, and in unison we nod, and I slide down.

"Oh, baby," he praises, and I get teary-eyed. He's being so soft and sweet it's overwhelming me. Theo is not this man, so for him to be it for me, it just hammers it home.

I slide up and down, using his shoulders as my anchor. He helps with his hands on my hips. They are lazy strokes. We aren't tearing and clawing at one another as if we're rabid. We are taking our time. I feel every vein of his thick length slide against the walls inside me.

"There has never been a better fit. How could you have been made for me so perfectly?" he questions, and I can't find words. I'm merely surviving while being held captive by the chokehold he has on me. There is no one in this world I will ever love more than this man. And one day, it could happen—he could hurt me. I could stop being perfectly made for him. So I choose silence in this moment. I choose to not let him know what I'm feeling.

My legs start to quiver and shake, trembling from the intense orgasm building and all the work I'm putting into going so slowly so I can absorb it all.

"So good. You feel so good. Ooh, fuck, baby," he moans, and it goes straight to my core. Reaching between us, he lightly plays with my clit. "You're mine. You know that, right? You're fucking mine in every way now."

I agree with a nod.

"No. You say it. You declare it now—that you belong to me. That I own all of you now."

I gulp, moaning so loud when he pinches my clit. "God! Yes! Oh! Yes! I'm yours."

"How many times do I have to tell you? I'm not God. The name is Theo, puppet. Now come. Come for your man."

I do as he says, so ready to orgasm. "Theo, baby, oh!" I scream out, throwing my head back and wrapping my arms around his shoulders. I come so fast and hard it's like a lightning bolt straight from my core, my walls trembling, and then reverberating in my clit. Who knew love could also create the most intense orgasms?

"Fuck. Fuck. Ohh, yeah. Shit!" He comes, and I feel all of it, his hot spurts of cum coating my walls and my insides. "Tell me you love me. Give me your ownership," he growls, his orgasm still riding its high as mine slows down.

"I love you. I hate it, but I do. I love you, Theo," I whisper, and he reaches down, circling my clit, and I come again. "Oh God! Choke me, please. I need it." He does, just like he's done since this started. Whether it be in an act of dominance, desire, or now in the name of claiming and love. I will never be able to live without that controlling touch.

We come down, and he lays us back, but then I stand, suddenly feeling something I can't explain. I don't know how to tell him, so I play it off. "Can we shower? My body is a little sore." That's true, but it's not what's really happening inside me. Something else that feels familiar, but I can't seem to place it. I almost feel like I've lost my mind. So all I can think to do is get us in the shower and not talking.

"How about a bath, baby?" he suggests, and I nod, making my way to the bathroom. He catches up to me and wraps his arms around my waist, kneading the softness of my stomach. "Why you rushing? You trying to get out of my hands or something?"

I just laugh, waving it off. What is happening to me right now? When he was telling me he loved me, I was on cloud nine, and now I'm a mess of emotions that don't feel like the good kind at all. I must be getting ready for my period. My PCOS makes them impossible to track they're so irregular. They tend to mess with my emotional state a little more than usual.

Yeah, that's it.

Twenty-Four

THEO

We finished our bath, sharing small talk. I can't believe it happened. I confessed to her what I swore I wouldn't. But the second she said it was over, I went mad. I even went as far as thinking I could lock her up in some fucking tower and keep her to myself, but I know that's not the right thing to do.

But was it right?

In the bath, I shared every minute thing with her—my Greek heritage, what high school was like for me, and a bunch of random things that didn't matter. Now that "I love you" has come out, there is a secret that dangles, and if I don't tell her soon, it will end us. But at the same time, telling her just might end us too.

Yet time is running out, and I can't hold off or protect her for much longer.

I leave her in the bathroom to do her skin care routine, and I lie in the bed watching her, taking in her beauty, while that nagging voice in the back of my head fills me with guilt.

Tell her. Take her somewhere she can't run, and tell her. Let her learn the truth, and give her a place to make her forgive you, I tell myself over and over again. Luckily, I'm interrupted when I notice she is staring at herself in the mirror, a look of pure distain in her eyes while looking over her reflection.

She looks ashamed. I don't miss it. She may think she's subtle when hiding her self-ridicule, but no. I see it, I loathe it, and it makes me seethe. Women like her should thrive when looking in the mirror, come alive with pride, and the image of her own body should even cause her to become arouse. But even after all the times I've fucked her, claimed her, and praised her under my hands, she still doesn't see it, feel it, or believe it.

"Hanna, come here." I watch her wipe at her tears, trying to hide the evidence, but it will do no good. Her face is stained and red with blotches of her pain.

"Yeah, just a second."

I stand then, not okay with her answer. I want her raw and without hiding. "Fuck this." I move to the bathroom, and she cowers a bit when my large, aggressive stature gains on her.

"You know I hate this, right?" My fist clenches at my side. I'm suddenly angry, fuming with rage at the world that made her see herself as anything less than a temptress. A siren. A goddess-like creature.

She blinks rapidly up at me, her thick lashes highlighting those beautiful green eyes that first captivated me.

"Wh—what?" Tugging at the loose band tee she wears, she

pulls it farther down her thighs.

"Lose the fucking shirt," I bark. She jumps back, my demand startling her. I can feel my chest rising and falling. I'm feral. Ready to take her and convince her of what I know. The woman who keeps me crawling back every night to devour her and who made me do what I said I never would—fall in love—is worthy of all things she would argue that she isn't.

"I don't want to when you seem so angry. What did I do?" Her eyes go doe-like, a deer in headlights, a beauty afraid of a beast, and I soften my approach.

"You and I are together now. I've told you I love you. You said you want to belong to me, and now you do. You know what you need to say if this is something you don't want."

"Theo, that's not fair. Clearly, I'm vulnerable right now," she points out, stating the exact reason I'm in here.

"I know that, greens. So you can trust me to take care of you, to know your limits. You can say your safe word, and I will back away and let you have the space you need." Her eyes search mine, a storm brewing as she decides exactly what she should do next. I keep my hands to myself, crossing my arms over my broad chest that is still flushed with rage.

Without a word, she removes her top, leaving her body bare to me, showcasing the bite marks and red blotches where my stubble scraped along her curves.

"Look in the mirror," I tell her, my voice even yet firm. Turning slowly, she faces the mirror, but her eyes stay lowered. "I said look in the mirror. You don't want to break the rules, do you?" Tears well in her eyes, and still she keeps her head down. Stepping behind her, I rub my hands together, watching her body react and tense in the mirror. She's aroused but scared; I feel it. That's the beauty of learning someone's body and what can come from them when you've trained it to be at the mercy of only your hands.

"One last time, baby. Look in the mirror." When she shakes her head and doesn't, I rear my hand back and slap her bare ass so hard it leaves my handprint instantly. Bracing herself, she grabs the lip of the counter and cries out, but the cry is mingled with a moan. Hanna needs this, loves it, lives for it. My control, my dominance, my ownership of her sexual satisfaction…is her greatest pleasure.

"Theo!" she hollers again when I bring my hand to her hip and slap it before gripping it and squeezing it.

"Eyes on the fucking mirror, greens," I growl in her ear, grabbing the column of her neck and forcing her eyes to meet mine in the mirror. Her chest rises and falls, her nipples peaking, and her face reddens. Arousal—she's gone. Completely gone and only feeling and hearing me.

"You look at yourself like you aren't a fucking sight to behold," I seethe, moving my hand from her hip to her breast and grabbing it just as vigorously as I did her hip. My other hand is still gripping her neck.

"You are not to look at yourself like that while under my care, puppet. You are to only desire yourself."

"No. I can't," she whimpers, and my hand on her throat grips tighter, restricting her breathing just a bit.

"Tsk, tsk." I suck my teeth. I move my hand from her breast to between her legs, finding her engorged clit aroused and begging for affection. Rubbing slow circles, I hear her whimper again, dropping her head once more and gripping the counter tighter, trying to remain upright.

"Eyes. Now," I bark, removing my finger from her clit. She screams out, the loss of my touch too much for her. I've never been with a woman who can take pleasure so deeply. Someone who can come with little to no effort. So under my hands, she reaches pure nirvana. With me, she cannot escape the euphoria.

"Please," she begs for me to keep going *and* to stop, but her urges to continue are much greater.

"Talk about your body. Tell me what you see." I slowly reach down and begin the lazy strokes against her clit, her cunt begging for more. She will get it...if she's a good girl.

"I see a body," she deflects, keeping her eyes on my hand between her thick, creamy thighs, her freshly shaved pussy looking delectable. I devoured it earlier, but I'm thirsty for more.

Later.

"No, what do you see?" I ask again, feeling her thighs quiver, letting me know she's close to coming. I move my hand, placing it on the sink just beside hers.

Hanna whimpers. "You're cruel," she tells me.

"No. I'm in control, and I don't like the games. Now tell me what you see."

"A body."

This time, it enrages me. She's being a defiant brat, and I won't tolerate it.

"Fine." I reach between us then, using two fingers to separate her swollen lips, and my free hand slaps her pussy hard.

She screams, toppling over so her ass is now at the right angle for my cock. Without a warmup or warning, I grab her hips and thrust into her, slapping her ass as I bottom out.

"Say it."

"No!" she screams, her face now pushed into the mirror as I slam into her without pause.

"Fucking tell me what you see!" I raise my voice and grit my teeth.

"I hate it! I hate the way I look! Okay?" she cries, her chest pounding with the sobs, and I stop my thrusts, watching her cry so hard she can't control it.

"Good girl." Pulling from her tight heat with great effort, I help move her so she's now upright and facing me.

"Up." I give her an order, and she continues to cry but knows she needs me. Needs the care that only I can supply. But little does she know I'm not done with her. She lifts one leg around my waist, and I lean to grab the other, leaving the bathroom with her slick cunt moving against my still hard cock. She drops her forehead to mine and cries, a little sound of pain and pleasure. "That feel good, baby?"

"Yes." She nods, her forehead against mine, moving her hips as best she can to keep rubbing her clit along my shaft.

"Good, enjoy it for a second longer, because I'm going to punish you for saying such a foul thing about the body I worship. I'm going to fuck you like you don't mean anything to me. Then you will know what it feels like to be hurt by something. The same way your words hurt me." And then I tell her in Greek, *"You cannot escape. You belong only to me."*

"What does that mean?" she cries, circling her hips and lazily draping her arms around my shoulders. When I tell her, she responds, "Oh God. I can't do this anymore, Theo. It's too much. Today, tonight, all the hours we've spent tonight at one another like we can't get enough...."

"You will have had enough when I say you have." I set her on her feet and turn her to face the window. Hanna braces herself with her hands against the glass, and I grab a fist of her hair to turn her head violently before pressing it to the cool surface.

"The neighbors could see you if I turned on the light," I tease, and she hollers.

"Theo, no! Don't you dare," she warns.

A sinister smile overtakes my face, and as I step away from her, she turns. I move to the bedroom light and flip it on, exposing both our bodies to the night outside. And I don't care who sees it. This will be the only time I will risk anyone seeing what belongs to me, but I need her to start seeing the worth in her body. Hanna can no longer hate herself. It just won't be an option in my world. The world I'm going to create with her.

"Theo," she warns again, and I stalk back to her, slowly stroking my cock at the sight of her entire body.

It reminds me of the first time I saw her. Those dents and winding curves made me hungry, and now I get to feast whenever I fucking want. "You have a word to end all of this." I stop a few feet from her.

She eyes me over, brows furrowed. "Don't." She starts to cry, the tears falling, and I would comfort her, but if I do that, she will not take this seriously. That she deserves the same things in this world as any woman, including the desire of a man she believes could never want her. Hanna should have always felt like she fit in, had a seat at the table with all the women she saw as better than her. In fact, she should have been at the head of the table, because she is the sexiest of them all.

"If I do that, I won't get you at all?" she asks with a plea.

I shake my head. "Correct."

"But I want you."

"And I want you. I need you to see a different narrative of yourself, baby. You have to believe that every fucking part of you is the wettest of my wet dreams."

"They will see what's yours," she tries to counter me.

"And after I'm done and I saw anyone watched you take cock like a good girl, I will pay them a little visit. How about that, baby?" I wait a pause or two, and she doesn't say anything as she turns and resumes the position I put her in before I turned the light off. "That's more like it."

"I ache for you. I would do anything for you. Because I love you." She sniffles.

"Baby, say the word, and I will stop," I remind against her ear, massaging her ass and hips, the love handles she has—fuck, I love touching those.

"I don't want to. Please. I just need you to fix me," she cries.

I debate telling her she can do that on her own because she has it all inside her, but I decide to show her.

"All right. I'll fuck you so good, make you come hard, but only if you play by the rules. You tell me the things you hate about your body—"

"That's easy," she inserts quickly.

That's what she thinks.

"Here we go. Safe word?"

"Sirius."

"Good girl." With that, I spread her ass and watch myself slide into her pussy.

"Yes," she moans. "Oh yes, you're so big."

I cease movement.

"No, please!"

"Follow the rules. First thing you hate."

"My stomach. It makes me sick. I—I don't fit into clothes like other women do."

I spank her ass and reach around, touching her stomach. "Say it's beautiful."

"It would be a lie," she says, and I stop. "No. Theo. I need you."

"Clearly you don't, since my opinions don't matter. You keep telling me my lust for your body is a lie. So clearly, Hanna, you don't care about my thoughts."

She pauses, her hands closing into fists against the window. "You know that's not true, baby." She looks over her shoulder.

"Then say you love your stomach like I do. I love the way it feels in my hands, against my lips, and the way it looks in tight jeans and dresses." I start to give her a little movement, rocking my hips, my cock sliding in and out.

"I love my stomach," she moans.

"Good girl. What else?" I keep that same pace, and she whimpers.

"My thighs. They have so many markings."

This sparks something in me. And it's going to possibly make her run, but even if it does, I would hunt her down and make her mine again.

I pull out, and she cries, "Why did you stop? I was honest!"

I move to my jeans and find my pocket knife. Moving back to her, I turn her around and drop to my knees. Immediately, I take her slick swollen cunt into my mouth and suck, licking in between each pull. I even give her small bites here and there. I flip open the knife, and that's when she sees what I have in my hand.

"Theo, what are you doing with that?"

"Giving you markings you will be able to look at and really love and admire." And then I bring the knife to her inner thigh and slide it against the skin.

She screams out. "Ow! Theo! What are you doing?" She's terrified yet aroused and still curious.

"You will wear my initials. You wanted my love. You got it. But that comes with something darker. I own you now." The T is small, but the blood runs down her leg, and I catch it with my tongue, lapping it up and swallowing it. She gasps at the sight, and then I stand.

"Palm," I order, and hesitantly, she slowly opens her palm, and I place the knife in her hand. "Your turn, puppet. Mark my body anywhere you want with an H."

"You're crazy," she gasps.

"Yes. I am. I wasn't lying when I told you I like control. And now I own you, and you own me. Mark me, Hanna," I bite out, and she jolts. Moving, she looks me over, up and down, and I know already where she is going to pick. Her eyes end on the V at my hips, and she does the same thing—dropping to her knees and carving an H in the skin there.

It doesn't hurt me, but the bite of the blade does make my cock twitch, and that doesn't go unnoticed. She takes me into her mouth, all the way to the back of her throat. I drop my head back and moan her name.

"Such a good girl." My head falls forward, and my hand finds her hair. I use it, making her take my cock so deep. The blood drips and mingles with her saliva and my pre-cum. What a fucking sight. She works me over, and it's not long before I slam her head down and let my cock gag her as I shoot my cum down her throat.

When she finishes, I return the favor tenfold, eating her for hours. It takes giving her three orgasms before I finally fuck her to sleep. Literally. I stroke in and out after our last set of climaxes, and she slowly doses off, spent, and I slide out, pulling her into me as I let slumber take me too.

Tonight, everything changed, and I can no longer lie. The truth is coming. It has to.

Twenty-Five

HANNA

"I WILL SEE YOU IN A LITTLE BIT. DRIVE SAFE," I TELL him.

Brenda asked me to come to dinner to meet her parents Sunday afternoon, and when Theo heard, he said we would go together and that he wants to introduce me. I suggested it be as friends, but he simply growled and smacked me on the ass. So there was no argument there.

"I will, baby. You too. Also, my parents may hound you. Just give me the look, and I will get us out of there."

I laugh. "I think I can handle it."

"Yeah, my parents are intense, and they're going through a divorce, so the tension might be thick."

I stay silent for a minute. He hadn't yet told me about his parents and their plan to divorce. "You know I'm here to listen—I mean, about your parents."

He doesn't make a sound on the other end. It's almost eerily silent.

Finally, he says, "Because there is nothing to say. Love doesn't always last."

I hold onto that, praying that he and I don't suffer that fate. Theo is made for me, everything I could want and more, and I could never picture a world where he and I aren't the same.

Especially after the other night, when he helped me finally see me—and I mean see me...as someone worth loving and deserving to be at all tables and in every category as the women I believed were better than me. That moment solidified this. He opened my eyes, and I saw sides of me that I wish I could have seen before him.

Then, when he carved his initial into my leg and I carved mine on him, it changed something in both of us. It made us even madder for one another. It turned love into insanity an unhealthy and dangerous obsession, but we both crave it.

"Okay, but I'm here," I add simply.

"I will see you in twenty minutes. We will get through this dinner, and then I need to be inside you. Got it?" he deflects, his signature trait.

"You will, since you're taking me away to some cabin this weekend. You aren't going to kidnap me and keep tied up, are you?"

"Puppet, don't tempt me."

"Maybe I want to, baby. Maybe I want to be tied down and punished really, really, badly."

"Mmm," he growls. "I packed cuffs, and now you're getting

them at all times when we're there."

I blush, now even more excited for the weekend away. "I'm counting on it. See you soon."

"Say it."

I roll my eyes. "I love you, Theo."

"I love you, greens." We end the call, and I finish up the paperwork for payroll.

The hour feels like three, but finally, I'm pulling up to Brenda and Theo's parents' house. Theo stands on the porch on his phone, and when he sees me, he gives me a smile. He looks delicious, wearing jeans, a white V-neck t-shirt and a ball cap. I rarely see him in hats, but the casual look is amazing on him.

Grabbing the pie, I climb out and right my outfit. I changed at work before leaving, not wanting to meet their parents in just jeans and my work shirt. I went with a romper that ends mid-thigh. It's a baby blue, and the shorts have one layer of frill, making it look like a skirt, and the top is a deep V that ends where there is a belt that I tied into a bow. My hair is down and curled, and I wore a medium amount of makeup.

"What the fuck are you wearing?" Theo growls when I shut the door. I didn't see him move from the porch to me while I was reaching into the passenger seat for the pie I made last night.

I look down at myself, suddenly insecure once again. "Does it look that bad? I can run home and change."

He pushes me against the car, and his erection nudges my stomach. "Does my cock say you look bad? You look so damn sexy

I want to fuck you against this car."

Blushing, I look up to the house, then back to him, putting my hand on his chest and smiling up at him. "After. I promise." Standing up on my tiptoes, I offer him my lips, and it's a lazy kiss, my top lip between his, and we linger.

"Damn, I had to fall in love with the biggest tease. Now I have to wait for my hard-on to go down before I take you inside."

"I'm sorry. It's just an outfit." I laugh.

"No, it's the girl making the outfit."

"Hanna!" Brenda hollers, coming down the stairs and heading toward us. I hurry and move in front of him, and he puts his hands on my hips, his cock already softening. "I'm so excited. My mom is too. She made a whole feast for you."

"They didn't have to do that. I'm trying to lose some weight."

"What?" they both say in unison, Theo's voice a little harsher and heavily laced with anger.

"I just want to get in a little better shape and eat food that's good for my body. Calm down, you two." I turn to look back and forth between the siblings. Theo's neck vein is protruding, and I know I'm going to have to explain this one to him.

"Brenda, you know the drill," he warns, and she and I both roll our eyes.

"Your broody, possessive alpha thing can be super annoying," she says while departing.

When she's gone, I turn and face him. "I am not doing it for body image issues. I just want to eat better. I need stamina to keep up with my insatiable boyfriend who can't seem to leave me alone," I tell him.

He eyes me, grabbing me around my lower waist, and he pulls me against him. I'm careful not to drop the pie in my hand. "Eating to fuel your body with better food is different. Doesn't mean you have to lose weight. Word it better next time, puppet."

I glare at him. "It is *my* body, and what if I do want to lose weight? What would that matter? You won't like me if I'm skinny?"

He grumbles, "You know what I mean. I know it's your body, but I just want it to be for purposes that aren't vain."

I sigh. "Theo, you have to let me have a say in my body and let me decide how I want it to look, work, and thrive. Whether it be for looks or health."

"As long as you don't do it because you've gone back to thinking I don't love you the way you are now."

"Oh, I won't. And I'm sure the neighbors don't want to see you teach me that lesson again."

"Dammit, temptress. You're making me hard again. Ass in the house." He turns me and slaps my ass. I start moving, and he catches up, grabbing my hand as he leads the way. When he opens the door, my senses are flooded with comfort food smells.

"Okay, that smells way too good. I can have a cheat night." I ignore his second grumble and some mumble about "fuck a stupid diet."

"Oh my! You must be Hanna. Brenda has told me so much about you!"

Theo stiffens next to me, going stone-like. What the hell is that? He drops my hand, takes the pie, and his mother hugs me.

"It's nice to meet you. She tells me about you too, and that food smells divine," I compliment her. I see mostly Brenda in her looks. Theo has some traits, but I'm assuming he looks more like his dad.

"Thank you. I made my famous casserole and mashed potatoes with homemade gravy. An old family recipe." Could she be any more Southern and adorable?

"Sounds great. Thank you for having me and making what I'm sure is a lovely meal." I turn a little red, getting a tad anxious. I've come into myself comfortably with Brenda and Theo, but before I came to South Carolina, I was never really a social person, so it can be a lot sometimes.

"All right, let's move it to the kitchen, Mom. Hanna made us a pie." Theo breaks up our exchange, and I silently thank him by reaching for and squeezing his hand.

"That looks wonderful. Brenda and Rob are in the kitchen." She leads the way, and I look up to Theo. He still looks so cold.

"Theo, I can leave if you don't want your parents to know about us."

He looks down, and I see the instant guilt consumes him when I give him a look of embarrassment.

"No, it's not that. I just try to not be too joyous around them. My parents can take a lot of energy out of me. And I don't want them to overwhelm you, greens."

I feel instantly better. "I will let you know if it's too much, trust me?"

He searches my eyes. "Yes. I trust you."

We make it into the kitchen, and I'm met with the same enthusiasm from Rob—Theo and Brenda's father.

"You're just as beautiful as my son let on."

I look up at Theo and raise my brows. He gives me a smile, rolling his eyes. "You're too kind. It's just a lot of makeup. Smoke and mirrors."

He comes up and scoops me up for a hug, and I was in fact right. Theo look more similar to his father.

"Dad, let my woman breathe."

My stomach flutters. That's the first he has called me his in front of anyone. Brenda knows we're a couple because I told her at work, but other than that, he hasn't said anything.

"Your woman. Did you hear that, Kerrin? His woman."

Kerrin gushes, making me laugh. "Never thought we would see the day, son. Can't believe this stone wall could make you fall for him."

I turn and look up at Theo. He is so tense, and I wonder what's really happening. Is it too soon for me to have met his family? Is he regretting it? I move a few inches away from him, thinking the space may help him calm down a bit. But I won't lie. It hurts me to think he is regretting this so soon.

"He really is kind to me. Very respectful. It wasn't hard. Anyway, I can help with anything." I leave him and move to Brenda, needing space because my feelings are hurt. He is treating me like I'm the problem and a huge shame. I have to hide the tears. I'm not the one who asked to meet his parents yet. Brenda invited me, and I told him I could go as just a friend of them both, but he insisted. Now, we're here, and he's being so cool toward me.

Before I get to Brenda, I feel the wall of muscle that I know well, the one I usually crave to feel but want to run from at the moment.

"Baby. You don't walk away from me." He grabs my hip and whispers this in my ear so only I can hear.

I move from him, annoyed by his whiplash of hot and cold. It could leave a damn mark at this point. This enrages him; I don't have to look to know. I feel the energy in the room. "Mom, Dad, Hanna and I need a minute." He grabs my hand, and I go to protest, but he is on a mission, dragging me with him, and I am stumbling until he puts us in the bathroom and shuts the door.

"You are such an ass. You could have went with my offer, and you didn't. You chose to bring me here as your girlfriend, and now you're ashamed and being so cold to me."

"No, Hanna. That's not it. Fuck." He turns and places his hands on his head, pacing the small space of the bathroom.

"Then what is it? Tell me."

He keeps pacing. I can sense his anxiety rising.

"I'm selfish. I need to tell you something, and it's eating me alive. Seeing you with my family is showing me I can't hide this anymore. I can't let this secret I've been holding in stay between us anymore." I look back and forth between his eyes, and my stomach drops. What did he do?

"Is there someone else?" My eyes fill with moisture, but I refuse to let them fall.

"What? God, no, baby. There is only you, but puppet...what I tell you could ruin what we have, and you might never want to see me again."

"Spit it out, Theo. I'm not going to stand here and beat myself up and think the worst. What is it?"

He goes to open his mouth and say something, but there is a knock.

"Dinner is ready. Dad is impatient, and I have to pee!" Brenda interrupts.

"Fuck. Okay. At the cabin, we can talk then, but promise me something."

The pit in my stomach grows, and I now feel like the entire afternoon will be filled with my assumptions and fear. What is he hiding that could be so bad it's eating at him? Nothing ever gets to him.

"You love me, and you will never leave. You have to hear what I say and understand why I did what I had to do."

That's so damn ominous I could vomit.

"I can't promise anything. I'm all out of trust and promises to spare." I open the door and leave it at that. Just as I step out, my phone rings, and I see Jack's name. "Shit," I whisper.

"What?" Theo asks.

"My phone just died, and Jack was calling," I tell him, watching the circle on my black screen disappear.

"I have a charger in my car. I can grab it," he says, and I shake my head.

"No. I will grab it. I need a minute to collect myself before I face your parents."

He takes the hint. "Glove compartment. Truck's unlocked," he tells me, and before he says anything else, I move out the door and to the truck. When I open the truck door, I pop the dash, and the charger falls out...and so do a bunch of papers.

"Shit." I hurry to grab them, but instantly I stop.

My face.

My name.

My address.

A report of me.

And so much more.

I read the words on the picture of me.

Possible stalker? Seems harmless. Wouldn't touch anyone? Doesn't have it in her. I throw that paper aside and grab the next one.

I believe Hanna to have no involvement with the Banks's missing daughter.

Missing daughter? What is this? What is happening? I keep sifting and find another paper, or what would be more like a report of me.

> Hired by the Banks family to look into Hanna Whittington for the disappearance of their daughter. Evidence in her apartment found. Seems to most likely have been planted. Why is there a connection? Why would he stalk her, then plant evidence? Stalker most likely the suspect in the case.

I drop the paper, and my stomach turns. I feel the bile rising in my throat. I lean out of the truck, and I vomit, the bile leaving me. I can't help it. Who is Theo, and what is he in my life for? I stumble a bit and search the pocket of my romper to pull out my keys.

Run. Get away. Run.

I repeat in my head the one thing I know to do, and when I unlock my car, I open the door and look up to see Theo bounding down the porch steps.

"Fuck! Hanna!" He must have forgotten about the papers, and before I slide into my car and lock the doors, he sees me crying, the pain etched onto me like permanent ink. He tries to open the locked door just as I turn the key in the ignition.

"Baby, open the door. Let me explain. Please. Come on, baby." I get the car on, and I shake my head.

"Leave me alone. Don't ever come near me again!" I scream, and he slams his fist down on the hood of my car. As I back out, he runs back into the house, I'm sure to grab his keys. I slam on the gas, accelerating like a bat out of hell.

What could it have been? Who is the Banks girl? Why am I person of interest? Why does Theo have those papers? So many questions run through my head. I plug my phone into the charger with shaky hands and look up to see I'm veering and almost hit the car coming the opposite way. They honk, and I swerve back over.

The only thing I can think to do is call Jack and have my bases covered. Ask him what to do, tell him what I saw. Is Theo a cop? Is that why he never talks about his job? I knew he wasn't the type to be in IT. Was I a job for him?

My phone turns on, and I pick it up and see Theo calling. I keep hitting Ignore, but he just calls again. I ignore it repeatedly until finally I answer. "Leave me alone and stay the hell away from me. I don't know who you are or what you are doing, but you just… stay the hell away!"

"Baby, it's me. Listen. I'm on my way to you, and I'm going to tell you everything. It's still me. The man you fell in love with. The man who loves you," he assures, but I'm too angry. I never want to see him again. Not only do I feel betrayed, but I'm heartbroken. I love him. He made me fall in love under the cover of lies and secrets.

"No, stay away—ahh!" I scream when my bumper is hit and I'm jolted forward.

"Hanna? Baby? What happened?" I look up in the rearview mirror and see the truck. The one that came to my house twice.

"No. No!" I cry. It's them. They found me. I knew it. I thought it was just my mind playing games. I eventually convinced myself the person was just casing the place, knowing my grandfather died and wanting to rob the place. But I'm now seeing I was wrong.

"Baby! Talk to me," Theo yells through the phone, and my fear leads me.

"The man. They *are* following me. They just bumped me, tried to push me off the road. Theo, I know it's the person from New York. It has to be." I lead-foot my gas pedal and speed as fast as I can.

"Hey, listen to me. I want you to drive as fast but carefully as you can. Put me on speaker and set the phone on the seat next to you." I may be livid, but if Theo is a cop, he is the only saving grace I have.

"Okay." I keep looking up, and they are on my tail. I try to see who it is, but the windows are so tinted I have no luck.

"Good, where are you?" he asks.

"A mile or so from my house. Theo, he is getting close again. He's trying to hit me." The truck is within feet and just getting closer.

"Good, I see him. I've almost caught up. Keep going and pull into your driveway. I will stay on him. You're safe, baby. He won't get to you."

"Theo, oh God. He's driving around me!" I scream, watching the truck move pull up beside me. He's going to push me off the road. I prepare for the impact, gripping the wheel and tucking my head into my lifted shoulders, but it doesn't come. The truck speeds up and gets in front of me. And within sixty seconds, he is out of sight.

"He's gone." I breathe heavily, my heart feeling like it will beat out of my chest.

"I know. I'm behind you." I look in the mirror and see him, and the anger I had for him just minutes ago boils to the surface. "I don't need you. I will call the police. You can leave now. For good," I tell him and pull into my driveway. I end the call after grabbing my phone and bag.

Theo pulls in and slams his truck into park. Jumping out, he meets me at the door. "Baby, hear—"

"No! You lost that right when you lied to me. Who the hell are you?"

"Let me come in and explain."

"No. You aren't ever stepping foot in my house again. Tell me who you are and why you really got involved in my life." I cross my arms and lift my chin, keeping the tears I want to let out at bay. I won't let him have that. No. I refuse.

"I was hired to follow you and check into your life. I'm a Private Investigator."

I shake my head. "Who are the Bankses, and why does this have anything to do with me? Why were you hired to come after me?" I ask. My back is on fire, the hairs on my neck standing on edge.

"I was hired, because the cops weren't doing their job fast enough for the family's liking, so they came to me."

"And how did you find me, and where the hell do I fit in? Who is the Banks's daughter?"

"The Banks family are popular jewelers in New York, and three months ago, their daughter vanished after leaving the gym." I don't say anything. "The cops hadn't had any leads, so they hired me. Well, when your boss called in and said you missed work for two days and couldn't reach you, he asked them to do a welfare check. The cops knew you had a record of calling them with reports of someone trying to break in, so they took it seriously and went immediately. When they got in there, in plain sight were items belonging to the missing girl, including her gym shirt she was last seen in."

My stomach drops, and I feel that bile rising again. "Oh God. How? I mean, how and why? I had nothing to do with it. I would never hurt someone or take them or anything."

"I know that. One of my friends, James, he is a cop and was there that day. He got word and called me, knowing I was working for the family. He knew I could track you down, and I did."

I look up at him and shake my head, more hurt than I think I've ever been. Betrayed in a way that is unmatched by anything from my past.

"So I was a job for you. You used me. Fucked me. Then pretended to love me for a job!" I scream but don't hold the tears back this time.

"When I first got here, yes. But, baby...." He pauses to touch my arms, but I stop him.

"No. I've heard enough. You are dead to me, Theo. How could you hurt me, knowing what I've been through? You could have just come to me and asked me. Or at least pretended to just be a good friend. But no! You made me your fuck toy and then tricked me into loving you. You never loved me at all, did you?" I wipe at the tears, hating that I'm showing him the pain he doesn't deserve to earn from me.

"No. Don't you dare question my feelings for you."

"No. Don't *you* dare tell me to not question you. All you are is a body of secrets that are now the center of the worst pain in my life. I loved you, Theo. Goddamn it, I loved you!" I push his chest, and he stumbles back a bit. I see tears well in his eyes. Good. I hope this hurts him. He deserves the pain.

"You still love me. I know you do. You're mine, Hanna. You belong to me." He clings to what little he has left, and I don't let him. He failed me. Broke me. Lied to me.

"No. It's over, and I will call Jack and get a lawyer. You and I are nothing. Leave me alone and go back to New York. Stay away." I unlock the door to go in, and he tries to follow.

"Baby, don't say it's over. Don't say something you will regret." He reaches for me, but I stop him once again, putting my hand up.

"Sirius!"

And just like that, he stumbles back, and in that moment, I watch his heart break. Just like mine is.

"Don't, please. Don't say that. Don't do this to us, baby."

"Sirius," I whisper again, letting the tears fall now without trying to stop them. He backs up, knowing he lost the battle. He can't touch me anymore. He can't control the situation, and all power is now gone from him too.

"Stay away. Goodbye, Theo." I slam the door, and I listen to him yell and curse. I slide down the door and cry through the pain, my body wracking in pure torture. Where do I go now? I'm now in the middle of some missing person's case. Lost the man who I loved, and now I'm alone. Alone again. Alone for always.

* * *

"HANNA, THIS IS DETECTIVE ARES OF THE NEW YORK City Police Department," Jack says, and a tall man with slicked-back hair that looks like it took an entire bottle of gel to do so comes in and sits in the seat next to me in Jack's office.

It's been two weeks. I called Jack after three days of sulking in bed, unplugging the house phone, and turning off my cell phone. I ignored everyone but Brenda, who stayed with me every night after work. She slept beside me as I cried through the night, waking up screaming and gripping at my chest because I missed Theo to the very core of me.

It felt like a death.

He hurt me, but before he did, he took all of me. He took my broken heart, began to mend it, and then shredded it. Jack told me the cops had reached out to him and said they wanted to set up a meeting to come talk to me. I agreed, having nothing to hide and wanting to clear my name and, honestly, find out more.

"Hello, nice to meet you, Detective. I'm Hanna Whittington." I reach over and shake his hand.

"Yes, hello, Ms. Whittington. Thank you for taking time to sit with me today."

"Please, call me Hanna." I give a half smile and tuck my hair behind my ears. My eyes are sunken in, and I look a mess I'm sure, but if I'm being honest, I don't care. It is what it is.

"Hanna. So I wanted to meet to ask you a few questions. Before you came to Cherry Hill, you made multiple calls to the police with reports of being stalked or hearing someone outside your apartment door, trying to get in, is that correct?"

Surprisingly, I'm not nervous around Ares. He has a calm demeanor, and maybe I'm just too broken to really be afraid of anything at this point. To feel anything really.

"Yes. All were ignored, and I was often told I was crazy and hearing things or that this was the downside of living in places like I did." My response is snarky, and I mean it to be. I knew I wasn't crazy, and now look at the mess we're in.

"Yes. I read the reports. I'm sorry about that," he says. "Did you know of anyone who would have any conflict with you or any ill feelings?"

I look down at my hands. "I didn't even have friends. There was no one to even give the chance to have any conflict with." How pathetic does that sound? I almost forgot that just a month and a half ago, I had a life with nothing and no one in it. But then I came here and was making friends...and falling in love. But now, with the exception of Brenda, I'm starting to see that lonely girl coming back, and I hate it. So much so, I almost start to pity myself.

"What about ex-boyfriends or any other family?"

I pause for a minute. "My ex is long gone and married, living on the West Coast. My parents dropped me off at the state's door and never looked back, and the only other family I had left was my grandfather, who is now dead." The last part hurts me. The last two weeks, I also spent time reading his letters to me.

He praised me. Talked about loving me so much and waiting for the day that I might give him the chance to be in my life. I learned my love of reading came from him. I learned that my grandmother died of cancer when my mother was a young girl. I learned that my parents were into drugs and stealing from him, and that's why he told them to leave and get their lives together before coming back. He apologized in a hundred and one different ways for things he shouldn't have ever had to.

The door opens then, and Theo appears.

"Theo," Detective Ares says in a not-so-surprised tone, as if he's not shocked he's here.

I look at him and he looks like me—like shit. Good, I hope he hurts. His eyes are sunken in just like mine, he now has a beard coming in, and he looks like he hasn't slept either.

"Hanna, I don't want you talking to them without me here."

"I don't need you. I have Jack as my lawyer, and Detective Ares has been very kind, given the matter of why he's here, so you can see yourself out," I tell him, but if I were to say what my heart was really thinking, it would have been more like, *I love you still. I miss you and hate you all at once. I want you here, because I'm so scared of what is happening. I want to feel you again. I want to be yours once more.*

No. I can't and won't. Not after his bed of lies. I can never be with someone who would betray me so thoroughly.

"I don't care. I want to make sure my messages and reports got back and that they know you aren't up to this and have nothing to do with the girl," he bites out, but it's toward Ares and not me.

"We know she isn't. She was cleared. There is video evidence of Hanna at work at the time and date Banks went missing, and we found fingerprints belonging to someone else. There was also some hair that was jet-black. Did you know anyone with that color hair?"

I think about it, trying to ignore Theo next to me with his arms crossed, looking down on me. His smell hits me, and it makes me want to cry. No matter the hurt, I can't deny the sense of home his scent brings. The safety it encompasses and just how much it makes me miss him. I close my eyes and redirect my focus.

"Yes." It dawns on me then. The only person I knew with black hair was my coworker. "Dax. He was a coworker. He asked me out multiple times, and I turned him down, but his hair was his main characteristic. It was as black as night."

Theo growls. It's the jealousy type, and I ignore it. He lost the right to be jealous over me.

"Was he ever aggressive when you turned down his advances?"

I shake my head. He was always pretty nice about it. "No, he just kept asking but never seemed upset with me saying no."

"Good to know. I will have my team look into him and find out more about him."

I wouldn't think Dax would be the type. But I'm not a detective, so what do I know?

"Can I show you some pictures?" Ares asks, pulling out a manilla folder.

"May I see them first?" Jack inserts, and the detective nods.

"Of course. Here you go."

Jack takes it, and Theo keeps his eyes on me. I feel them, but I can't look at him. If I do, I will break down, lose it in front of all three of them.

"Oh my word," Jack says.

I expect Theo to jump to see what the images show, but he doesn't. Nope. He stays in place. Arms crossed over his chest. Feet crossed at the ankles. His eyes glued on me.

"What is it?" I ask and Jack looks up to Ares, then to me. Closing the folder, he stands, leans forward, and hands me the folder. I take it and open it. When I do, my jaw almost unhinges.

The woman in the picture looks similar to me. Blonde hair, thicker build, and green eyes. I would even say we could be sisters.

Is that possible?

I can't go down that rabbit hole. No. Not a chance.

"Who is this?" I ask.

"That is the missing women, Angelic Banks. We believe the person who is responsible for her disappearance may be the person after you. Jack let us know you've had a few instances that resemble the ones you had back in New York, is that correct?"

"Yes, I had the same truck appear at my house twice. Once, it just parked for a minute or two with their lights on, and then another time, they actually broke the window and nearly got in. Theo, my—" I stop, almost calling him boyfriend. I have to close my eyes and rein myself back in.

"Her boyfriend," Theo growls. "I came by, and he was gone before I came. Then he tried to run her off the road two weeks ago." He finishes what I was going to say, but I want so badly to stand up and slap him across the face. To come here like a knight in shining armor, even though he broke me and did the opposite of what a knight would do—protect the one he loves without secrets so painful they are unforgiveable.

"I see. And did you ever get a glimpse of him or anything?" Ares asks.

"No. It was either nighttime, or the last time, he had very tinted windows. I'm sorry. I know that doesn't help."

"It's okay, Hanna. We just want to figure this out and find who is doing this. Until then, we will have an officer outside your house each night, making sure you're safe. Sound like a plan?"

I go to answer in the affirmative, but Theo once again butts in. "No need. I'll be there at the house with her. The small-town cops here do no good. But I want you to find this man before I do, because I will end him if you don't."

"Theo, you can't say things like. I can arrest you."

"Freedom of speech." He shrugs as if he didn't just tell a detective he would murder whoever this person is.

"Not when it's a death threat," Ares counters.

"I will take the officer. Theo will not be staying with me."

"The hell I won't. Hanna, there is someone framing you for a missing person and fucking stalking you. They have come close to getting to you three times now. I'll be damned if I let them hurt what's mine."

"Too bad I'm not yours to worry about anymore."

The pain in his eyes matches the one in my chest, but I don't spare him or his feelings. "You're letting me stay. End of discussion."

"Hanna, for what it's worth, he is the safest option. He has worked for us a few times on cases, and he is trained well in self-defense. Maybe it wouldn't be a bad idea."

This can't be real right now. Did the detective just say that Theo is the safest bet? Over a *cop*?

"Uh. Fine, whatever. Just please find whoever is doing this... and find Angelic. I can't imagine what her family is feeling." I focus on the real issue at hand—that someone is already a victim to my stalker—and I just hope she's safe and still alive.

"We will do our best. If anything happens, contact Jack and me. We will keep you posted." Ares stands. "Jack," he says, shaking his hand. Turning, he breathes out a grumbled, "Theo." And then he's gone.

Glad to see I'm not the only one who is annoyed by Theo's persistence.

I stand and thank Jack. He says he will keep me posted, and then I hurry out. I need away from Theo. Now.

I get to my car, and before I can get the door open all the way, he slams it shut, caging me in with his big body. "I'm fucking dying here, Hanna. You won't talk to me. You won't answer my calls. You won't do anything to let me in." I turn and look up at him, missing the way that this stance used to hold connection, love, and trust. Now, it's a reminder of all he broke and everything I don't get to call mine anymore. My hands impulsively want to reach out and touch the skin just under his shirt.

"You are hurting me, Theo. Please, just let me move on," I cry, turning and dropping my head to the top of my car.

He pushes up against me, nuzzling his face into my neck. "Please don't cry. I can't take it. I will do anything to get you back. Anything, Hanna. I'm not going to stop. God, you smell like mine. You smell like home. I miss this. I need us back," he tells me, and I break free, pushing back.

"You broke this. You can beg and plead, but you broke us, and I'm not yours anymore." I open the door and get in, slamming it shut. He stands there and watches me go.

Twenty-Six

THEO

TWO WEEKS. I HAVE BEEN WITHOUT HER FOR TWO whole weeks. I called nonstop. Sent a million unanswered texts. Showed up and begged her to let me in. I even spent the night in my truck outside her house, hoping she would just wake up and miss me so much that she would forgive me and take me back. It didn't happen, so I did the only logical thing I could think of. I forced myself in.

I once told her that if she ever left me, I would go to great lengths to keep her.

Now, I will be watching over her until they find out who is doing this. And the second she mentioned that coworker who pursued her after her many turn-downs, I knew he had to be behind this. Also, I don't care if I wasn't in the picture yet; I want to remove every limb from any man who ever wanted what is mine.

Watching her drive away should hurt, but since I now have an in and a way to crawl on my hands and knees to beg her for forgiveness, I feel some relief.

Getting in my truck, I make my way to her place and see she is already there. She had to have known I was coming. I'm surprised she didn't go to my sister's.

Guess she knew I would have gone there too. I also haven't talked to Brenda much in the past two weeks, since the news of my real job and what I did was also new information for her. She felt betrayed but told me she just needed time.

Going up to the door, I twist the knob and find it's locked. At least she's persistent and safe. I knock.

"Kick rocks, Theo!" she yells from inside, and I can't help but smile, missing her sass.

"Baby, I can pick locks. Open the door."

"Nope. That's breaking and entering."

"I'm sure Ares will let that go." She doesn't say anything back, and I shrug. "All right." I head back to the truck, grab my tools, and return to the door. Seconds later, I'm in the house.

"You jerk! Can't you just leave me alone? Why do you keep doing this to me?" she bitches at the top of the stairs.

"Because I love you, and I told you I wouldn't let you go once I admitted it."

She huffs, groaning annoyedly, then walks to the bedroom, slamming her door shut. I make my way to the kitchen and start cooking us dinner.

A FEW HOURS LATER, I HEAR THE BEDROOM DOOR OPEN after she ignored me trying to get her to eat. I stand in front of the sink and wash the dishes, waiting for her to enter the kitchen. But when I hear the front door open and close, I shut the water off, dry my hands, and run to the door. The hell she think she's going? Opening the door, I see my sister's car take off, and I curse and grab my cell to text her.

> Me: Where the hell are you going?

> Hanna: To burn down a house. Calm down. I'm going out dancing with your sister, and it's not like it's your business. I don't have to answer to you anymore.

> Me: The fuck you don't, puppet. You're missing the whole point. You will be mine. Actually, fuck that. You ARE mine, and you better stop with this shit.

> Hanna: Or what? You'll break my heart again?

> Me: I deserve that. But I'll do you one better. I'll smack your ass red and leave you cuffed to the bed, where I can fuck my apologies into you until you can't help but want me back. Try me.

> Hanna: Maybe tonight, after I'm done dancing in this dress, with the body I learned to love right before you lost it, I will let another man do things like that to me.

I see red. Pure, burning red. Like an inferno.

> Me: What did you just fucking say to me? You think I'm just a simple man

who wouldn't do anything, don't you?

Hanna: No. I know you're a man very capable of secrets and breaking something that didn't deserve it.

I laugh sinisterly.

Me: I'm also a man who will empty a clip into a man for ever touching you the way I do.

Hanna: You're a psychopath.

Me: Yeah, puppet. Your psychopath. And I will find you tonight. Watch me.

Hanna: Sure, good luck. Hopefully, I'm not gone and at home with a man who picks me up by then.

Instantly, I put on my leather jacket and boots, grab my keys, and head out. The only place they would go here is Dean's, and I know they wouldn't be dumb enough to do that. So I head to the next city over. There is a new club opening, and Brenda let it slip that she had an in with the owner. I've never driven so fast in my life with so much rage coursing through my body.

I find the club, pay the valet, and go to the door. There is a line, but I hand the bouncer a hundred-dollar bill. He lets me in, seeing that I don't look like I'm staying long. People are dressed up for a nice dance club. I'm wearing jeans, a tee, a leather jacket, and boots. I came for one thing and will leave with her in minutes, freeing up two spaces in this new club.

I walk in and search the bar first, seeing if they're ordering drinks, but find nothing. Next, I eye all the booths quickly and come up empty-handed. But then, bullseye. In the middle of the dance floor, wearing a strapless skin-tight dress ending midthigh with a thick black choker around her neck, Hanna is dancing with my sister.

She doesn't see me, but I watch her, take in the sight of her actually loving her body, feeling free and sexy in her skin for the first time. I watch men attempt to touch and hit on her, but she turns them all down.

Thank God.

I am packing tonight and don't feel like putting a gun to anyone's temple. It just proves to me that she wants me. She can't replace me. She can't stop thinking about what I said before all this happened—that I would ruin her for all other men—and I did just that.

A new song—one I've heard—starts, "Ocean Drive," and she starts dancing, tossing her long dirty-blonde hair to one side, and that's when we lock eyes. I move to her like she's prey, and I'm the hunter. She doesn't attempt to turn and run. No, she feels the music, dancing and tempting me with her body. She has never looked more desirable than she does now—confident, sexy, and still missing me.

When I reach her, she turns and presses her back to my front, grinding against me with a purpose. She moves like a skilled dancer, ready to show me what I lost. That's what she thinks. Really, she's just showing me what I'm going to get back.

My greatest possession.

Her.

We dance to the beat, and when my hands find her hips on the crescendo of the song, I lean down, bite her ear, and growl, "I'm going to ruin you in this dress. Fuck you in it, then tear it to shreds while I take you over and over. Until your cunt hurts and you forgive me." On that note, she turns, and I think she's going to leave, but she doesn't. She leans up and kisses me, taking my mouth, and I return the kiss with a hundred percent conviction that I have won her back.

Our tongues punish each other, and we fight for dominance. I kiss her, bite at her, lick at her tongue, and she does the same. It's messy but calculated. When the song stops, so does she, leaving me wanting more, and then she turns and heads for the exit. I hurry after her, and once we're outside and hit the pavement, I chase after her.

"Come on, baby. Where are you going? You think you can just leave me?"

"Exactly, you stubborn son of a bitch!" she yells, passersby giving us judging looks.

"You kissed me back there. You want this too. I know you do, so tell me what I can do to get you back! Fuck!"

This stops her, and she turns on me, poking me in the chest. "I was a fucking job. You fucked me as a job. How could you think I would ever take you back?"

"Because," I say.

"Because what?" she yells, her voice cracking with heavy emotion.

"I betrayed you. Lied to you. Tore your heart down the middle when it was already broken, but the lie led me to you. *This* lie...gave me *this* love. And I'm sorry this lie destroyed your trust."

She stops, stunned. There isn't anything said for a solid minute or two, but then she speaks. "Goddamn you! Damn you!" She brings her fist down repeatedly on my chest, crying and screaming how mad she is. "I loved you."

Past tense? She said that past tense.

"No, you still love me. I just fucked up, and I will do that from time to time, but Hanna, before you, I didn't know happiness or love. And because of you, I do, and I'm not sorry about how we started. I'm not. I'm sorry it hurt you and broke your heart, but I'm not fucking sorry that it gave me you. But you have the words to say to end it all. In fact, all it takes is that *one* word, and if you say it now, I will go and leave you alone. If you don't, then I will spend the rest of my days proving to you that the secrets I held and the shadows you ran from were worth it. Because it gave us the greatest goddamn love the world has ever seen. Your call, baby." I'm two feet from her, and I wait it out.

There's a pregnant pause, and finally, she speaks.

"Sirius."

And my world crumbles around me. Hanna isn't going to forgive me. I fight the tears I have never cried until Hanna. I've never loved until her. I never had something worth fighting for until her, and now I have none of her.

"Okay. I set you free." I turn and start to walk away.

"Sirius," she says again, and I stop, looking up at the night sky, hurt that she said it again. "The brightest burning star. The hottest flame. The most explosive star there is. Sirius. You are my everything, Theo," she whispers and it hits me. She is using it as a safe word as forgiveness.

"You are my greatest fucking love, Hanna." And like that, we collide in a few strides, her body melting into mine, and we kiss, my hands around her neck and hers on my hips. I devour her mouth, reclaiming what is mine. Tearing myself free, I kiss her cheek.

"I'm sorry," I whisper. I kiss her jaw. "I'm sorry." I move over her collarbone, from one end to the other, leaving open-mouthed kisses. "I'm sorry. I'm sorry. I'm sorry," I repeat as I kiss all the skin I can that shows.

She cries with my apologies. "Take me home. Please." She doesn't have to ask me twice. I get us to the truck and grab her thigh, pulling her next to me. Up against me. She is texting Brenda, while I start up the truck and get us out of here.

"Is she alone?" I don't want to leave my sister by herself.

"No, she has some of the other girls with her, and the guy she's seeing owns the club, and he's there tonight."

I look to her. "She is seeing a nightclub owner? Great." Another thing I will need to worry about—some sleezeball club owner breaking my sister's heart.

"He is a nice guy, and they seem happy. But can we not talk

about them? Can we just focus on us?"

She's right. "I want nothing more than to focus on us," I tell her. We slowly make our way out of town and hit the highway home, and when the city is in the rearview, she asks me to pull over somewhere secluded. "Why, baby?"

"I can't wait to get home. I need your sorrys now," she tells me, unbuckling my pants and kissing my neck. I'm hard instantly, and I do as she says. Finding a side road, I take it until we are in a grove of trees in the darkness. Putting the car in park, I let the music play, the song "All I Want" by Kodaline starts to ring out as I help her straddle me, lifting her dress and ripping her panties to shreds. I don't waste time; I impale her on my cock, and we both let out a mixture of cries and groans.

"I've missed you," I tell her.

"I've felt so empty. I've cried every night. Woken up in fits from missing you so badly," she admits.

"I'm sorry, baby."

She slowly moves her hips. "Say it again."

I kiss the tops of her breasts, then pull down the fabric of her strapless bra, kissing each nipple. "I'm sorry. I'm sorry. I'm sorry." I will say it over and over, as many times as she may need, to make her understand I will never break what we have again.

"You feel so good, princess. I've missed this. I needed your body. I craved it since the last time you let me have you," I confess to her, watching her slide up and down, up and down so slowly it's almost torture.

"You promise you will love me with no more lies? You promise...because my heart is more fragile than before...that you will not shatter the glass it's made of?" she asks in between moans.

"Oh God. Yes, puppet. I will protect not only you but especially your heart."

"Ohh!" she moans, grinding her clit against my pelvis on her downward thrust.

"So—fuck, fuck—so damn good."

"Yes!" she gasps, bearing down on me.

"Tell me— fuck." She tightens her walls around me, and it chokes my cock, nearly making me come. "Did you wear this dress, knowing I would come find you and beg for you to take me back? To make love to you in it? To make me jealous?"

Her eyes lock on mine, and she nods slowly.

"Bad girl. Such a fucking bad girl. Bounce on this cock and apologize to your man. It's your turn," I tell her, and that lust, that heat that overtakes her eyes, comes full-force, and I'm reminded how much I missed that. When she goes from shy and reserved to unhinged with wild inhibitions.

"I'm sorry. But I'm glad it worked. I— oh!" she yelps with a high-pitched sound, when I smack her gorgeous ass. "I wanted you to feel an ounce of the pain I felt when you did what you did to me."

That's fair, and she knew just how to do it. "You won. Fuck, did you win." I take over, fucking up into her and bringing her down on my shaft over and over again.

"Ah! There, I'm there. Come for me. Fill me. Please."

"Oh yeah, dirty girl. Right there with you. Choke your man's cock."

She does just that, and together, we explode, our orgasms in sync, and they feel like they roll on and on.

Once we settle, our breathing not so labored, she grabs my throat with her hand, switching the rolls, taking control. "Theo. Don't ever hurt me again. Ever. There will be no third chances. Please." Her face doesn't flinch.

I match her and grab her throat, both of us doing this now. "I won't, if you promise to let me always keep you."

She smiles. "I never had anyone who wanted to keep me. You are the master who holds all the keys. I will forever be yours, always. I love you, Theo."

And with those words, we start the mending process.

Twenty-Seven

HANNA

Three Months Later

We have mended, for the most part. Some days, I still feel the pain of the secrets Theo held from me. But he always makes it up to me. Spoils me with touch and words and acts of kindness.

Dax has not been found. Theo asked to help on the case, but I told him I didn't want him to. I want him safe, and I don't want to lose the one good thing I have left. If Dax weren't missing and nowhere to be found, I wouldn't have thought he was up to this, but it does seem suspicious.

But why? Why would he want me? Why would he have taken Angelic? I think of her daily. Pray she is okay, that she is out there and safe. But this doesn't ever make my stomach feel at ease. Theo moved in, and I feel safer, but all bumps in the night still scare me.

Theo says I need to trust and move forward. Let the cops handle it and let him take care of my safety. I started writing again.

It felt good, so good to put pen to paper and words into sentences. I started a novel that I hope to publish. I doubt I will, because I'm wildly insecure my work won't be loved by many. It's my story, actually. One where I tell the tale of a lost child, growing into a lonely and confused young adult, to a woman who found love and a life in a town that changed her life.

It opened a lot of wounds, some I forgot, and ones that it helped me close and heal. Theo said he is going to look into working on the police force here. I keep telling him to go back to co-owning the business with Brenda, but he is so stubborn. I want the man I love to be safe. If I don't have Theo, I don't have the biggest part of me other than my self-discovery.

"Hey, I need to go over to my parents' to help dad pack up some things." Theo pulls me from my wayward thoughts.

I sit in my grandfather's office, typing away. The divorce between his parents was finalized. Theo still doesn't talk about it, so I don't bug him on the issue.

"That works great. Brenda will be there, so I'm covering for her." I look at the time and say, "Oh shoot. I need to get ready. I have to be there in an hour."

"Perfect, we should be done by the afternoon. You think you'll be home by then?"

"Oh yeah, I get off at four, so it's the afternoon shift. Why? Can't go a minute without me?"

He walks up and leans over the desk in front of me. His fist prop up his frame. "Yes, but I recall someone saying she wanted to be cuffed to the bed and have her cunt feasted on like a delicacy. And baby, that's all I want to do, and it's all I'm going to be thinking of today."

I blush, scandalized. "I was a little tipsy."

"We don't have to then." He stands again and moves to the door.

"Wait! No. I mean...I want that. It's been a minute since we've been able to do anything." I had the heaviest period this past week, and the cramps were out of this world, so we put a hold on our intimacy.

"Such a slut for me." He winks, and like a caterpillar, I flourish into a butterfly under his dirty talk. Who would have thought that would be me?

He comes to me, grabbing my throat and kissing me firmly, tugging my lip at the end. I moan, and then he's gone, leaving me missing him already.

Getting in the shower, I play some music and sing along, in an embarrassingly good mood. I don't know why, but everything seems too good to be true, and for once, I'm not questioning it. I'm living in it. Shutting off the water, I wrap myself in my towel and pull out all my makeup.

I hear the front door open, so I call out to Theo. "Did you forget something?" He doesn't answer, but I hear him in the kitchen. He must not have heard me. Walking down the stairs, I move toward where he stands by the kitchen window and open my mouth to say something, but my voice is lost when I see him.

Dax.

When he turns, I see the man I barely knew, who seemed to know me and wanted me too much. He looks awful. His clothes are raggedy, his face unshaven. He looks like he hasn't showered in a long time.

"Hello, princess. Or is it puppet? I hear that's what your boyfriend likes to call you." He has a mad look in his eyes.

I'm terrified, my blood chilled. "Dax, you need to leave, and if you do so quietly, I won't say anything to the police."

It's a lie, but it's the only thing I can think to do. I start backing up slowly as he starts moving toward me. That's when I see the gun in his hand. I look around for anything I can use as a weapon, and I look to the door, seeing if I have a chance to escape. It's maybe fifteen feet away. If I run fast, I can make it out. I don't care if I'm in nothing but a towel. I need out.

He eyes me, then the door, catching on, and when he sets into motion, gaining speed, I run. Right as my hand twists the knob and the door opens slightly, he grabs my wet hair and pulls it, yanking me back into the house. Kicking the door shut with his foot, he throws me to the floor, and I hit my elbow so hard I scream.

"You stupid little bitch. I could have had you, and you had to mess it all up. Now I have to end you both!"

My eyes widen, and I look at him rub the gun against his temple, his eyes manic. "What? Why are you doing this?"

"You turned me down. Over and over and over. Thinking you were too good for me. Ha! Look at you. You're lucky a man like me would even consider a girl like you."

If it were Theo saying this, that would hurt, but given that it's this psychotic man, it doesn't sting, not even in the slightest.

"Dax, I didn't want to be friends with anyone or have anybody in my life. I didn't want to get hurt," I try to reason with him, giving him the sad truth of the real reason I wasn't interested.

"Bullshit! You come here, and within a week you're fucking that piece of shit like some slut!" he yells, waving the gun at me. I scuttle back, my body reaching the bottom of the stairs. "So when you turned me down, I saw her, Angelic. She looked just like you. I needed to feel what it would be like to have you. So I took the next best thing," he admits, the sick theory making my stomach turn.

"Is she alive?" I question, knowing the answer will most likely be one I don't want to hear.

"Yes. For now. But because you had to come to this fucking town and leave nothing for me to follow, I had to do some dirty work. So I planted her shit in your place. Used our access as writers for the papers to hack into the system, and I tried to find out where you were, but the cops didn't know." He steps closer, and I try to scurry away, but I have nowhere else to go. If I move to run up the stairs, he just might shoot me.

"So I had to find your parents." He pauses and laughs. "Man, do they hate you, and holy hell did that work in my favor. I told them I was a friend and that you left in the middle of the night, and we were worried. They were hesitant. Didn't see why they should say anything or even care for that matter. But then they said they believed you were here, taking the money they clearly felt they deserved. The disdain they had for you—God, no wonder you were such a sad, miserable bitch." He takes the gun and runs it over my naked calf, my blood going colder, and I didn't think that was possible.

"So when they said that, I saw an in. If they told me where you were, I would take you and make you sign over all the inheritance. They bought it, and boom—I found you. But then that fucker found you first."

The way he talks about Theo makes my blood boil. I don't care what he says about me, but what he says about the man I love makes me want to hurt him. Yes, actually cause him pain. A swift kick to the fucking nuts.

Am I shocked my parents would do this? No. When I finished all the letters from my grandfather, especially the ones between them, I knew they would do anything for my inheritance. But they didn't get a dime. Selling *my* soul for money isn't something I would put past them.

"But now, the cops are on to me, and I don't have time to do this with you anymore, so I think there is only one option." He leans in, tucking my wet hair behind my head, the touch repulsing me.

"What's that?" I dare to ask him this, knowing the answer will be sinister.

He laughs. "Oh, sweet Hanna. That would be to kill you both and then myself."

No.

Twenty-Eight

THEO

"THE AMOUNT OF BOXES YOU HAVE IS A BIT MUCH, Dad," Brenda complains as I load another one into the moving truck.

"That's thirty-plus years. What do you expect?" my dad counters. I'm not engaging. All I can think about is getting home to Hanna and making up for lost time.

"You could toss some stuff. Hoarding is a real problem, you know." Her phone rings, and she hands me the box she was toting.

"Hey, Big Mike, what's up?" I put the box down, then turn back to her, while Dad goes to get another box from the house. "Wait, she didn't show? That's not like Hanna." My eyes hone in on my sister. Hanna would never miss work or be late, and she hasn't called, so she can't be having car trouble or something typical like that. "No, I will call her. I'm sorry. Thanks, Big Mike." She turns to me. "Hanna didn't show up. I'm going to call her. If I can't get a hold of her, you're on your own with helping pack up."

I already have my phone out, calling her, and it keeps going to voicemail. It hits me then—something in the pit of my stomach.

"Fuck!" Running to the truck, I'm out of there in seconds, ignoring Brenda and my father yelling after me. I speed, calling her over and over and still getting nothing. When I'm just able to see over the hill, I spot the black truck, and my heart sinks.

"No, baby. Fuck." I park the truck in the ditch a hundred yards up the road. I don't want him knowing I'm here. Reaching over, I grab my Glock out of the glove compartment, and I climb out. I approach the house quietly, going around the back. The dogs are in the house still, but they must be locked up, because I hear them barking from the bedroom window.

Approaching the back door, I open it quietly—so quiet I almost don't hear it. I step in and shut the door just as silently as I opened it. I hear voices coming from the foyer, and I cling to the wall of the hallway and slowly move along it, not wanting the wood to creak.

"You're a vicious little bitch. We could have been so good together. You think he fucks good? No, baby. I do. But now we have to end it. If I don't get you, no one can, and no one can stay on the run forever."

I'm now clinging to the wall midway of the stairs, and I can see them. He towers over her, and she is on the floor by the bottom step in only a towel.

"Fuck you for informing them of me, you self-centered bitch. I'll see you on the other fucking side, then we can finally be together.

He cocks the gun, but before he pulls the trigger, I point mine toward him. "Not a fucking chance, piss-ant." And I pull the trigger, hitting him right in the temple. Instantly, he falls, and I know it's a shot that ended him. I aimed to finish the man who was going to kill Hanna. To kill my woman. My one and only thing I'm fucking living right for.

"Theo!" she screams, opening her eyes, and I run to her. She sits there, covered in splatters of his blood, her hair wet from a shower.

I pull out my cell, and I call the cops. I hold her in my arms against me, and she clings so tightly, as if I'll evaporate into thin air.

"You're safe. You are safe," I tell her when I end the call, and within five minutes, the cops are here.

I covered her up with my jacket and blankets while they asked her questions. I have to listen to what he said, and if I could, I'd bring him back from the dead and kill him again. When they checked his truck, they found a bound Angelic. She was terribly emaciated, but she was alive.

The cops finish with their statements, and then we have to call and talk to Detective Ares, which took far too long. My family all showed up and rallied around Hanna, but I just wanted them all gone. She hasn't showered the blood off, and she's spent.

By the time I get them out the door, it's nearing midnight. I carry her bridal-style up to the shower. She still has splatters of him on her, and when I finish unwrapping her, she is on me, kissing me and ripping at my clothes.

"Whoa, whoa, baby." I stop her and take her face in my hands. "What are you doing?"

Her eyes well with tears, and she whispers. "You saved my life. And I want to make love to you. I don't care about his blood. I need you." And that has my chest swelling with twisted desire.

"To be fucked while wearing the blood of your fallen enemy?"

She nods, and suddenly we're tearing at each other. She claws at me, trying to get as close as possible. It doesn't seem to be enough. I lift her up on the counter and violently spread her legs, slamming into her—her fully naked and me still fully clothed but my cock free.

"Oh God, yes. Theo! Don't stop! Fuck me, please!" She's humming, begging for praise and freedom.

"Take it like a good slut. Like your keeper's good little slut."

She brings her head forward again and looks down, watching my cock disappear into her repeatedly, animalistically.

We reach the highest euphoria together, fucking with foul words and loud moans.

"I would die for you, but what's more is I would kill for you. Anyone who would ever dare to— Fuck!" She clamps down on my cock. "If they ever dare to touch or hurt you, I will be their ending," I tell her, using one hand to squeeze her breast, the blood smearing a bit. My free hand then pinches her clit, and she comes in that instant, but I don't let up. No, I keep going and going until she's had enough to beg me to stop. I finally give in and come.

"Fuck. Take all of it. Each drop. Good girl." Her pussy sucks me dry, and when we're done, I move us to the shower. I wash her clean of him.

The water goes cold eventually, and we have to get out, then I towel us dry.

"Theo?"

"Yes, baby?" My voice is low and deep.

"Thank you."

"For what?"

"Saving me. Loving me."

I smirk. "I don't just love you. I fucking breathe for you, Hanna."

"I love you so much," she whispers, running her hands through my hair as I drop to my haunches and dry between her legs and down to her feet.

She lets me tend to her. Aftercare but with a whole new meaning. I watched a man nearly pull the trigger on her and take away the most precious thing I own. I make a vow to never let anything or anyone make Hanna walk in the shadows again.

I will make the shadows fear her. She's learned so much already under my touch, but my puppet—God, my sweet puppet—still has so much to learn. And I have a fucking lifetime to show it to her.

Epilogue

ONE YEAR LATER

Staring in the mirror, I look myself over, surprised that I'm here now. Standing in front of it in a lacy baby-pink bodysuit, which is see-through and showing every inch of my body that once offended not only the world around me but myself too. I'm brushing out my curls, giving my hair volume, and I start applying my makeup.

How am I here? How did I learn to love my body? To see it as a force to be reckoned with versus a sore sight to my eyes? I want to credit it all to the man who showed me how to open up intimately and explores my curves like they were crafted by Picasso. As if I'm his muse, painted in a way only a real man could see worth in a real woman.

I was never a real woman. I was deemed a waste. It's the truth. The honest to God truth. No one can tell you different. Even the most confident women in bodies like mine have had to fight to love their bodies. All women, in fact, not just ones shaped like me.

But in my case, in scenarios like mine, women had to fake it 'til we made it. We were never enough, so we loudly became enough for ourselves. That's never an easy feat, and many may come and try to help you in the journey to love yourself, to see yourself as sexy, beautiful, and as a woman, but the real work has to come from within.

Theo gave me the tools, but I had to give myself the grace. The faith. The courage. And now, I stand her, in all my flaws, loving them and having them loved by a man I can never see me being without.

I see him enter, not saying anything as I apply my bronzer. He looks me up and down. Usually, it's in a predatory way, but there is something deeper, a longing for me. He steps up to me without a word, taking his arms and wrapping them around me.

I used to dread this. Arms around me. It was like a grenade being tossed into the pit of my stomach. But when it's him, it feels like I'm a part of him, something he needs to cling to in order to breathe. He always told me about the control he has to have, and now I'm the center of that control but with something more, a deep, deep need to be the core of his obsession. He massages the fat on my stomach, kneading it, then moves his hand to my neck and moves my hair so he can kiss and lick slowly at the column.

"Theo, I have to get ready," I tell him, smiling and placing my hands on his and letting my head fall back on his shoulder. Moving his lips from my neck, he places his chin on my shoulder, reaching his hand down my thighs, rubbing softly at the skin.

"I need you to need me right now. Please, baby," he begs me, and that's not something he usually does.

Turning, I grow worried. I clasp my hands on his jaw and peer up into his soft brown eyes. "What's wrong? Did something happen?"

He keeps touching me, all the spots that make me most insecure but have slowly learned to let him have access to without stopping him. "No, just that I want you and need you. You look so beautiful. God, look at your gorgeous ass in my hands."

I peer over my shoulder at our reflection and watch him grasp two handfuls of my ass that is covered in cellulite. It may be big and round, but it's filled with indentations, and Theo eats…it…up.

"I'm addicted. I feel like I need to be this close. Fucking inside here." He leans in and kisses my chest, above my heart. Theo never had this in him, truly, but just like he flipped my world on its axis, I did the same for him.

Something I learned about Theo—he needs me close. So close most would find it suffocating, but for me—I thrive on it. His obsession with me makes us feel vital to one another.

"Where do you want me?" I know he needs me, needs to be inside me, and I want that just as much.

"Bed, now." I look at him as I walk away, and he bites his lip, taking in the sight of me. I start to remove the sexy bodysuit, but he halts me. "Leave it on. I want to fuck you in it."

My core tightens, my stomach coiling into knots. God. He makes me mad with lust. I get to the bed and stand on one side as he stands on the other. We face one another, intensely staring as I wonder what to do next, but I'm no fool. I see it in his eyes. He has a plan, and it's a sinister one.

"Nightstand drawer. My knife, get it out."

I swallow thickly, my legs beginning to tremble. "What am I going to do with that?"

He gives me a sly grin. "Whatever you want, puppet. You are in control tonight. Use that control wisely. I won't give it away often." I look at the H I already carved into the V of his waist a year ago. He gets naked and crawls on the bed, lying there bare and waiting for me to make the next move.

"You want me to mark you?" I ask with a shaky voice.

"If you want to, you can do that again. You can do whatever."

I nod slowly, looking at the blade, the shiny silver a stark contrast in my innocent hands. I'm still new to a lot of the things Theo likes, in and out of the bedroom, and knife play is one of them. But I can't say I hate it. Then it comes to me. The day he used the knife to get me off, then made me declare his ownership over me.

Slowly, I climb on the bed and straddle him. Immediately, his hands go to my thick thighs, and he kneads the skin. It feels good, but I can't let that distract me.

"Move my bodysuit to the side, Theo. Show my pussy to your big cock."

"Fuck," he growls, aroused by my orders. Even I am, but dirty talk is a personal favorite of mine, and what else? Control. Being able to control the man deemed uncontrollable.

He does as I say, and when he does, I take the blade to his neck. "Now, fuck me and tell me you're mine, Theo. Tell me I own you. And that you belong to me."

He tilts his head up when the blade touches the scruff and skin of his neck, and he chuckles and licks his lips. "You fucking insane little slut. I knew you would thrive in this."

I nod and lift, careful that the blade doesn't cut him; that's not my plan. I just want the dominance for once. To see a man crumble and quake in my hands for once in my life.

I slowly bring myself down on his thick shaft, and this causes us both to groan out our pleasure.

"Say it, Theo," I moan loudly, grinding and circling my hips.

He keeps rubbing at my thighs, groaning, "You are mine, and I'm yours. You own this cock, this man, this armor." I gasp when he thrusts up into me and throw my head back. "Not so good at control when you're being dicked down by my big cock in that tight pussy, are you?"

I realize I'm not fully as in control as I wanted to be, but I can't help it. Regaining it, I reel in the pleasure and focus myself again.

I keep a tight hold on the knife and lean forward. "Worship me then. Tell me all the things you love about me."

"You want words? Or actions?" He hisses when I tighten the grip on the knife and bend to bite his chin.

"Both." And before I can even blink, he moves us, fast, flipping us and taking the knife from me. This time, repeating the action, he fucks up into me with so much force I feel I will be split in half.

He drags the knife down between my breasts and to my stomach. "I love this belly. So beautiful. So perfect. The feel of it in my hands." He's sitting up now, using one strong arm to have my hips lifted enough for him to start slowly sliding in and out of me. "To know it's mine. To know you hated it and now love it. Your confidence fuels my desire for you, Hanna. You came into your own skin, puppet."

He moves the knife to my thighs, tracing it along the T he carved, and all over my indentations. I cry out, suddenly insecure. How come? I don't know, but in this state, I am drowning in my insecurities. Moments ago, I was proud and loving the body I'm in, but seeing the type of man Theo is, strong, muscular, and leaning above me with not one flaw, I start to cry.

"You think I'm lying?" He takes the knife, puts it to his palm, and cuts it.

I immediately panic. "Theo, baby! What are you doing?"

He starts bleeding and lets the fresh blood hit my skin.

"Theo!" He doesn't answer, and when I try to sit up, he pushes me back down and grabs my hand, still thrusting into me, but then he does something—something I wasn't ready for. He takes the blade and nicks my hand a little, and I yelp out.

He clasps our hands and mixes our blood together, entwining us as he takes it and smears our joined blood over my thighs.

"You're mine, and I'm yours. Your body is my temple, and I'll fucking worship it." He rubs it into my thighs, and the sight is disturbing but beautiful.

He then takes our hands and places them above my head and begins to fuck me mercilessly.

"You're everything I waited for. No one compared. And no one will. You're mine. Blood with blood. Marks with marks. And even in death, I'm yours, and you. Are. Mine." He enunciates as he pounds into me, and with that, we both reach the peak, bliss claiming us and spreading from head to toe, through my body and into his.

Now, we really are one.

"Even in my shadows, I found your light," I whisper, my bloody hand cupping his face when the dust settles and we come down from our high.

"And my secrets brought me to you." He drops his forehead to mine, and we breathe heavily in tandem. And with a kiss, we seal our fate I hope we never escape.

I'm his, and he is mine.

● ● ●

HEY, GRANDPA. TODAY IS THE ANNIVERSARY OF THE DAY you left here. I wish you knew how much I miss you." I sit in front of my grandfather's headstone like I do once every month. Theo sometimes sits with me, but other times, I ask him to wait by the truck, because I need some moments alone.

"I know we never met, but the letters you wrote me, I read them over and over, and it makes me miss you." I laugh lowly. "I mean, I tell you this all the time. But I just thought you could use the reminder."

I play with the ring on my finger, the one Theo proposed to me with just weeks earlier. "He asked me, Grandpa. The crazy man who said he could never love anyone asked me to marry him. I hope you approve. God, I wish you were here to tell me you approve." I pause.

Glancing behind me, I look at Theo. He leans against the truck with his ankles crossed and his arms folded, watching me, I'm sure. Even with his sunglasses, I can feel his eyes on me. That simple posture—maddening. It still gets me every time. Everything he does still gets to me.

"He taught me how to love. He gave me love. He was the first. Besides you...." I trail off, remembering each time he said he loved me in the letters.

"I wrote a book. I'm calling it *The Girl Who Belonged to Cherry Hill*. I mention you a lot. I wanted to read you a couple lines that I wrote about you before I go." I wait a minute, close my eyes, and let the breeze sweep over me.

"'I learned of the man who would have loved me so fiercely... when it was too late. But I knew his love ran so deep that he wouldn't let me go a lifetime without experiencing some sort of love. When he brought me to Cherry Hill, he knew I would meet *him*—meet the man who would change for me. Live for me. Breathe for me. My grandfather never left me, even in death. He helped me find what I wish I always had. Love. My grandfather brought me to Cherry Hill, where the girl who never knew love found the greatest love of all.'

"Thank you for loving me when you didn't have to. I love you, Grandpa. See you someday." I kiss my hand, then bring it to the grave stone, leaving it there for a few brief moments. Finally, I stand and move to Theo, but of course I'm not fast enough. With two fingers, he summons me to move faster. Picking up speed, I jump up into his arms.

He kisses my forehead and then my lips. "Want to tell me what you two talked about?"

I shake my head.

"That's not fair. What happened to the no-secrets rule?"

I laugh, climbing in his truck and letting him buckle me in. "Let's just say we're even now." I wink, and he gives me a devilishly handsome smile.

"You sly minx. Now let's get home. I want to get to practicing."

My stomach flips. "You really ready to be a dad?"

"I'm ready to do anything that tethers you to me permanently."

Aren't we both?

The End

Acknowledgments

Lashelle. I really couldn't imagine a life without you in it. You are the best aunt to my sons, the best friend to my broken vessel. You are the light in a world that seems so dark to me. I used to hate the shadows, but now I face them because of you. Thank you for being here since the day I started this journey and doing whatever you could to help me get here and continue this ride. May you always know you are loved and cherished. I hope our time never runs out.

Todd. You are always a guiding force in my chaotic world. You center me and ground me. You keep me wrapped in love I never believed I would find and be able to have for all eternity. Thank you, my King.

Heather. You are always here, even when time steals from us, it never dulls the power of our friendship. Forever and Always we will ride or die. You're so amazing to me. Never stop being the rock in our life.

Kayla. Thank you for being a sister-wife. A co author. My

tits. You are always there to tell me when I spell a word wrong or start talking in past tense. But you're there even more when I need someone to just let it all out with. You are a blessing in my life. You are always going to be in my life. Too bad for you. But yay for me ;D Also, thank you for being my biggest cheerleader. Commenting and posting up. Love you!

Ness. You are truly a kind soul. You speak to mine in a way many cant. I adore you. I hope you know how special you are. Every Rose has its Monroe is more than a show. It's the truth. I wouldn't be the Monroe I am without you Rose. To the years ahead, may we race for the moon and back hand in hand. Here we go.

Jules. You are the one person I call when my world spins too fast. You don't seem to think it and you always tell me you aren't the person to call when you need advice or a shoulder, cause you ain't the one, but you don't see what I do. You always make me feel better. You make me feel like I can conquer so much and fight anything I'm too afraid to. You are a smart ass, but you're my smart ass. You, ma, and Matteo are near to my heart always. You are family now.

My Queens. You are the OG's the ones I love the most. You keep me so motivated, and my heart filled with eternal joy that never seems to dull when I spend time in your presence. You are the reason I will continue to ride out that imposter syndrome and push through.

To all the authors, bloggers, booktokers, creators and friends I have made along the way. Thank you for believing in me enough to support me. Thank you for giving me a chance and not making me feel like I wasn't good enough. You changed my career. I owe you a thousand and one thank you's!

About the Author

USA Today Bestselling Author, CC Monroe spends her days working and her nights writing spicy romance novels, that will leave you blushing during the steamy scenes and crying when romance gets a little angsty! Living in the snowy state of Utah with her husband and two sons, she enjoys reading, music, movies and the outdoors.

When she isn't writing or working, she is making people laugh with her mad sense of humor and tip of the tongue one liners.

Printed in Great Britain
by Amazon